69

Anton Marks

Marksman Studios
London, United Kingdom

Copyright © 2016 by Anton Marks

All rights reserved. No part of this publication may be reproduced, distributed or transmitted in any form or by any means, including photocopying, recording, or other electronic or mechanical methods, without the prior written permission of the publisher, except in the case of brief quotations embodied in critical reviews and certain other noncommercial uses permitted by copyright law. For permission requests, write to the publisher, addressed 'Attention: Permissions Coordinator,' at the address below.

Marksman Studios
Marksmanstudios1@gmail.com
www.anton-marks.com

Publisher's Note: This is a work of fiction. Names, characters, places, and incidents are a product of the author's imagination. Locales and public names are sometimes used for atmospheric purposes. Any resemblance to actual people, living or dead, or to businesses, companies, events, institutions, or locales is completely coincidental.

Book Layout & Design ©2013 - BookDesignTemplates.com

Ordering Information:
Quantity sales. Special discounts are available on quantity purchases by corporations, associations, and others. For details, contact the 'Special Sales Department' at the address above.

69 – Anton Marks. – 2nd ed.
ISBN 978-1-9029345-0-1

In Dedication to the Talented, Sexy and Revolutionary Josephine Baker

I don't stop when I'm tired, I stop when I'm done.

-James Bond

Prologue

AS YOU CAN SEE I'VE GOT THIS SHIT UNDER CONTROL. I know I make it look easy but you wanna-be-playas whose game ain't tight, watch, learn and tighten up your game. The seconds disappear from my mind like a weapons countdown and this inebriated motherfucker right here, yeah, the one in front of me trying his utmost to stay upright, is running out of a very precious commodity - time. Please forgive my black ass in advance for not being captivated by this Mickey Mouse performance but you see I've seen this shit done before and with a lot more finesse. I know what he's gonna do before mo' fucker here knows he's gonna do it. In my circles, I'm an OG, a legend of sorts and that means, I've seen it, done it and bought the goddamn T-shirt. Nothing he does or will ever do can phase me, so:

I watch his flapping lips, unaffected by the meaningless bullshit spitting from his mouth, hey everyone deserves a say, right? A listening ear. Sometimes I even take in a sentence or two, allowing their sibilance to play in my ears but inevitably they're discounted. Ma Campbell taught me to have respect, but just like how my subject is running out of time, I'm also about to run out of patience.

'What did you call me zute?' The wankster in front of me grunts in my direction, knowing full well I ain't said shit. 'You come into my backyard from your glass tower calling me a cunt! Is that what you calling me? You think you better than me, zute?' He ranted on.

His turn of phrase tells me he's from the South Zones, where Zute in their parlance means a well-off city worker: a suit. I'm flattered. He's obviously not tagged, or he'd have a split second of twenty thousand volts lighting up his unlucky ass as soon as he'd left his hood.

The Corporate Councils are good like that.

Let's play devil's advocate and say he had a level nine intellect and corporate contacts. Let's stretch our imagination further and say he could wander the big city freely. Deactivating the biometric offender leash would alert, every Met APB grid in a five-mile diameter. He'd have so many Five-O crawling up his ass he'd be shitting blue for weeks.

Nah, his dumb ass was just another anonymous face in the multitude of L-Town, a Saturday night special, an identikit brawler. Either a potential criminal thinking of crossing the line from petty crime to big boy felonies, or a free civilian who had joined one of these Fight Club's springing up around the metropolis. For substantial credits, you could dip your toe into the murky cesspit of L-Town crime with minimal consequences. This dipshit was just under two meters tall with the physique of a swimmer, Coral jeans, chain mail T's with Kevlar webbing to protect him from knife attacks, dark lank hair tied back, cowboy hat atop a head with scant brain cells to rub together to make a coherent thought. This was the kinda dude who needs the adrenaline rush of a punch up to give his dumb ass significance and meaning. Probably paying a hefty monthly subscription to the numerous fight clubs springing up around L-Town for the privilege of combatants-on-call. Pity he doesn't know that all his preparation won't save his raggedy ass tonight of all nights. Tonight, he's a willing participant in a spectacle that happens to be my hustle, a prop reacting per my script and usually that's the way shit slides.

Yow! He doesn't have to take part if he doesn't want to, I can't force his involvement. This opera is consensual. He only needs to pause, take a deep breath and listen. Open his goddamn eyes and watch my body language very carefully. I'm giving him an upper hand but nah, the dumb fuck, is too caught up to see that I'm giving him a way out. Still, it could all backfire. He could apologize and move on, then I'd have to deal with a disappointed client who'd paid good money to see shit pop off. But I ain't tripping 'cos I know his sort well. I'll give him exactly five seconds more, after that his chances to save face and walk away with his homies disappears.

Two........one......... time's up, playa. He's two steps away from me, still pointing and shooting off his mouth. This motherfucker is sweating me but I remain cool, I can feel his dilemma. Nobody is paying us the slightest attention anyway. We're just part of the overall background of rucks, drunken disorder, arguments and general badass behavior.

Coming into Rodeo ten minutes ago with my client I'd passed some guys chatting loudly. I knew a manufactured beef when I saw it, so my shortie and I ignored them. I'm flirting with my hottie for the evening, sipping juice, all the while playing the game. The guy picks his moment to waltz over. Less than five minutes and I had a willing stooge. Must have been a personal record but in my game convenience makes me nervous. My situational awareness is on auto just in case some whacked out freak tries their luck while my mind is engaged.

You see amongst orchestrating chaos and making my client horny and wet. I'm looking back at tonight and putting together previously ignored, unrelated shit that only makes sense when I'm in a controlled hyper state. Things I experienced days or hours ago, begin to make connections. That sleek BMW that was tailing me from the East, for example. I glimpse a familiar female face but keep it on the down-low. I've had a few real stalkers in my time, probably due to my natural charm, but now I'm starting to think it's something else. Never enter a joint without taking stock of your surroundings and the obvious focal points.

I eyeball an old Hell's Angel looking cat and a distinguished woman trying her hardest to blend in but failing. The bro smiles and interacts with a group of younger men while the older woman focuses on the band and then me when she thinks my back is turned. She's self-assured with no sign of nerves, obviously been around flowing testosterone before. But there are question marks all over this portrait because I've seen her before, on the motorway, my gut tells me. She has the same poise, air, and Hairdo as the woman in the Beemer.

Something's going on. First the distinguished lady and now these dudes? I repeat to myself that there are no co-incidences. But for now, I let that simmer on the back burner of my consciousness and focussed on a badly played score to some fucked up horror movie, this dude in front of me was a part of. Pity he couldn't play his part with the volume turned down because his threats were annoying the hell out of me and intruded on my other thoughts. I hesitantly let it slide and focus on the last spray of words that burst from his flapping lips. What is a playa to do except encourage his fall from grace with some fake ass sincerity?

'I've come up in the club for a quiet drink with my woman, and you're disturbing the peace, man. There a problem blood?' I say.

Not bad. Sincere enough for him to think I'm bothered by his threats but with enough authority to warn him that I ain't gonna curl up at the first harsh word and admit defeat. I'm willing this asshole on because he's a financial instrument, his violent predictability my pension plan. I'm miles ahead of him because I know from the off what his problem is. Hell, I'd be tripping too if I looked and smelt he did.

Damn.

A half smile crosses my lips cos baby boy had made the worst choice of venues no self-respecting playa would make – unless you were a maestro such as myself but that is another story. No ladies in sight, except the one I'm with. The bitches in here are low down and dirty, like a scene from a yesteryear flick of crack whores in a snow driven, decaying zone. Standing around a drum packed with debris from the neighborhood, crackling flames spitting out heat sparks as they warm their hands and stamp their feet, voices as harsh as gravel, their addicted eyes vacant. This joint is not my kind of place, so I'm doing these motherfuckers a favour. Oh, and let's not forget my client.

The shortie sitting at my table rubbing my thighs and dick, is like a laser beam piercing the fabric of the night, a harsh reminder that there is life beyond this whack joint.

My date is a statuesque, drop dead gorgeous red head. Oxford educated class breeding and CEO of a very successful internet business. And hot damn, to add insult to injury, she's just waltzed into the club, arm in arm with a real smooth nigga. To tell the truth, if I was him, if I was watching how a real man handles himself, I'd be pissed off too, but I'd have the good sense to keep my mouth shut and learn from an OG. That's precisely why I don't drink, dawg. Lose your judgment and could lose your life.

He fixes me with a hard stare. 'You're my problem cunt. You spilled my drink all over my facking shirt then looking at me like you just stepped on shit.'

Now ain't that a shame. I smile disarmingly and beg forgiveness even though I'm a whole five inches taller than the little runt. He doesn't have the brains to know he's being played.

'Look homie, if I've spilled your drink I'm sorry, I'll buy you another and even pay for your dry-cleaning bill.'

'Fuck off with your money zute!' He spits. 'You did that on purpose! Tryin to see how far you can go. You think you're a hot shit Exzek, right?'

Damn, this mo fucker has issues! Calm down partner. I don't want your insecure ass to blow just yet, I think. Another bout of consoling should rub him up the wrong way, so I liberally apply the bullshit.

I was wondering if Millwall had lost at home and the pain of loss was too much for his delicate soul to bear. Or was it the thought of me pushing my length and breadth between this beautiful sister's alabaster legs just too much for his feeble mind to accept. Fuck knows. Predictably the fool gets physical. He knocks me forcibly on my shoulder with his knuckles.

Oh shit, you done did It now, dawg.

Okay, this is not my normal line of work and contrary to how things look, I do have standards, but my client is a regular who'd paid damn good money for the spectacle

I would provide. My gig is to give her what she wants. That is good customer service. Leaving nothing to chance.

My friend and business partner, stationed in a hi-tech tram yard that I've never been to, messing about with scientific stuff way beyond me, is about to win our friendly wager, again. I'm street slick, but he's old school Oxford University slick. James Marsden, aka Digital, professor, businessman and brains behind this enterprise with an annoying tendency to be right whenever he uses his goddamn models of probability.

'The Rodeo is the place,' Digital had advised me earlier. 'Scotland Yard has secure files on all sorts of wonderful crimes committed and this Pub consistently hits the top five for weekend call outs. It's outside of the Zones, but this place will seriously test your skills and should titillate your more discerning clients.'

Test my skills? 'Fuck that!' I had said in reply.

And I fell for it. Hook line and sinker.

'A thousand credits.' Digital had offered, a half smile on his lips. We shook on it. When would I learn to stop falling for Digital's smooth ass way of putting me in situations that would 'sharpen my skills and improve the customer experience?'

The drunk makes enough noise to attract his mates who stagger over, also in an advanced stage of intoxication. Where are the automated security guards you may ask? Wake up and smell the caffeine homies. This is the wild, wild west, despite being an area that Met1 has designated safe for the average law abiding citizen. Rodeo management prides itself on being as close to the danger of the Zones without being in one. The place is modelled on an old western saloon with sawdust on the floor to absorb the spit, blood, and beer. Nothing less than a pub brawl would pique management's interest, and for me, that's a license to get Matrix on their punk asses.

I stand, and so does my date. My date grips my arm her nails digging into my flesh, her voice a husky whisper as she told me what she wanted done to her in the bedroom. This is what turns on this breed of woman. Violence. Fear. Excitement. I work in a world of vices and fetishes that would make your head spin. Weird and freaky shit that even a home-grown boy like me, took time to get used to. I nod, acknowledging her request. I couldn't have arranged this better if I'd hired stunt men. From her profile, this is exactly what Ms. Huntley has paid handsomely for, but there's one flaw, no-one has my back. The cardinal rule is; stay in contact at all times, but tonight, there's no wireless video feed, or concealed two-way communication link. Luckily my gut tells me I have nothing to worry about.

The drunk's four mates eyeball me again.

'What's his problem?' They ask the pathetic piece a shit who'd challenged me in the first place.

'He called me a white cunt and threatened to glass me. Said he used Zone scum like me to wipe his ass.'

And so, spits the lying mo' fucker in the England rugby strip.

What a punk. Doesn't he know that anything not screwed down in here is made from plastic? My hands were covering my clients backside; I gently move Ms. Huntley behind me and sit her down.

'When I call, you come, no questions. We clear?' I say. She nods. 'In the meantime, sit tight and enjoy the ride.'

She smiles nervously touching my back lightly. I sip my carrot juice slowly, aware that the wankster and his posse are waiting. I'm ignoring the music, the laughter, and all the bullshit, calm as the surface of a lake at dawn. My twenty-twenty is keen. I slip my right hand into the pocket of my slacks and set my dick into conflict position - straight up and to attention. Then I turn the whole situation up a notch by turning my back on the cowardly assholes.

A hand grips my shoulder. The fool attached to it is babbling, when my perfect center renders his attempts to shift me useless. I come about to face him.

'I want a piece a you, Zute shit!'

Ah! The sound of angst. Music to my ears.

Ever since I was a peewee, I've had a finely tuned sixth sense, always knowing intuitively when situations were dangerous. Over the last year or so it has significantly evolved. Drop my ass in any threatening situation and my perception goes all Steve Austin and shit. That's my twenty-twenty. Never told Digital about it. Wasn't sure it had anything to do with the vitamin shots he insists I take. Didn't want him to think I was developing a kind of Spiderman psychosis. At first, it was strange, but now it's so familiar it's normal, narrowing my focus to such a degree that everyone around me slows down. When it's switched on, it gives me a distinct advantage; I don't worry about how, it just does.

I'm facing four men excluding the drunk with not an ounce of commonsense between them. Dim-witted mo' fuckers. I move low and spin to face the drunk. He receives a rapid double tap to his abdomen that lifts him off his feet. Beer spews from his mouth as he staggers backward, smashing into his two drinking partners. I duck avoiding a crazy swing to my head, which I'd seen before the idiot decided to throw it. I plant my size ten and a half between his legs expecting his balls to come spitting out of his mouth but he just looks at me, mumbling incoherently before I push his head backward, sending him into the sawdust below. The punters make way, a signal that the conflict is about to spread. I look past the faces; some frightened some admiring. My date is gripped by my display of prowess and skills, her eyes flashing, her lips wet as the chaos fuels her excitement.

'Debbie let's bounce baby!'

Every woman's fantasy is different. Some pay for the sheer excitement, upfront, and personal or from afar. Some want to be hurt, their scars sexual reminders of what they've experienced. I insist on establishing how far they want to go before enacting any fantasies. Ms. Huntley is not a sadomasochist, and I don't want her touched. She's off the stool quickly, squeezing through the crowd, reaching out to me as the drunk appears from nowhere and makes a beeline for her.

I slide through two bar tables, my Versace trousers soaking up spilled alcohol and sawdust. I scissor the drunk's legs from under him. He rises struggling against gravity before dropping, taking down a table filled with drinks. I spin back to my feet like a body-popper busting a move side-stepping the tsunami of alcohol and plastic cups. I pull Ms. Huntley close to me, reassuring her with the warmth of my body and the calmness in my tone.

'Easy.' I rasp. 'One more thing to do.'

My twenty-twenty screams. I look to my left to see the pussy with the four musketeers steaming towards me, a bottle of Bacardi white in his hand previously swiped from the bar. A group of revellers spots their menacing approach and fragment into small groups. I shadow a group of two men and a woman feigning panic with them. Then suddenly I stop, whirl back and give my stalker the Adonis forearm, neck level. You need a camera for this shot, dawg, trust me. I catch him just right, his whole body takes flight, laying almost horizontal in mid-air, some Wachowski brothers shit, then he crashes to the floor, the rum bottle twirling into the distance. His flunkies see this and decide against pursuing him. It ends as quickly as it had begun.

Everything returns to normal speed; people scatter in all directions and the drunk, looks at me, from his prone position on the floor, surrounded by his mates, just like in the movies, he drops his head in defeat. Done.

My body is still, only my eyes move as I hunt for my shorty. Instead, I contact the mystery woman who's calm and smiling amidst the pandemonium. Like someone who knew what was going to happen before it did. Maybe I'm tripping, but there's no time to make up my mind because she disappears in a sea of panicked humanity. I sight my peeps on the fringes and our eyes meet. We merge with the flow of excited bodies as they depart, a small remaining crowd converging on the vacuum my presence has left. I brush past the doormen unprepared for the cold wall of air that hits me. CIO Debbie Huntley hangs on as I head to my G-ride. I'm considering my escalating bank balance while she has nothing but rampant sex on her mind.

1.

69

One Week Later

DIGITAL IS PISSED OFF, AND I DON'T BLAME HIM. We're in a Soho bar sipping shorts from slightly dirty glasses. He should have been grinning from ear to ear since a large sum of money had been deposited to our offshore accounts in the Bahamas, but for a multimillionaire like him, money ain't a thang. He let the young bucks like me trip about achieving my fourth million. While his focus is Sixty-Nine and the longevity of his company Steel Erection. But you can't get longevity if your ass is in a sling.

Hence the mean mugging.

I'm an asset worth fifteen million credits a year. My body is insured for thirty million, five million of that covering damage just to my dick - I ain't playin. I would be no use to the company's future profits fried from plasma rounds or punctured from knife wounds.

Yow, I'm your boy Adonis Campbell - yeah you know, named after that handsome dude from Greek mythology - and although some of you women are ready to judge me, I fulfil your fantasies at a very high price. Women ain't just a leisurely past time; they are my love, my passion, and my business. I'm no gigolo, get that straight from the get-go, that honor goes to the sucker who advertises at the back of the Penthouse Suite digital magazine, all dick, and no gimmick. Don't mistake us or worse still, confuse us. You won't see my service promoted anywhere 'cos we operate a strictly word of mouth business amongst the high roller circles.

Coz when we roll, we roll VIP.

If you're extremely well connected or just lucky you could have the name Sixty-Nine whispered in your ear or one of our smart cards pressed into your palm. I'm an artist, not a cocksman; there's a world of difference between the two believe dat. There is so much more to making love to a woman than you'd expect and I've learned my art well. Sex is the easy part; my prowess extends way beyond what I can do between the sheets.

The Art of Seduction requires a gimmick whether you're seducing your wife, your shortie or an illicit lover. James Bond had a gimmick. Casanova had a gimmick. Don Juan had a sweet gimmick. Sixty-Nine has a hell of a fucking gimmick.

Without it, you become a common playa on the street scraping the barrel while the Creme de la Creme drift towards the more enlightened pussy and I say that with the highest regard to the female anatomy. More business for me so I ain't complaining. No hype, just facts kid. Digital wants his dawg looked after. His dawg.

That's why I'm here with the man who helped make the dream a reality for me, apologizing like a bitch.

'Should I make this bloody Com smaller? Is that it?' Digital holds the modified V-Comm unit, ebony flesh coloured, between his manicured fingers.

'If you make it any smaller man, I won't be able to find it.' Adonis takes it from him and slips it over his ear.

'You do have your dog tags on though right?' Anxiety fills his voice. He's tripping about a diamond encircled, platinum enriched compound, meteorite shit, ten times more expensive than diamond, which is woven into the matrix of the dog tag interferes with low and high-frequency light. Meaning I can't be photographed or captured on video footage and if the conditions are right, I practically disappear.

'Yes,' I reply, 'never leave home without them, man.'

'Good,' he sighs. 'Then next time you go on a Scenario, even one I recommend, make sure you stay in contact. Remember we have enemies and competitors who will go to any length to topple our monopoly. You could be being systematically observed or worse, targeted. It's the difference between life and death. Do you understand?'

'Aight,' I'm tired of his tongue lashing, 'I'll do better.'

'Good,' he extends his hand. And I look at his manicured fingernails quizzically. 'We had a wager did we not?'

'Damn!' I transfer credits to his account using my V-Comm and a practiced gesture my communication rig understands. 'You know you just keeping that shit safe for me 'til I win it back.'

'Whenever you feel the need, son.' Digital smiles slyly.

I've come to expect his genuine and sometimes abrasive concern. It's not that he doesn't expect me to do dangerous shit, sometimes he even gives me some dicey scenarios to keep me in form, but he's a control freak, a quirk which enables him to mitigate against fuck ups where I might get hurt. Strange how two men with different philosophies just click? My past life was parties, popularity, and risk, all the things he yearned for in his understated, reserved way. Meanwhile, he has money, a creative mind and a thirst for discovery, the things I yearn for. Opposites attract.

I stare at him absently as the tip of his match glows red from the pressure of his fingers on the pseudo-wood shaft and lights his cigar. The glowing tip illuminates his large eyes. His features are tight as if nature didn't want to waste a morsel of flesh on his manufacture. His face, understatedly striking, a no-nonsense uplifted nose that seemed to say, he was blunt and to the point. His hair is smoothed down. He's handsome in an understated kinda way, with a stockbroker's sense of dress; Pin stripe suit from Prada, a shirt straight from Saville Row and red silk tie. Immaculate, not that he gives a shit and underneath it all he's a veritable dynamo of brainpower. His punctilious attention to detail and his obsessive concern for security are the two reasons why I admire him.

'Money doesn't solve every problem after all, does it, Adonis?' He pulls elegantly on his smoke, not caring that he's gone all cryptic on me. I shrug trying to stay upbeat. Digital's personal wealth is calculated in the hundreds of millions so when he says things like that you tend to take note. But we're seeing wealth from two different ends of the spectrum.

'Maybe not,' I say after a while. 'But it goes a long way to ease the pain, and if you wanna make amends for a past fuck up, there's nothing quite like it.'

'I've always imagined my family would be with me every step of the way. Never thought I'd be alone again.' Digital is still distant. I listen keenly, privileged at being let into his personal thoughts.

'You've got us, the business and some of the most beautiful women in the world. You can never be alone.' I pipe up, still on a positive tip.

Digital's grin is mercurial. He's back to the days before he lost his daughter to some incurable congenital illness, after which his wife left. The time his life went to shit. It was a memorable time because my son was christened that month and we asked Digital to be his bona fide Godfather. He spent more time with Adonis junior than I ever could because of my restraining order. I like to think that helped him come to terms with his grief. Now we're, sitting in a dingy Soho joint, drinking bad whiskey, chain smoking and remembering some of the most painful episodes of our lives.

'Whaddup nigga? Look like you got the world on your shoulders, man!'

I look up from my thoughts to see Milton Macgregor aka Popeye grinning down at me. I'd forgotten the reprobate had disappeared to the 'john' for a leak. Popeye earned his name from being a strict vegetarian. He's our logistics man, doing the research for our little team, checking the feasibility of our more elaborate fantasies and making sure all the technical details ran smoothly. Popeye had felt the pub gig was too risky, and just like Digital wanted to express his concerns, even though he's only heard the last five seconds of our talk.

'Have a drink and sit your ass down.' I shush him, worried in case his off-kilter mindset throws an already sensitive discussion into a tailspin. Fortunately, he complies. I turn back to Digital searching for the words I know he needs to hear. I think about telling him that his remaining daughter adores him, but the words sound flat. Digital is purpose driven. I need to give him something with more substance.

A lauded professor of both biochemistry and biotechnology he'd had to stand by helplessly watching his eldest daughter die. Crippled with grief, he looked into his shit and stepped up his game. He still tries to convince me that there's no point to his life and qualifications if he couldn't save his flesh and blood. I'd always felt there was something else behind his decision to make such a radical change in his life, but I never dug deeper. He was cagey about that aspect of his story even when his ass was tipsy. Hey, a man needed some secrets, and if I respected him, I could allow him that at least. Sex became his focus, and he became a multimillionaire genius who designed and manufactured some of the most innovative sex toys in the world. You've heard of the Giraffe - the only vibrator on the market that can locate and stimulate the G-spot every time? Yeah, that's my man. What about the Whisper? A handheld device that fired pockets of air at varying temperatures straight to the clitoris guaranteeing orgasms on demand. Five million joints selling worldwide and counting. Then there's his piece de resistance, the G-ring. My man worked out that when it came to contraception a lot of people weren't into keyhole vasectomy, the pill popping thing or even some messy application. The G-ring gave off a patented frequency rendering sperm cells ineffectual in ninety-eight percent of cases. It had one side effect though It made your dick bigger with constant use. His innovation blew all the other pretenders dead in the water. It sells fifty million units and rising per annum. Pure genius.

    Still, for all his international success Sixty-Nine was his labour of love, his baby that had grown beyond his wildest dreams aided by an injection of my ghetto charisma. Maybe it was time for Digital to take stock. A few drinks later and

Digital's melancholy is gone. 'You're right, life is too short, why worry about something I have no control over?' He sits up and smoothes out his jacket, brushing away barely noticeable wrinkles.

'True word. And on that note, fill me up.'

Digital leaves to collect another round. Popeye shoots me a stare wanting to know what's gonna happen next. He always did hate to feel left out.

'We on a roll, turf boy!' My reply is accompanied by a careless shrug and a mischievous grin. 'Whatever we do next is going to be big. Trust Uncle Campbell.'

Popeye mouths off with some ideas, but the part of my brain that gives a fuck has long gone on lockdown. My earlier energy is depleted, and I'm in kick-back mode. I appraise my surroundings noticing the diehard, hopeless washouts trying to round up the dwindling amount of skirt in the bar. That's when I hear the crack. Short and sharp. Five fingers across a jawbone. I know that sound well. I look over to a dimly lit corner and see an inebriated punter stagger out of the darkness, tie dangling around his neck, shirt out of his trousers. The only thing stopping him from ending up on the floor is a drink-filled table. The woman who comes after him is definitely a working girl - tight jeans, shocking red blouse barely containing her breasts and her outfit finished off by a shiny pale blue organza fitted skirt. No matter how society tries to demonize prostitutes they bravely provide a service, often going against their particular preferences to maintain professionalism. The recipient of the slap obviously thought that he was dealing with something less than a woman.

Huge mistake, homie.

Drinks spill all over the floor as the pitiful playa apologizes but his words are drowned out by an angry tirade. I consider enlightening him, but I prefer to be entertained tonight.

'Remind me why we always meet in this shit hole?' I pose the question to Digital on his return, my eyes still on the debacle.

'The ambiance.' Digital's humor is dry enough to scuff glass.

'Yeah dawg,' I agree, 'the ambiance.'

Then for the second time in one night, some dude considers a woman less than him, and once again all hell breaks loose.

The 69-cadre parted at the end of the night reluctantly, the warmth of our camaraderie was unable to bear up to tiredness and mild inebriation. Standing on shaky legs Digital was the first to admit defeat and called Austin his ex-SAS chauffeur who was in a holding pattern half a K above their heads and who immediately descended to earth. Five minutes later the driver docked the Bentley into a ground parking space on Thread Needle Street and had the pressurized doors cushioning open. I ushered my boss out and guided him by his elbows making sure he was comfortably seated before bidding him good night, in return, I received a garbled ardor in response as the doors sucked shut. Popeye had taken the hint as we stood up and started to depart heading outback for the wagon. In minutes, he pulled up to the front from the parking bay in the 69-surveillance van just as Digitals ride hit the air lanes. Big man seemed especially pleased with himself tonight with the window down, and his elbow cocked through it. Leaning back in his seat he lets out a long old sigh of pure contentment that whistled through his teeth. I guessed all that green shit he eats was finally messing with his head. I stand with my hands in my pocket watching him expecting one of his end of night pronouncements.

'Are you thankful for your life?' He asks.

'Nigger, please! It's three thirty in the morning.'

'I'm serious, man.' I look into his eyes wondering where he's coming from.

'I'm thankful,' I say honestly. 'I'm not the best or the worst, but I count my blessings.' I decide to keep the details to myself.

'Good.' He looks relieved. 'Karma is a big thing for us Buddhists.'

My face is a blank canvas, but he's undeterred. 'If you do ill, ill will follow you, right? So why am I enjoying what I'm doing so much? Good health, a good woman, friends. Why aren't I paying for my past?'

I respond quickly, even though I'm tired. 'Because you're more thankful than most.'

He pouts his lips as if that makes sense. My heart goes out to him:

But it was a friggin accident, my friend.

The couple may have been young, but they were drugged-out, staggering around in the middle of the blacktop on a rainy night. You were tired. The road was slick. Shit happens. The memory of that unfortunate incident has dimmed but remains, never too far from his mind.

'Did you check out the microdisk footage?' I switch Popeye on again. An abrupt contact that matches my newfound sudden state of alertness. The sparkle immediately returns to his eyes.

'Quality!' he laughs. 'You're well equipped for the job boss, fo sure.'

I laugh along.

'What's in the jeans is in the genes, dawg!'

Popeye's mood brightens considerably. 'Your client is going to appreciate the footage privately or with friends. You've got screen presence man, pity your identity has to remain secret.'

'Hey, a guy needs something to fall back on, right?'

We grip hands gully style and part company.

Am I thankful for my life?

The question burrows under my skin and incubates there, coaxing out the harsh memories and the elation entwined in my life all at once.

Released from San Quentin on trumped up charges from the presiding Judge John Cracker – I shit you not - with a sentence that did not fit the crime, I got out of the US before the shit hit the fan. But that's what you get from a judicial system – and a government - that over decades had insidiously become fundamentalist Christian and racially intolerant. My ass was judged more or less from the dictates of the Old Testament, and you know the good books position on fornication.

Fire and brimstone.

The only reason why I wasn't still languishing in lock up was it so happened that Hallelujah land had an out of control crime problem - even with the highest density of churches in the world and that required reshuffling resources. They came to realize that me fucking rich married bitches and leaving them in orgasmic dementia then fleecing them of some loose paper did not warrant twenty-five years in jail. I was perfecting my survival tactics for five years amongst gang bangers, terrorists, sexual predators and some plain grimy mo' fuckers when they came to their senses. So, my sentence was commuted, and I was handed my pass out of Dodge. I've pissed off Uncle Sam and his tambourine clapping brethren, so my green card is revoked and a lifetime criminal record hangs over my head. They deport me to the UK, and I end up in London, holes in my pockets and homeless. Ma Campbell – rest in peace Ma - wants to take me in but I can't let her do that. So instead I lie and tell her everything is cool.

My journey back to health, wholeness, and riches starts with my climb from one of the most notorious Zones of North

West London. A hell hole with a population of eighty-five percent electronically tagged, hardcore, savage, criminal minded sons-of-bitches – and I say that with the greatest of respect while living amongst the law-abiding poor. I get the paper as a guinea pig for some scientific gig. Nothing taxing or dangerous, then I do some stripping and make some credits, always ensuring that my hustle is clean and crispy. Finally, one day I say it; Fuck the Zones, I'm outta here.

At the same time, lady providence smiles on me setting a series of fortuitous events in motion. First, I meet Maria. I tell her my brilliant idea, and she agrees to bankroll it. Then a chance meeting with Digital and my determination to make something of my life increases significantly. Sixty-Nine is born and the rest, as they say, is history.

Playas lifestyle and I mean P. L. A. Y. A. S, is what I'm used to these days. Penthouse flat in an exclusive block in the docks. I'm an investor stocks and bonds and in precious stones from Earth and Venus. I have a silver Aston Martin chilling on my drive; a fire engine red Ducati languishing like a bad bitch in the underground lock-up and an ultra-healthy bank balance in the Cayman Islands. A picture-perfect chalet in Negril Jamaica is one place I decompress from the grind, but my pride and joy is a small island in the World development in Dubai replicating the shape of Jamaica, trust me, Ms. Campbell's son wasn't born dumb. If you've been through what I've been through and not learned from experience, then you would deserve to end up in the Zones, copping benefits, nothing but a broke ass menace to society. Not me turf boy, not me. I whisper thanks to the big city, lady luck and the higher powers.

I drive to the Docklands in silence, the only music in my ears as I come down from the high of the night is the tinkle of good memories resonating in my head. Endorphins explode inside me with decreasing frequency. I sink into my leather seat, appreciating London, its savage cityscape, its vibrant energy, its contradictions and allow it to seep into me. The city that never sleeps is wide awake. The ariel lanes busy with hover cars, ground huggers, like me, determined to get to our destinations as quickly as possible. I couldn't have done this anywhere else. London, L-Town, tag it anyway you see fit dawg, a place of boundless energy and unlimited potential for success. I'm living proof.

I yawn. Years of clean living have allowed me to keep going for so long but after sixty hours without sleep, I'm feeling the pinch. One block away from my crib, I turn on my autopilot. My bed calls me, just like the Sirens of Greek mythology and I can't wait to get there.

2.

FIVE FINGER SHUFFLE

THE FAMILIAR DECORATIONS ON my bedroom wall transform into a digital tableau of the weather predictions, traffic density, trading statistics and of course the time flashing 6.40AM with a soothing rhythm? Five minutes later, like the undead, I'm suspended upside down from the rafters of my personal gym, air con belting, sweating like a mo' fucker, grunting to finish my fiftieth rep, my ab's and thighs are on fire, but it feels good. With a hearty expulsion of air, I'm done. I hang there for a moment longer coated with sweat, muscles aching, my stomach empty and unhappy.' Feel good' endorphins pump into my bloodstream and once again I'm back on point.

I press a switch in the rail that's holding me up which turns off the electromagnets in my boots. Holding my position, arms supporting my body, legs outstretched, I swing. As soon as I've got enough angular momentum I dismount with a somersault landing deftly on my feet. I grin at the applause from the imaginary audience, the judges' scoreboards showing perfect tens. I laugh lapping up fantasy cheers and adulation. Hey, imagine life if you took shit too seriously? Fuck ups aside, I fully appreciate all of life's blessings.

I feign a left hook then let fly a ferocious right hand ready to tear the leather punch bag from its elasticized restraints. I bob and weave from its rebound trajectory and slam it good, then dance nimbly away. Float like a butterfly, sting like a bee. A natural pugilist Digital once concluded.

You got that right, playa.

I pad down the corridor toward the kitchen and stop off at my study. It's neat and organised with books, lining the three walls and computer equipment in front of my comfortable leather chair. My stuff is well worn but the children's titles on the bottom shelf remain in pristine condition except for the dust. I developed the habit for reading as a means of surviving prison life.

I reach out and disturb the photons in the Holo image, situated in pride of place in my study.

When I got out, I was desperate to turn my life around, because of you. I love you more than life, cowboy. Adonis Junior smiles back at me. I look at the cute features, big eyes, and an even bigger smile. A carbon copy of myself. Only your

Ma thinks I'm a worthless piece a shit. Even when I was dedicated to pulling us out of hardship, she couldn't see beyond what I did, beyond the hype. Now the bitch is trying to take you out of my life, trying to prove I'm irresponsible. But that shit ain't gonna happen.

I stroke his face with my fingertips. Nobody writes me off, son. They've been trying that shit from time, but I always pull something outta the hat. From Primary school, they said; pretty looks will get you nowhere. Well, fuck you, Miss Jenkins. It was your duty to mold my young, impressionable mind but instead, you constantly told me I wasn't worth shit. That good for nothing Zone kid is doing pretty well for himself. Never signed on in my life and you can count on me not relying on a personal pension or worrying about any of my financial instruments performance over fifty years. Nah man. And I won't be moonlighting at sixty to maintain my lifestyle either. I did it the hard way or did it just to prove cocksuckers like you wrong. Live well and prosper bitch because I'm gonna.

My rant over, I walk into the small adjoining room. The twenty-first century is obsessed with convenience. The written word has become digital like so many other things, but a few diehards like myself still prefer tree pulp and ink. The books in my library look crisp and untouched but don't think that they're just there for show. Like my dick, knowledge is an essential tool. The women I meet are movers and shakers, classy and moneyed. So, in or out of bed. I must be able to converse intelligently on current events and relevant shit, keep them engrossed with some esoteric joints I've learned or experienced. I must be the eternal student because the Art of Seduction requires no less.

Hey fuck the Art of Seduction, my stomach complains during my introspection. Soon I'm in hovering distance from the interface of my HMCR - Home Multi-Format Communication Rig that is in every room; a digital voice message has been recorded, and it tells me so by showing me the telephone icon projected on every glass surface I pass near to. I smile again, it's Sunday morning, after all, trust Jessica to remember. The thought is pleasurable but it conflicts with another woman who's waiting in my bed. I decide to replay Jessica's message at a less sensitive time.

Maria is all wrapped up in my white silk sheets like a little kitten. Breasts, hips, legs, her proportions are just perfect. I always tease her about her heritage. No Chinese chick I know has a backyard like you girl. That's black baby, through an' through. Although she's petite, she has the assets of a sister. Blame that lying mama of yours, I keep telling her, your old lady has been playing away in the hood. I smile unable to resist rubbing my fingertips over her feet. Small and well formed, just how I like them. 'Nevah check a gal with bigger feet than you', my Yard cousin had drilled that maxim in my head, you could find out she has a bigger prick than you too.

I shudder.

Maria and I understand each other. I make no demands on her; she makes no demands on me. Our relationship is some experimental shit that the sisters I dealt with previously wouldn't consider in a million years. They would have laughed their asses off at the suggestion of what Maria calls, 'flexible commitment.' The freedom to sleep with other people, which I do anyway because that's my business, but with the important proviso of treating our relationship as a priority. Would I sleep around if I was just another average Joe and I didn't do what I do now? I'd like to think not, except for the one or two stray pussy that stumbled and inadvertently fell on my dick.

Maria stirs. She could still be tired but, if I know her at all, when she wakes up she's going to be very hungry. The urge to join her under the sheets is strong but I let my little Chinese flower sleep.

I work the kitchen without apology and in no time the Ackee and salt fish is simmering, the plantains have just finished frying, and festivals are turning golden brown in the Dutchie. I'm in the mood for some Yard food. I'm not a tea person, a glass of carrot juice and I'm cool, but my shortie likes the Earl Grey stuff. Hers is brewed, mine is chilling. My Smeg cooker gleams, showing off my reflection on the aluminium housing. I'm bare-chested wearing one of those punk ass, novelty kitchen bibs. A birthday present from Maria. I must be a woman's worst nightmare, good in the kitchen and the bedroom; money ain't a thang, and I'm ambitious. I'm also enough of a gentleman to smooth out my thug tendencies. How could one woman hold me to emotional ransom? It's just not possible. Maybe that's why I still struggle to maintain a relationship beyond five months, present company notwithstanding. I guess that could be where my problem lies. I'm just not hot on showing my vulnerable side. I'm an OG cooking breakfast for a woman. My shortie has done what a select few have managed to; gotten under my skin. The urge to fall in love is almost overpowering. You know what I'm talking about? You're defenseless, your knees are knocking, your balls quiver, and it feels like you're butt ass naked in public, all the while kidding yourself that you're in control. She is special even though I don't really know her. I'm curious, but I never pry. She's one of the most selfless people I've ever met, and I respect her enough to allow her that freedom.

I take the last fried dumpling out of the frying pan and my home V-Comm goes off. I beep up the cordless and the conversation is piped to the kitchen. The usual visuals are blocked letting me know it can only be one man.

'Yeah, yeah!'

'I didn't wake you, did I?' His formal Oxford educated twang confirms that it's Digital in business mode.

'Whaddup, nigga!'

'A deal has surfaced.' He says ignoring my crassness. 'We need to meet.' As usual he's all business. 'As much as I'd love to stare into your baby blue eyes over lunch, the timing sucks. Just e-mail me the details, dawg.'

'No can do. Even with your razor-sharp mind,' he joshes. 'We need to plan this in detail. The first step is your agreement.'

'Five finger shuffle?' I ask.

'Like nothing we've done ever before.' I can practically see him nodding his head. I tingle with nerves or maybe excitement.

'A challenge huh? I figured one would never come around, man.'

Digital responded with a smile in his voice.

'Life has a way of giving you what you sincerely ask for.'

'True story. Where and when?'

There's silence as Digital considers the best place for our rendezvous.

'The Depot, tomorrow about noon. It's more secure there and anyway you're due for your regular check-up.'

I'm flattered and surprised. The Depot is Digital's Research and Development centre. No one is ever invited. We all know what goes on there, but I have never stepped foot in the place. My previous medicals have taken place on Harley Street or Casanova House, the administrative offices in L-Towns financial district, where the rest of the world considers Steel Erection Ltd to be based, Shit, I didn't even realize he had healthcare facilities there.

'Aight!' I respond nonchalantly but I'm wondering what's going on. Why such a sudden change in procedure?

'Maybe you should discuss it with Maria or better yet put her on and I'll quickly go over the remuneration package I'm currently negotiating.' Digital breaks into my thoughts. Son-of-a-bitch.

'What makes you think she's here?'

'The chime,' he answers, a little too sure of himself for my liking.

'What fucking chime?'

'The one that patterns your voice whenever she's around.' Suddenly I feel very vulnerable. I make a last-ditch attempt to throw him off course. 'You're hearing things rude bwoy.'

'My voice analyser doesn't seem to think so. Should I talk to her later then?'

I give in knowing when my dunce ass is beaten.

'She's still asleep.'

'Tell her to call me.'

'Aight.'

'Food smells good,' Digital can't resist fucking with my head one last time before he signs off.

'Ackee and Salt fish.' I don't bother to test his skills of deduction, 'I know,' he says, with a 'what else could it be?' certainty. 'Are you ready for tonight's scenario?'

'Ready and waiting,' I nod.

'Do a good job and this could lead to even bigger and better things.'

'Don't I always?'

His silence tells me he's nodding his head in agreement.

'We'll talk soon, son.' Once again, I hear the smile in his voice before he disengages the line.

No talking goes on when my baby is filling her tank. She doesn't talk, don't read, don't watch the TV, just gives the food her undivided attention, like it's the most important thing in the world. I know the 411 on this, so I don't front by disturbing her ritual. I break out into a punk smile at how comfortable she is in bed downing the Ackee and salt fish, plantain, fried dumplings and Earl Grey tea.

Peeps looks good draped in white. The silk sheets cover her from the ankles up to her waist, her breasts are small but much more than a mouthful, I watch them jiggle along with her well-formed toes. I'm bugging but I love having her around me and, as much as she won't openly admit how important this down time is, I know she wouldn't miss it for nothing. Finished she lays her knife and fork neatly in her plate.

'What's so funny?' She asks.

Obviously, I'm still wearing that pansy ass smile.

'Goddamn girl! Where do you put it all?'

Her smile, framed by small but full perfect lips, lights up my room. 'You know you're a fantastic cook and, you also know the way to my heart is through my stomach.'

'And to other parts too...,' I mumble under my breath.

'You seemed to think I had multiple routes to my heart last night!'

'Damn, right.' I laugh at her sense of humour. 'And I found them too.'

'Compliments to the chef,' she beckons me over.

This is how we do shit. I watch her from my position at the head of the bed wearing only my silk boxers. She slowly reaches inside my shorts like she's taking the winning lottery ticket out of its envelope. Gently, and with some effort, she nudges the meat and grizzle into the palm of her little hands. She holds me for a moment as if she measures weight and consistency. Eventually, she puts me in her mouth and takes a long drag like she's pulling on a big ass blunt. Ten inches' length, four inches' girth and that, playa, is on a cold L-Town morning. A sigh of satisfaction escapes from my peeps slightly open mouth. She kisses my member and watches it stir majestically. She doesn't know it, but she's holding tradition in her hands.

The males of the Campbell clan hailing from Burnt Savannah, Frome and Toll Gate, Westmoreland, Jamaica, were all gifted. My grand pappy an old-school scholar said he genetically traced our family lineage to some Ivory Coast royalty. A long line of big woods men it seems. My good for nothing Pops was no different, and the old lady couldn't mention his name without a curse first and a twinkle in her eye last. Hell, I thought everyone was as gifted as my cousins and me. Imagine my goddamn surprise when I came to England, and started using changing rooms with the football team. That's when the rumours spread in all the girl's locker rooms and to the private girl's school down the road. Hot damn.

Those girls were as horny as fuck and from the beginning to the end of Sixth form I was flush with pussy. Soon I was like a High School Hugh Hefner. Can you imagine the confidence that gave my black ass?

'Richard called this morning, how is he?' Maria drags me back to the present and tries to tuck me back into my boxer shorts but it ain't happening. She makes do with stroking it instead.

'Oh yeah,' my erection interferes with my thoughts. 'He called all hyper about a new scenario we've got to create. Never heard him so excited before. He thinks this is gonna take us to the next level.'

She raises her eyebrows. 'I'll pencil him in for a meeting, the sooner the better don't you think?' Maria kicks into business mode, searching for her Touchstone.

'Best do that before he explodes all over his Saville Row suit with excitement. What are you looking for baby?' I already know the answer, but I love messing with her. Maria's Personal Digital Assistant has everything she needs to run her business on the move; her client base, her plans, her past, her future. She gives me a 'don't mess with me boy' look. I reach under her discarded lace panties and hand her the personal organizer that looks and feels like a five-centimeter across pebble. Once the Touchstone connects with her skin, a holographic interface circles it and all her previous notes show up on every interactive surface from a drinking glass to a massive mirror on the wall. She condenses her files onto a transparent tablet at the foot of her bed. Next, she's looking around for her diary, a hard copy of her electronic notes. Her business dealings are meticulously organized, but she's hopelessly wack at finding her stuff.

'Adonis baby I think I know where I left it.' She looks up at me.

'Where?'

'My locker at the gym. I'm there on Friday anyway, I'll collect it then.'

'You do that and in the meantime.........' I lean over to suck her nipples. 'I got business to attend to.' The dark knobs become hard as she giggles. I trail my tongue slowly down her chest, over her stomach through the dark tangle of her pubic hairs to her very wet and very willing coochie.

3.

CORKSCREW

SUNDAY NIGHT AND I IMMERSE MYSELF IN THE exuberance of the West End with all my senses engaged. Where else in the world could I do what, I do and enjoy every goddamn minute of it? I'm chillin' with the freaks in Piccadilly Circus, and everything is everything. I left my Ducati parked in a secure bay in Leicester Square, then strolled up here deep in thought. Eros holds his pose as always, seeking to shoot his arrows into willing hearts. Nobody's told him times have changed. In today's world love is more elusive than ever, even with the influence of the gods.

I watch the image sharp holographic displays advertising the myriad products from the corporate giants as if it's all new to me. I inhale the hydrogen discharges, the body odors, the stink of burning meat and onions. And I'm aware too of the shrill laughs, coughs, screams, and whispers.

Every shop you pass calls to you by name. Its sensors read the part of your personal ID that specifically targets your shopping preferences. Images of films, perfumes, the most recent lick in fashion, an exposé of some political figure taking the country by storm; a mass of information force fed into your personal space but I love it, 'cos I helped to build this shit. I'm contributing to the economy of this great city.

The CyberMesh is sixty-five percent porn driven while the sex industry contributes to nearly 30% of this local district's cash turnover alone. It provides thousands of jobs and is a hotbed for entrepreneurs. Ironically, but not surprising really, the real estate in this part of town is mainly owned by the Porn Kings of Europe, another testament to the adage that sex sells.

As usual, I'm one of the most dapper freaks out tonight. I'm thugged out in an ankle length black Versace leather coat. Under that, I'm in loose easy on, easy off slacks and top. Now under that, a leather thong clutches my prime black ass. My personal tastes are less flamboyant, but my client has a preference for leather.

The Li-Fi wireless rig sits snugly on my bald head. Telescopic mike close to my lips and headphone sensors around my ears. Momentarily I think of my team, who are an unseen part of my landscape. Popeye is in the mobile command centre, somewhere in the bustle of the night, constantly testing for communication clarity. He's always a nervous wreck when we ready ourselves for a Scenario. Popeye's a perfectionist, and although his insistence can be a pain in the ass, he is a communications genius. He's been quiet for, oh five minutes after I'd told him to relax. The Scenario starts in fifteen minutes, and I'm close to our start point, so there's no rush.

I stroll slowly up Regent Street with Piccadilly behind me. I check my watch, aware that I'm approaching my rendezvous point. Right on cue Popeye does a comm-check.

'Having a leisurely stroll, are we?'

'Yeah, ETA three minutes.' I respond.

He ignores my optimism with good reason. Even with such meticulous planning we both know a thousand things could still go wrong, but what the hell. I'm in an enviable position. When Johnny Gigolo clocks in for his shift, he has no idea what manner of Frankenstein monsters he'll be whining and dining for the night. Whereas me, I can pick and choose the kind of clientele I accept.

If 69 weren't such a success, I wouldn't have that luxury, hence the main reason for the underground popularity of the business. I get to know my women through their dossiers; elaborate and honest profiles of their lives. When we meet, I'm already feeling them and my excitement is the genuine article. Everyone knows that the female psyche can spot the frauds from a hundred paces. Lumping me into that category would be bad for business.

Popeye gives me a Sit Rep; in clipped tones. 'The driver has just reported to me that he has POB. From what I can figure' traffic is a bit heavy but he should pass your point of entry plus, or minus two minutes from now.'

I check the digital display under the skin of my wrist and prepare. Positioning is everything if you want to avoid looking suspicious. I stand several feet away from some night owls waiting for a Black Cab to slide down the way with its available light on. These guys are in for a long wait. They're completely ignorant of who I am or why I'm there. I keep my eyes on the traffic lights, mentally reciting my operating list for the night while simultaneously eavesdropping on my companions. Out-of-towner's obviously. The Mexican meal was great, and they're about to catch Dr. Jekyll and Mr. Hyde at Shaftesbury Avenue.

Popeye crackles in my ear again. 'Remote-cam check?'

I adjust the micro-lense in my earring, raise my head and grin broadly.

'Smile!' I say to the group, flashing a pen that's not even remotely related to a camera. 'You could be in tomorrow's edition of the Evening Standard!' They huddle together presenting a portrait of a smiling, enthusiastic family, apart from the baby who looked somewhat uncertain. 'Brilliant!' From Master of Seduction to fake-ass paparazzi, I can do it all baby.

Popeye chuckles enjoying my little game with the tourists. 'Remote-cam, good. All systems online and by the way, your carriage awaits.'

I spot the gleaming body as it approaches. The limo idles to a stop at the traffic lights. Black and shiny glass like a hi-tech dildo, tinted and stretched to an abnormal length. At least I'm not boarding a floater. When your ass is five thousand feet from ground zero, amidst computer controlled airborne traffic, you need an entirely different sort of mental preparation for that. Thankfully this is by the numbers.

As soon as the lights change and the vehicle pulls away, I'm beside it. Ground car or not, we take no chances with our Scenarios. Everything is practiced to perfection, either virtually or on real life mockups. Ninety percent of the time the rendezvous are smooth thanks to Digital's exhaustive research.

It takes a particular kind of character profile to appreciate our rules, so we know our clientele well. Firstly, a vague warning that the game will be played anytime in a specified three-day period is communicated to the client or sponsor. The ambiguity is never a problem; the free-spirited women who return to 69, time and time again thrive on the element of surprise. Neither is the cost. Once we've fulfilled their fantasy and blown their minds, our five-figure fee becomes insignificant.

As the limo picks up speed, I casually try the door and feel it give. My stride becomes wider as the stretch accelerates. Two quick steps and the door is fully open. My right leg is on the step plate, I'm off the road and we're cruising at fifty miles per hour until the driver puts his foot down. I shimmy around the door - note: if I fall I'm fucked. I swing out slightly, duck down and gracefully take a seat in the plush leather, my jacket flapping in the wind, enhancing the illusion of risk. Like a classic martial arts master, I twine the offending material around my wrist and lap it under my thigh. I pull the door with my index finger and look away from it to focus on my client. In this business style is important. It only takes me five seamless movements to enter the limo. Gotta say it; I'm goddam proud of my work!

Phuck-kuk!

That is the sound of top marque engineering as the door locks, and then the outside world becomes silent.

The beautiful woman is on her mobile phone. She cuts her conversation short as I slither beside her, my hand placed gently over her mouth before she can squeal. The Sixty-Nine smart card materializes between the fingers of my right hand, a trick I picked up from magician brethren in LA. I place it flat on the arm rest and watch its underside light up like photon engines. Less than a second later the hologram blinks into existence. The image, which faces you from every angle, is that of an attractive, mature woman. Her whole demeanor screams authority. A department head, I surmise, who respects hard work. We listen to the personal message that now comes through.

'Fernanda, congratulations on securing the account with the three military Juntas in the Amazon basin. Our commission cheque should go a long way in saying job well done but this gentleman beside you is a token of our appreciation. Relax and let him treat you well, you deserve it.'

The eyes of the beauty beside me shine recognition, and her lips hint at a smile.

The energy cell depleted, the imagery collapses into itself like a genie sucked back into a magic lamp. Fernanda's eyes widen but then relax. Her mobile disengages exactly as the memory cell falls to the floor. Discreetly looking around I automatically ensure that my working environment is safe. I catch the chauffeur looking at me through the mirror. His cold grey eyes are hard, and I immediately dislike him. As I move towards him, he averts his gaze, not wanting a confrontation. I trip the switch, and he disappears.

Private party, homie and you ain't invited.

I drop the remote miniature camera to the floor and although I don't see it sprout spider-like legs, it will. And in its own time will crawl to an optimal position and record everything it sees. A memento of our exploits will be on micro disc for her at a later date. I get comfortable and shrug off my overcoat like a cobra shedding its skin. I scope the inside of the luxury carriage for the first time, but I pay the most attention to her. My surveillance routine seems drawn out but in reality, takes less than a minute.

Miss Fernanda Figueredo a Brazilian Commodity trader on secondment from Rio with Connaught, Younge, and Speakes. A woman who single-handedly pulled off one of the biggest financial coop's in the South American market this year but also a woman with important needs left unfulfilled. Her corporate perks mean that as well as a healthy bonus she finally gets her sexual fantasies realized.

I absorb everything about her. Long, golden brown hair and piercing brown eyes, the subtle mix of Indian and African heritage evident. Her short black evening dress made from bio-engineered material designed to cling to every delightful curve, has ridden up her thigh. My eyes linger on a platinum pendant that rests between her substantial cleavage, noticing with pleasure the rise and fall of her breasts as she breathes. It's a pity Digital hadn't been able to convey these sensory impressions over the Net.

Fernanda's smell is overpowering. A mixture of her natural scent and some mind-bending perfume that even I don't recognise. Her shoes land on my calves as she flicks them off. The supple leather of the seat easily accommodates her form as she reclines. I take charge reaching for two chilled glasses from the cabinet. I pop the cork on a bottle of Don Perignon and pour. My final touch is one of Fernanda's favourites; The Isley Brothers, courtesy of my memory stick that is already downloading the tunes.

"Play,' I say huskily to the AI and the sweet sounds ease through the speakers. Now I'm good to go.

The interior of the limo is infused with the sounds of classic soul. Moving in time to the soft beat I'm soon on my knees. I caress her waist then lift her further along the seat, and she's not a small woman, making sure she's comfortable. I watch her sip the champagne trying to ignore Popeye's squawking on my head rig.

'You okay?'

'Don't I look okay?' I whisper back. My hands drift under her black dress, sliding over her skin which is soft and smooth. My fingers come to her waist, and I snap her thong dragging it off. She's glistening wet and fragrant, gasping as my finger glances over her clitoris. My movements are slow and teasing.

'Okay, activating the remote camera,' Popeye is still talking. I look up and see the video's link light turn green.

'Remote is activated.' I confirm.

'Time?' He goes on, but I'm focussed totally on my client.

Carefully she removes the set from around my head and throws it to the side by my jacket. She kisses my neck and reaches into my slacks, trying to ease me out of them. She shudders when she touches the leather, her psychological associations now causing her to lose control. Fernanda's not interested in slow and considered foreplay. She wants me now. She reaches again into wonderland touching the legendary length and width in its erect glory.

Eventually, she exhales in a long husky-drawn out breath, and I'm content.

Coz that's what I'm about, customer satisfaction. Can't buy that dawg. The artist in me strives to be heard, but the uncultured cock's man is shouting just as loud; 'time now'. Fernanda's nipples push taut against her dress; warmth flows from between her thighs. She's ready. I gently turn her over and raise her dress using my finger nails to excite further the goose bumps on her booty. I ease into her slick tight kitty and, grinning like a Cheshire cat she hisses my greatness in Portuguese. I hope, for modesty sake, the cab is soundproofed, but somehow, I don't think she cares.

4.

LOCK N' LOAD

I'M ALWAYS LATE FOR MY MEDICAL. It's unusual because generally, I'm a punctual kinda dude, a discipline drilled into my head from my old lady and years in the Pen. Even when I was fleecing the rich bitches in Los Angeles, my jobs were carried out on time and to completion. Orgasm to order almost. Subconsciously I like to see Digital flap, but this time it couldn't be helped. I haven't replayed his message since he'd recorded it on Sunday. I'd been so busy I haven't had the time to listen to it in detail. I deal with my messages the same way I make love, slow and unhurried. Anyway, today I'm taking the time.

I request playback, and before Digitals regimental tones march through the air to my ears, he is upstaged by the tinkle of Jessica's voice dancing from the hidden speakers of my apartment. At the sound of her voice, I remember the saying: When the pupil is ready the teacher will appear. I've been lucky enough to come across some bona fide human beings in my time. People with good hearts ready to sacrifice without asking what's in it for them. Jessica was my most recent teacher who came to me from nowhere just when I needed her.

    I had just laid Ma Campbell to rest under her favorite mango tree at Burnt Savannah back-a-yard in Jamaica. When I returned to London, I was at the lowest point in my life. I couldn't bear the thought of being alone, so I dumped my bags in the apartment and was out through the door before my Home Avatar realized I was gone. I ended up at Paradise Child Club where I'm a member, and the manager is a friend. I knew the girls well and my compulsive need to be around beautiful women with very few inhibitions was always met there.

    I'd sat at my table nursing a glass of Cristal, trying nicely to repel the honeys, concerned friends really, who'd wanted to dance for me. The DJ dropped a hardcore R&B track, and I must admit, these new sista's knew the moves, but in my state of mind, they'd become little more than blurred background images. I don't know how long I was submerged in my little world of hurt, but when I came up for air I saw a vision of a young woman, slither down the pole and land in a very graceful split.

    Pow!

I was trapped in the warmth of her hazel eyes, and suddenly I'm calm and collected. No memories of Ma Campbell's funeral. Only peace. When I'd snapped back to reality, she'd exited the stage.

Shit.

Disappointment had flooded through me, and I'd sat there wishing I could recapture that feeling of safety, put it in my pocket and take it home. I thought I was the only one who felt it but moments later I felt her hand in mine gently pulling me from my seat. 'I'll dance for you,' she'd whispered in my ear. Her voice husky.

Chills ran up and down my spine, playa. Hey, I know what you're thinking. What happened to the professional detachment, this is supposed to be business, a financial transaction between two willing parties, right? But sometimes the mask slips and your humanness shines through. That was the moment when I showed my vulnerability. The dark-skinned angel shed the little she had on and danced for me like we were lovers. She laid my head on the silken skin of her stomach as I cried. Yeah, you heard me. I cried. We hugged and I'd told her how much I missed my best friend in the world.

Jessica had simply listened, allowing me the liberation of speech and when I was done she'd promised to call me every Sunday night after work. I left Paradise Child, a different man. I'd been touched by something unfamiliar yet significant. Now I had a yearning for more and for the last seven weeks Jessica has kept her promise.

I smile and focus on the road.

A gleaming black Bentley pulls out of the depot swinging out of my path just as I angle my Aston Martin into Digital's R & D headquarters. It accelerates before taking off into the sky lanes. I strain to see who's in the back seat but I can only distinguish a silhouette of a female. Strange. My mood darkens at the sight of a black unmarked van, oddly positioned across the road until I descend the drive and glimpse it pulling away through my rear-view monitor. Coincidence? Digital would never extend invitations to his research facilities or offices on a whim. I could rest assured whoever was here; they were supposed to be here. He disliked investors and hated banks, always complaining about their tendency to turn up as and when they wished. Digital's obsession with security and privacy wouldn't allow it.

So, who is the high-profile bitch visiting my man's crib and why am I edgy about someone I don't even know?

I accelerate towards the secondary gates which open on my approach. My senses are still spooked. I slide past the copper sculpture of an ancient Briton majestically stroking an awesome hard on and a laser light sculpture representing the company's logo. I'm eager entering Digital's little Shangri-la of innovation. I patiently submit to the phalanx of Biometric and standard security checks, the question of why I have finally been invited here still bugging me. I'd even tried some personal surveillance –

succumbing to my inquisitiveness - but his security blanket was extensive and covert. Not even the address was Global SatNav listed and Google's eyes in Sky could not monitor his comings and goings. And that playa took connections. The luxury car eventually disappeared from my view just as it dawns on me that if something was amiss, then the prime suspect has just disappeared into the bustle of L-Town. I lock the Aston Martin with the laser beep on my ignition key and hustle towards the shed noticing immediately that the car park is full. I'd expected to see Digital's Bentley floater squatting there on its lonesome. Sometimes I forget that he's the CEO of a multinational company, staff, and their cars included. I drift along the well-defined paths and islands of manicured grass following the directions of the holographic pointers. Suddenly an old Railtrack depot looms in front of me. It's been restored to sparkling functionality and is surrounded by greenery. Whoever designed this obviously had an appreciation for space and colour. It was positioned just beside the mainline with working manual points for trackside exit and entry. Its reconditioned rails and platforms were now there to make the working life of Steel Erection staff more comfortable.

I'm not sure where I'm going, and I don't care. I'm simply amazed by the old-school quaintness of this place. Ahead of me are three two-car carriages stabled on lines two, three and four, behind them a building four stories high with tinted glass and white brickwork, the classic nondescript architecture associated with mundane scientific research. My money is on Digital using the carriages for his R&D centres and personal administration. I follow my nose towards the sheds just as someone in a shirt and tie peeps out of one of the carriages and motions me over, must have seen me on hidden CCTV cameras. I keep my guard up because my twenty-twenty says things are not what they seem. Paranoia, you think?

Nah, playa.

I'm gifted with a highly-evolved preservation instinct. I've no idea why my innate early warning system is so acute, all I know is that when my twenty-twenty screams at me or gives me a gentle reminder I take note of its good advice. Like keeping my ass right here, outside of the office for a moment longer. After a second I hear Digital's voice from the inside.

'Are you coming in or what?'

I nod and step up.

Digital's PA, David Banks, ushers me through a scanner and into the main office. Dr. Marsden's bright-eyed boy is wearing a dark blue, fitted Valentino suit, his blonde hair highlighted, salon fresh, his gay poster boy looks more serious than his normally jovial attitude. I shudder when his hand inadvertently touches my shoulder. I'm cool with all the other staff, but this dude can immediately alter my mood for the worst and creeping me out in the process.

Superficially he's okay, apart from being too organised and efficient for my personal liking. There was just something about this cat I couldn't put my finger on. Whenever he was around Digital, I'd stare at him behind his back, hoping and waiting for him to slip up so I could be the one to bust his smooth ass down, but so far, he'd never put a foot wrong. Perhaps it was jealousy, after all, he does have access to areas of Digital's business which I'll never see. Whatever it is, I just don't trust the dude, never have, never will. I push those observations to the back of my mind and take stock of my surroundings.

I'd forgotten just how punctilious Digital is about his living environment. The orderliness of his workspace and his love for the finer things in life are self-evident as always. Genius requires all the trappings money can buy; he'd boasted, and you couldn't grudge a playa that. My eyes are everywhere, surreptitiously soaking in as much about my mysterious boss as I can. I'm drawn to two old school photographs which take pride of place in his display cabinet. The images speak volumes on how Digital dealt with the vagaries of life and death. Crammed with the snapshots are little mementos. A baby-grow, a small blanket, a rattle, and a teddy bear among other things. The smaller of the two images is a picture of Digital and his ten-year-old daughter in a park. They hug with broad smiles. The other image shows his deceased daughter as a baby and again as a young adult. Digital never stopped blaming himself and the bureaucracy of the drug corporations, who forced him to stand by helplessly while she suffered and then died at thirteen years old. The Heamophage had not just claimed another life, but one Digital felt he could have prevented. Now he makes recompense I guessed with this shrine created in her memory.

I turn to the old Oxford Don. He's integrating data from online into a virtual PowerPoint that everyone was raptly focused on. He glanced at me and showed me five fingers before smiling weakly and returning to his guests who're all seated across the room from me.

Three men in dark, sombre business suits mess up the ambiance with some ugly Karma. Popeye would empathize with me on this one. Suddenly everything takes on a murky, despondent vibe as my internal security system alerts me to danger entangled within these dudes.

My twenty-twenty goes into overdrive when my eyes rest on the big yellow nigger. Yeah, that's right, a hulking, African-Caribbean bro with yellowish bleached features. The other men revolve around the albino like he's got gravitational pull on them. They turn to him for constant approval of their contribution to the discussion. His Saville Row suit is designed and fitted to accommodate his big chest and thick dangling arms. His diamond-encrusted Rolex, single plain graduation ring his only jewellery. His manicured nails add a surprising finish to his thick fingers. This boy is working hard to dispel the image of being a thug, but his efforts are wasted on me. I can easily discern his true nature. He throws back his head and laughs with gusto, barring his teeth, the smile lingering for far too long. It's almost funny. This motherfucker is a gangster through and through, and no manner of cosmetic preening can hide that fact from me.

I want to hear exactly what they're rapping about but if I move any closer my intentions will be obvious. So, not wanting to appear rude I stand at a discreet distance and wait. I don't want this cat clocking my face, so I turn my back as they all shake hands and depart. He slides past me, the aroma of his cologne strong, the trail of his corrupt aura even stronger. I shiver but hold it together and wait until they leave the room before I throw my ass down in a muscular leather chair close to Digital's expansive desk. Numerous plaques and statuettes adorn one wall, scientific stuff, mainly for achievements in Human Physiology Modification. Very impressive, whatever the hell that is. The development and sale of innovative sex toys aren't such a massive departure from what he's used to. Sixty-Nine simply fills the gap while allowing him to keep shit real.

Digital navigates the smooth swirls of his desk, takes a seat and leans back, pressing his pointed fingers together and looks directly at me from his seat behind his desk.

'Looking good boss,' I open the conversation with sincere flattery.

'Feeling good Adonis. You looked surprised to be here.'

'Nah man. You know me, I'm not gonna start tripping because it's my first time in your domain.'

I'm lying of course, and he knows it. I want to ask him why those guys are here and if there's anything going on that I should know about; who the fuck was yellow nigger and what did he want. But I keep my mouth shut. If shit were serious he would tell me, right? Besides, we have other business to discuss.

'Let me explain what's on our agenda. First,' a thoughtful pause from Digital, '... your regular medical. Second, a gift from me to you and third, the new account that I'm excited about.'

'Where's Dr. Patel at?' I ask my face aglow. 'I'm forever thankful to you for headhunting her away from Harley Street dawg; you know that, right?'

Digital's brows go up. Not a good sign. 'Unfortunately, the good doctor is away for five weeks in Kashmir. Her replacement is the very accomplished Dr. Benson. Mister.'

Accomplished in what, I wonder. Motherfucker won't have an ass like my regular doctor, won't possess a size forty bust or smell of honeysuckle. He had a dick and was probably fit and gay. I'd been looking forward to being examined and tested by the single, Sikh princess with the healing hands. Giving blood and urine samples had always been a pleasurable experience. Digital's lips twitch at my obvious disappointment. I give him my poker face and wait. Maybe his mystery gift will redeem his sorry ass.

Digital pulls out an envelope from deep within his top draw and pushes it over to me. I stop it from sliding off the end of the table feeling the expensive clamminess of the paper, smelling the refinement of the fibre. I open it and extract a gold leaf card. Subtle colours in the form of hundreds of points of light twirl off the paper, regimentally forming a corporate logo which floats inches above the card. It's a formally worded invite to a pharmaceutical industry soiree being held downtown in two weeks. Digital outlines its importance. 'I've been invited by my peers to present an opening speech at their annual event, and I want to show you off to them. These are powerful people who can help you continue to grow especially after I've moved on to other things. Clear your diary.'

My guts tighten. We've talked about where I go from here on many occasions; like making me a partner and giving me more involvement on the management side of things. When I'd brought up the matter, he'd always said when I was ready he'd let me know. But it seems like he was going to make things happen now, not some hazy time in the distant future, funny but all I could think about was my son.

My solicitor had warned me that although prostitution was legal, the courts still held an old-fashioned view of it. For me to become joint guardian of Adonis junior I needed to be something more than a glorified sex worker. But what else could I do, that would fulfil my need for adventure and give me the lifestyle and security I'd grown so accustomed to?

Then it had dawned on me in the shower of all places. A partnership with Digital. Director would look good on my business card and maybe even have the power to impress the paternity judge. Now, with Digital's personal invitation my hard work could now be about to pay off.

'I'll be there.' Excitement threatens to explode within me, but I lock that shit down till it's well and truly under control. Digital's eyes mist over for a second, but then a smile emerges.

'Did you see that car leaving the secured compound when you came in?' I nod, he's still smiling. 'That charming woman being driven away is Ms. Lorraine Van Horne. She's on the board of one of the City of London's biggest scientific consulting firms. The gentlemen you saw when you came in are her associates. They've used Sixty-Nine in the past, but this is the first time they'll be using us as an incentive scheme for some of their top-flight employees. Times are changing Adonis rapidly, and I like to think that we're a lean, super adaptive animal that can thrive and survive in this economic jungle because we're able to evolve rapidly.' The passion flares in his eyes and the hairs on his head almost stand on end. My man is on fire. But he's preaching to the converted, his only disciple who truly believes in his brand of sexual capitalism. David the PA places a cup of herbal tea in front of him and offers me a glass of chilled fruit juice. I sip and keep listening.

'The women in the corporate world are powerful proponents of what we stand for. Barriers are lifting, inhibitions dissolving and we are poised to take advantage. Futurists had thought that sex robots would take the market share of our business. The uptake was enthusiastic, but many purists want flesh and blood. And if packaged correctly will pay a premium. This is our opportunity. But we still need to prove ourselves.'

'How?' I ask, eager to hear his solutions to anything that could stand in our way.

'When most people think of sex now-a-days they think of technology. They try to replace the human interaction and touch with some joyless, virtual reality, mind fuck machine or a mechanical contraption that provides a cold, impersonal orgasm. Much as I hated the trend. I knew there would always be users who would prefer flesh and blood. While the sex industry churned out the same vapid nonsense, Sixty-Nine would flourish. Do you know why?'

His question is rhetorical. I wait for him to continue.

'The human touch, Adonis. You. I've enhanced it with cutting edge technology and given it that all important missing sense of the romantic and adventurous. A stark difference to what is out there wouldn't you say? Our job is to construct fantasy scenario's which will swing the apathy of Lorraine Van Horne's staff and company.'

'What's she looking for?' I try to ask the right questions, aware that I'm being tested.

Digital drums his finger to some stupid-ass marching song playing in his head and then smiles, flicking his thick hair over his ears. He can sense my eagerness. The smug bastard knows me too well.

'Fortunately, your Brazilian client spoke highly of you to the right people, namely the female CEO of her company who's obviously passed on your praises to her colleagues. Ms. Van Horn knew exactly how she wanted it done and even wanted to take part to a lesser degree. So, armed with that information, I've constructed a feasibility model. Want to see it?'

'Hell yeah!' I say.

A 3D presentation unit rises from the belly of the desk. Photons arrange and a computer-generated image floats in space showing how one of five scenarios could go down. I watch in silence for a moment as the facsimile of me goes through its predetermined actions, and even in animation, I'm slick. Contrary to popular belief, self-praise is every recommendation.

'That's sick!' I say finally. 'I'm in.

5.

TEQUILA SUNRISE

I SIT IN MY CAR, THE MUSIC LOW AND I RECITE his shoe size, his clothes size, his class number, and then his teacher's name while I peer through the glass. I watch my son in the playground screaming his head off as he and his boys let loose and in my imagination, he's just materialized into the seat beside me.

'Your ass is grass!' I tease him in my mind as I continue to dazzle his five-year-old brain with my memory, winning the game we've invented together called, Guess What?

I smile because there is nothing else I can do except curse the day I had dealings with the Battersea bitch. His mother. How could she ever have left me? The man whose business is the pleasuring woman in the most creative ways possible? She left me. Not because I wasn't a good father, not because I didn't provide for my family. That would be a reason enough. But nah, It was the green-eyed monster of all things. Her jealousy fucked up a good thing, and now she's trying to punish me for her rash decision.

Yvette thought that if she kept us apart, Adonis Campbell II would forget about his old pops. Big mistake. What the bitch forgot I was in the operating room when the doctor's laser scalpel, sliced her at the navel and took him out. They wrapped him up like a loaf of bread and gave him to me. His eyes never left mine. How could she forget I took him to the nursery for the first time and at three years old Adonis reminded me to come back for him. Don't forget me, daddy. I'd cried. I would never forget the look of relief on his little face when he saw me. A connection like that is for life, dawg, a gift, but even that doesn't give me any consolation. Instead, I'm reduced to watching my flesh and blood in secret like some desperate pedophile.

Just after the break up with his mom I'd turned up at his school and explained the situation to him. Stuff like how I'd meet him at school because we didn't want to upset his mother. His teacher knew I was his father and everything was smooth. I didn't need to worry because my little man understood. He's always been wise beyond his five years. It was his teacher who let slip our little arrangement, and as soon as she found out, the crazy bitch slapped a restraining order on my ass. Met-1 threatened to electronically tag me if I was within three hundred yards of my boy, my brief was being paid a small fortune to keep them off my back, but still, I had to be careful. At least Yvette allowed me to rap with little man every week or so online.

In the time, it took my mind to dredge up the unsavory shit I'm going through, the play fighting in the school yard gets a bit rougher but Junior wards off kicks and punches just like I showed him, putting two of the little tearaways on their ass. In my heart, I bid him farewell.

Later, little man. I got some business to attend to.

False starts and fuck ups notwithstanding, I've always had the knack of being in the right place at the right time. 21st Century London brims with wonder and opportunity and on the cusp of all of that is where the big bucks lie. There's been a tangible swing in people's perception of how they're expected to live. Cancer was treatable. AIDS is now almost unheard of; except for isolated cases in the Deep South of Hallelujah Land – a major spanner in the works of Christian Conservative bible bashers who thought the US was blessed by the hand of God himself. Instead, a rampant blood disorder called the Heamophage – the same one that claimed Digitals daughter - was rearing its ugly head in Mega cities across the globe, attacking individuals with an unknown genetic predisposition for it. Family planning has become an exact science. Yow, for the right amount of credits, I can pick the colour of my baby's eyes or play with the uncertain science of improving my child's intelligence. Earth is a much smaller place with instant connectivity to any resource conceivable, and we are going beyond. Eve1 is the most luxurious holiday resort conceived, and it's positioned 35,786 kilometers from the earth in geostationary orbit. Our first manned expedition to Mars is already five years into its ten-year journey and as we relentlessly discover and conquer our down time becomes more important. And that's where I fill in the cracks for the female movers and shakers, Adonis Campbell at your service.

I'm crouched uncomfortably in an auxiliary computer room, a small space used by HVAC engineers and mainframe technicians to access vital systems that intersect at this point, making it an ideal area to run system diagnostics for the seventy-storey building. There is no way you could know this little cubby-hole even existed without detailed knowledge of the buildings schematics – of which I have access – so the chances of being disturbed are slim to none. I can do what I got to do without looking over my shoulders. Popeye, my operational support, is outside in the van twiddling his thumbs. Five-star establishments like these protect their privacy with religious zeal. They adopted state of the art technology borrowed from MI5 to deter electronic eavesdropping on guests. Consequently, my only means of contacting Popeye if anything went wrong would be a rock through his windshield from fifty storeys up. Digital won't know until the last minute what had happened. In the meantime, he'd be shitting cows underneath his calm, reserved exterior. Maybe that's why I'm all tingly.

The insertion was simple enough. Enter the room through the air ducts - leaving the hired hands at the entrance none the wiser. Then here's where it gets weird. The client has this fetish thing for secured areas. Digital's psychologists have already given it some psychobabble Latin name, I can't dredge up from my mind right now. I'm told the turn on is the fact that the client is bound and housed somewhere that seems impossible to break into.

With my Cristal, karats, and coochey lifestyle, there are still some things I will not do, not even if you offer me seven-figure digits. I'm about pleasure and entertainment, anything that crosses that line, and believe me it can be a thin line in this business, I question. Case in point dangles on the monitors in front of me.

The client's head is covered with a bondage mask; all cut eye holes and zipper where the mouth should be. She's bound in a rope that's been tied by an erotic Japanese knot master and suspended courtesy of a complex system of pulleys. I've been watching her for the last ten minutes, wondering what's on her mind as she swings in the metaphorical breeze. I've been told that when this specialized type of bondage is done by professionals, it's safe, looking at it makes me unsure. Practitioners of this freaky shit can orgasm simply from the fact that an intruder has broken into their home undetected. Thief, friend or murderer, it really wouldn't matter they'd cum anyway.

Chi-ching!

There's no turning back. The funds are already snugly deposited in Swiss accounts, and the client is ready for me to complete her fantasy. A scenario like this can't just be abandoned because you've suddenly acquired morals. It's not like I've got to free-fall from a helicopter, smash through toughened glass security shutters or use suction cups to scale the sheer face of a skyscraper. I've done stupid shit like that before, so this should be a walk in the park.

I crook my arm and check my watch, which is showing me the scene beyond where I'm hidden. Five minutes before I enter the room and do my thang, I see it - a splash of sweat. I'm on five times magnification watching the droplet dislodge from somewhere on the client's face and fall slowly, frame by frame.

Nah dawg.

Then it dawns on me. It can't be sweat. All the rooms are monitored to compliment body temperature, constantly adjusting to match the occupant's unique metabolism. Saliva maybe? Some people salivate when they're sexually excited, right? If I believe that, then I'll believe any goddamn thing.

I crawl my way along the familiar network of vents, and in moments my face is pressed against the grill peering into the darkened bedroom. I flick on the twin lights, attached to my headgear and substitute fear with enthusiasm. I force myself to breathe easy. I reach for my hip pouch, fingering my multi-purpose tool and power it to life. It squeals weakly, and I undo the screws in the four corners of the grill. A moment later I'm inside back against the wall checking the place out.

Its times like this that I'm thankful I did as Mama said and ate my vegetables. My eyes adapt quickly to the darkness, my pupils dilating to make the most of the available light. The schematic of the suite flashes through my mind, and I waste no time finding the bedroom. But for reasons I couldn't explain the eagerness suddenly evaporated and it's as if I'm struggling through a field of molasses my feet straining against imaginary tendrils of sticky sweet stuff that eventually brings me to a stop. I'm standing outside of the door for fuck knows how long, the concentric grains in the real wood standing out like an artist's finishing touch. Something is not right. My twenty-twenty is humming expectantly in the background having Shanghaied my motor neuron system and brought me to a stand. The hairs at the nape of my neck are at attention, and although I may not be in immediate danger, something is up.

I place my palm on the touch pad; the door opens, and I step into the twilight zone.

The room is how it was twenty minutes ago, on the CCTV. I stand rooted at the doorway noticing a faint coppery smell mingled with a floral essence. I'm surprised that my ability to distinguish the fragrances is so acute, but I let that revelation slide. I walk over to the centre of the room, my panic level rising although I can't put my finger on the reason, I'm spooked. I figure the client must have heard the door slide open so why is she unresponsive?

The coppery smell is more pronounced now, making my stomach turn. I look down as though trying to see inside my guts but my eyes scope the floor. You remember the drop of sweat I was freaking out about on the monitor, the one I thought was saliva? It's not saliva dawg, but blood, her blood. Sticky crimson Claret drips from a gash to the client's throat. Now I'm fucking freaking out, and the sensible thing would be to abort this shit and go. But for some unknown reason, I reach for the mask and peel it off inch by inch trying hard not to touch the blood or her cold skin. Perhaps if I see the client's face, I'll understand what went down here. Maybe the eyes would reveal something to me, but in the meantime the chill hand of ominous expectation was nudging at me, scratching at the inside of my skull for attention. The gimp mask falls away from the head, and a tangle of long dark hair falls out. My heart surges in my chest like an ocean breaker, and I freeze for an eternity.

Jesus H Christ, no, Jesaaaas! I stumble backward like I've been pole-axed. An awful recognition came screaming up from some dark place inside of me, a horrific reality my conscious mind did not want to acknowledge existed. My thoughts evaporate into nothingness. Rationale and reason depart me as I lose my ability to speak and move.

M..

A bruised and beaten body.

Ma....

A cruel red smile ripped into her throat.

Mar.....

A fucking bullet to the head.

Maria.

My Maria.

My legs collapse, and I hit the floor shaking like I'm a junky in withdrawal. My tongue flaps loose in the cavern of my mouth. I think I'm sobbing, but I don't know for sure. I can just hear a pathetic whimper that felt as if it was being fed into this drama from someplace else. From someone else but it was me.

Oh God, no! Maria, here? Jesus fucking Christ it can't be! I look at the tortured corpse again. The stats of the woman who should have been here is reeling through my head. I'm on my knees, my shoulders heaving, the contents of my guts deposited in front of me with whips of bile and saliva hanging from my lips. I look up hoping I'm wrong but the nightmare persists. Christ no! I wipe my sour mouth with the back of my hand. We were going to meet tomorrow for lunch, spend the evening together, make love...

I'm trembling all over; my vision tunneled, and my sense of balance has seen better days. I try in vain to undo the knot holding her, but it's too complex, so I just slice through it with my knife, a knife I don't even remember picking up.

Lights! I scream, and my gloomy hell turns a brilliant yellow. I position myself under her body as it falls, gently lowering my lover to the floor. My eyes cloud with tears; I place my fingers firmly over her carotid artery hoping for a miracle, but none appears.

She's dead.

And the only thing keeping me grounded was the prickly nerve-jangling alert of my twenty-twenty lighting up my ass and imploring me to leave. The trigger for my sudden alertness is beyond my comprehension; I was alone. Maybe some level of danger outside of my awareness, a signal from Met-1 or the killer returning to the scene of the crime. Who knows?

I jump up from my kneeling position, my physiology already decided for or against fight or flight, and I make my way out of the bedroom. My eyes are drawn to the blood on my hands, the only thing I have left of her. Reluctantly I wipe it away on the front of my slacks. Muscles bunched, teeth gritted, I turn in time to see the front door vibrate and then begin its opening sequence. One dude silently wiggles through and takes cover in the lounge area. I see fingers clasp the door from the other side and I think just can't afford for his partner to squeeze through too. I estimate the distance between me and the door to be about fifteen meters in a smooth arc and I lock on to it.

I explode like I'm coming out of the blocks at a world class athletic meet, head down; sprinting with every ounce of strength I can muster. I'm an arm's length away when one man slips through; homeboy shows his head and shoulders just as I kick the door shut. Wood slams into flesh and blood with a bone-crunching impact, eliciting a long drawn out grunt as if he was clearing his bowels from a bout of constipation then nothing. I use my heel to try and clear his unconscious body from the door. But he's heavier than he looks, so I lower myself to lever him out of the way.

I flinch as something rips the fabric of the air above my bald head.

I hear an angry crackle and the space where my head had previously been exploded into a spray of superheated splinters. This unconscious cocksucker had just saved my life. I blow him a kiss of gratitude and look up at the smoldering hole. They're using plasma weapons, the sole reserve of the military instead of the standard metal jacketed ordinance, leaving me at a distinct disadvantage.

I frisk the asshole on the deck, admiring his weapon which I've snatched from his shoulder holster like I've got time on my hands! Another volley rips into the door frame and adjoining wall threatening to peel my skin from my bones, and I drop to the floor on my hands and knees scuttling backward. My ears ring from the awesome report and the smell of ionized air irritates my throat sending me into a spasm of coughing. Bracing myself, I realize that with all this mayhem going on I never checked the environs outside where there more of these guys targeting my ass. The corridor is in darkness as all lights had been disabled, but I could only guess the room was situated at a junction with multiple access points because of where the slugs had impacted. I give it the green cross code. Look right, clear. Look left.........Shit.

Company.

Busting the corner is; surprise, surprise, Yellow Nigga. Two men to either side of his broad shoulders, all three with their guns at the ready, casually strolling my way. As soon as they see me and their felled partner, their heaters rise. I think fast. The corridor is about to get hot but inside the room is hotter. At least from the inside, I can probably find a way out. I half slide, half dive back into the maelstrom to be greeted by more heat seekers, itching to incinerate my sorry ass from the wankster in the lounge. I'm about to be severely outnumbered and outgunned as I roll for cover. Out of the corner of my eye, I notice hit man drawing out from behind an ornate lounger back into view. Sheathing my nuts in steel, I pimp walk steadily in his direction my plasma gun aimed at where I'd last seen his head.

Fuck dis, I'm the impatient type. I ain't got time to wait for him to show himself. I fire my weapon high and low, left to right, the sweeping superheated pellets punching through the prefabricated walls like they're Kleenex. Paint peels and bubbles as the plaster is pulverized, the once tasteful decor blown to hell in a hand basket. I keep on taking his silence and the repugnant stench of burning flesh as an indication that he's been hit.

Behind me, Yellow Nigger barks orders. I picture them, like the three stooges, trying to enter the room at the same time, the bubble bursting as I hear feet on broken glass. I'm up and into the Air vent like a chimpanzee, only my head visible as I turn back to look. One end of the grill is attached; the other screw is waiting for my attention, but I'm fixated with the surreal picture. Questions crowd my mind, threatening to burst and haemorrhage out through my skull. But one thing in all that confusion takes centre stage.

Protocol DEADBOLT.

The one thing that I would never have thought, I would need. Digital had insisted from day one, that it was required for a worst-case scenario, I just thought his upper-class upbringing and his life's journey had made him paranoid. Now I understand. I reach for a clip at my back and undo it. The thermite bomb feels cold to my touch. It's what it can do that makes me hesitate.

Maria is still in there; I'm thinking.

I file away the memory of her in vibrant life, trying to erase the horror I left behind and depressed the button on the bomb. I take one last lingering look before tossing it inside and closing the vent. I scuttle away from the impending explosion.

Popeye watches my frantic gait approach the driver's side of the van, looking at me as if I'm Met-1's most wanted. I glimpse the shadow of my former self in passing a wing mirror and understand why. My body language speaks volumes about my recent fear and shock. I weave my way through cars in the guest's parking space. Popeye's parked as inconspicuously as is possible for a black transit van. The blood drains from his face, and he tenses as I draw up beside him, watching me mumbling incoherently.

'We're fucked.' I open my mouth to elaborate, but I'm lost for words. 'We are royally fucked, dawg.'

The big man checks his watch and attempts to step out of the van, but I raise a trembling hand to stop him.

'There's CCTV cameras in the lot, stay hidden.'

'What's up man?'

A messed-up part of my psyche thinks that this shit is hilarious. Where do I even start to answer Popeye's question?

'Cuz, we in a world of shit.'

He waits for clarity, his mouth wide open. I give it to him raw. 'Client's dead, man. Murdered and they tried to waste my ass in the process.' His eyebrows rise as if pulled up by invisible fish hooks.

I pause for what feels like an eternity, an image of Maria floating to the forefront of my mind. Then I lose it. My knees buckle, and I crumple onto the driver's door, almost denting the paint work. A burden of grief like a ton of bricks fucks me inside and out. I sob uncontrollably, a rising nausea threatening to bring me further down. I bang my head on the window frame expressing grief and sorrow in my own personal ritual. Popeye waits, staring as if he's expecting me to say, got yah!

'What the fuck man! Calm down. What's going on?' The welts on my forehead tighten as blood rushes to my head. Popeye's big hands cushion the blows as I continue to slam my head between metal and glass. 'Get your shit together boss!' The big man is frantic in a way I've never seen before. Hell, he's never seen me so spazzed out before either.

Clarity slowly forces its way through my synapses. I straighten up, my gaze gradually becoming clearer. My throat hurts when I speak it feels like I'm chewing broken glass. 'Digital.......have you hooked up with him in the last hour?'

Popeye shakes his head, totally confused. 'I thought that was weird, but all his lines are dead.'

I pause to gather my buck wild thoughts. 'I tried to contact him on the fly but nothing either.' My stomach tightens with the realization of what was happening here.

'What do you want me to do?' Popeye asks, his fear a treacherous ice-slick road that he had to steer with the utmost care and respect.

'Keep trying, when you do get him, tell him to be careful. I'll be in contact.'

Popeye's lips quiver with nervousness. I can see the questions burning in his mind. 'Who did this to us, man?'

'I don't know, but I know we're all in danger. You've gotta leave London straight away. Meet me in Manchester. Remember the Carlton Towers? Forty-eight hours from now. In the meantime, don't even try to contact me.' I look deep into Popeye's eyes, signaling him to hold down his resistance to my plan along with his many unasked questions. 'Just trust me.' He nods then guns the engine. I walk away before he drives off, the screech of tires behind me followed by the banshee squeals of the hotel's fire alarms.

I should be alarmed, but I'm not, as I've done enough to destroy any DNA traces of me ever being there. I clutch the micro-disc from the evening's recordings and merge with the guests evacuating the building.

6.

CUNNILINGUS

I'M STILL NOT SURE HOW THE HELL I even got here. My memory is fragmented like shattered pieces of stained glass window. Lights, horns, the interior of my car, phone calls, ringtones, electronic voice messages and then... here. Some things trickle back, like making calls to the few people I trust and no-one being available.

My subconscious struggle for answers has led me to Michelle. A solid rock who'd be there for me while also giving me much needed space to get myself through any crisis. Much as I didn't want to burden her I just couldn't face the thought of being alone. I didn't want to go back to my pad or any of the vacant properties I owned, not yet. The only other alternative was to find a hotel, but that was not such a good idea either. To book in, they'd need my details, the system automatically cross-referencing my stats. The hotel would have digital footing of a ghost entering or leaving their establishment, remember my dog tag renders my slick ass invisible to any electronic recording. Hell, I might as well walk into Five - O and hand myself in. What I need is neutral ground away from any prying eyes until I can know for sure what I'm up against. Time to get myself together and Michelle, a lady with a keen mind housed in the body of an athlete, would understand. I had to shake off this cloud surrounding me so when I see her, I can construct a bullshit story that's plausible but not accurate.

Images of Maria oozing her lifeblood all over the glass floor play on a grotesque loop in my head. And every time my mental projectionist plays it I crumble, a feeling like pieces of me being torn from the body politic and flung to the flies. Scornfully extracted and flung to the wind without a care. It was a terrible image trapped in a freeze frame just for me, a torment for every waking second until I learn to deal with it or I destroy myself. I lean on the wall of the corridor sobbing again. My world is caving in on me, the burden of questions is threatening to put me down on my ass and leave me there. But Miss Campbell's one son is made from sterner stuff than this. I wipe away the tears and stand upright just as Michelle's front door sniff's me out and belts out a funky chime. I catch sight of my reflection in a nearby pane of glass. My eyes are red, and I brush off traces of dust from my outfit. I shift uneasily hoping that the chinks in my armour aren't too apparent. A quick bath and a change of clothes and I'll be good to go I try to tell myself, but I know it won't be so easy.

A shadow flits inside, and the door opens. A man stands at the door unmoving, one hand in his gym slacks fondling his nuts and posing as if he's expecting me to take his photo.

He's wearing a pristine white wife beater he has no hope in hell of ever filling out, even with Steroid treatments, a white gold chain around his Popeye scrawny neck and long spindly arms that end in the most elegant male hands I'd ever seen. This motherfucker had been shy of hard work for years.

Your turn, I think giving him time. He eyes me leisurely, finishing off his appraisal with a growl which comes from the back of his throat. I half expect him to strut around pissing in the dirt to mark out his territory but remains the 21st century. His attempts at keeping his expression neutral fail when his hooded eyes flood with suspicion and his guard flies up like a security shutter. Whoosh! Too late motherfucker, I've already got your ticket. His body language is fucking him up big time, but I act unawares and patient.

'Waddup homie. Michelle, is she around? I'm a friend,' I explain.

'She's sleeping,' he replies. 'What is it?'

I didn't like him, and I don't like his tone, hell I don't like the air he's breathing. 'I just need to talk to her, partner.' My voice is hollow.

Michelle's new man realizes I'm not moving. 'Hold on.' He goes back inside. Homeboy takes longer than I expect. In the meantime, I overhear conversation that's not meant for me; Michelle's voice, his agitated bass tones. Short bursts of conversation like gunfire, then nothing. Some strange shit is going down. Soon after, homeboy returns, a hint of amusement on his face. 'She's asleep,' he drawls. 'And I don't think she wants to be woken up.'

He's either fucking with me or homeboy's a retard. Michelle doesn't want to talk to me? I take a step towards him but then catch myself.

Calm the fuck down, Adonis.

So, Michelle hasn't truly forgiven me despite all her chat about remaining friends. I'd explained to her, sat her down and thrashed out the reasons why an intimate relationship would be complicated, why it wouldn't work, and at the time she'd been in full agreement.

Bullshit. Girlfriend had been waiting for the right time to sting me, and I'd just provided her with the ideal opportunity. The numbness envelopes me again soaking up the hurt, but I can still feel the chill hand of betrayal. The same pain that I had meted out to women in the past had just come back to bite me on the ass. Karma, motherfucker. I want to lash out and smash the self-assured smirk from his comic book face, but I just nod and muster a sour smile acknowledging the irony of this shit. I hobble, or maybe I stumble, by now I'm past caring back out into the streets where it feels safer.

I sit up and stare wide-eyed into the darkness, sweat moistening my face. I inhale the smell of my panic ground in with fear and vomit. An overpowering amalgamation of smells that overcomes my aftershave. I'd needed to get off the streets. That's why I'm here. It comes flooding back to me along with aching muscles, a pounding head, and desert-dry mouth. I'm parked in the shadows at the back entrance to Paradise Child Lap Dancing Club. The digital timer in my car tells me I've been here for about three hours, drifting in and out of sleep, tormented by feature-length nightmares, crammed into minutes of disturbed shut eye.

But despite my hazy state of mind the decision to be here is a calculated one. The shock is subsiding and I'm regaining clarity, or so I keep telling myself. It's hard to concentrate, but I keep my eyes fixed on the building across the way. My mind wants to stop and examine what's happened, to get answers and work out just what the fuck is going on. At some point, I'll have to obey the demands of my very soul but not now, some other time, partner. I punch in a Refresh Program into my onboard computer, letting it scrub the bad smells and possibly the bad Karma from the car's interior. I scrub up with some Antibacterial wet wipes while I watch.

Fluorescent lights flicker on illuminating the yard throbbing to my pain. The secured door opens outward, and two young women step out into the crisp night. I'm so close to the passenger window that the glass fogs when I breathe. I can't let her disappear without seeing me, not even an Aston Martin can compete with a soft, warm bed. I need to be with someone tonight, not necessarily in the same bed, hell, just the same house will do.

I stare unblinking, trying to recognize someone I'd only seen once in person but many times on my Smartphone. I'm sure I'll recognize her, even if it's on some level that I can't explain.

More girls exit. Suited and booted bouncers scan the area making sure everything is everything. Cars pull up whisking away girls while others walk to the main street. A car horn beeps and then I see her, Jessica, arm in arm with some dude. My heart sinks.

So, I'm still feeling like a pussy assed wuss.?

This is one homeboy getting in touch with his feminine side, my frailties showing up like pubescent acne. Maybe my Aston Martin will be my bed for the night after all when the guy peels off from her with a kiss, waving goodbye as they go in opposite directions, leaving behind a lush oasis of hope for a tired ass traveler in need of water and shade. You don't have to tell me twice. Like a man on fire, I'm out of the car and jogging up behind her.

'How about a lift home angel?' My voice is calm, taking even me by surprise. The old senses kick back in, bringing with them my normal sexy demeanor.

Jessica stops. Her shoulders relax, and she smiles with her whole body. She turns to me and takes me in her arms.

'How are you?'

'Not good, angel.' I can't lie. 'Goddamn it, not good at all.'

She shivers a little. 'We can work it out.' Her voice is so hopeful, pumping my numb and dreary ass with a much-needed dose of optimism.

Wordlessly I give thanks, but this is going to be a cocksucker to work out. I feel it in every fibre of my being. This shit is going to test me, from head to mo' fucking toe.

I'm still holding her, not wanting to let go. She smells of fresh flowing rivers and aromatic plants. I remember Pop-eye's words and they bring new meaning to all this shit;

Are you thankful, homes? I'm thankful, man. I owe her a piece of my sanity. Now it's my time to exhale.

7.

THE HITCH

I AWAKE. SWEATING, WOUND UP TIGHT, AFRAID that my nightmares have opened the door and invited in my terrors to put up their feet and stay awhile. I breathe steadily; clean air in, stale air out. In moments, a reassuring reality settles over me like a freshly laundered sheet as I realize that my fears have no power, it's the meat and grizzle of the human Wraiths that I had to worry about.

I'm safe in Jessica's spare room, and if it weren't for the fact that I instinctively trusted her, I would have thought she'd drugged me, but all that had been administered was a comfortable bed and a warm and cosy spare room. I'm rested, aching and still a little fuzzy round the edges but my energy levels are high. I look around for my watch, finding it on the side table. Jesus! More than twenty-four hours have passed since I parked up outside

Paradise Child. Jessica would have left to go to work by now.

I spring up, a fresh wave of questions bombarding my mind, I let them churn away in the background. I ding Digital from my V-Comm, auto-dialling all his numbers, including the scrambled ones, but coming up blank every time. This is not like him. I cast around for solutions. Maybe I need to be more hands on in my approach.

The streets are calling, nigga.

My clothes are folded neatly on the back of the chair, smelling fresh with an attached note: 'Food is in the refrigerator, and there's a swipe card for the front door. I hope we can talk some more, later.'

I push naked into the hallway. Jessica brings a smile to my face, not an easy job considering the circumstances. The floor is warmed by convection pipes, eliminating the need for slippers. Jessica's flat is small but orderly; a near miracle when you consider that she has a kid. I step on a cuddly toy and wonder if I've inconvenienced her baby by taking its room for the night. I sit the toy neatly in the sofa thinking of Adonis junior. The colour scheme is bright and breezy with a hint of lavender in every room. Jessica loves metal; sculptures, appliances and decorations. You would have thought it would make the place cold, but far from it, this was a place of heartfelt the warmth.

In the shower cubicle, I switch the wall monitor to local London news. I punch in a vigorous bath program, and breath deep when jets of water blast my body from every angle. Hot water streams down my face obscuring my view of the Tele-Vid while the splash of the water makes it impossible to hear what's being said. I move my dripping fingers over the sensors, and the volume amps up. The weather is mundane as always; only the weather girl makes it interesting viewing. Seems like she's putting on weight in all the right places, or maybe, her flesh augmentation surgeon is giving her a helping hand.

I wait for breaking news about Maria's murder but instead there's just a litany of the usual work disputes, armed robbery, and domestic homicides. I skip backward a day for the recorded news headlines. Nothing. Not even a report on a fire at the downtown Sheraton.

It's a cover-up, big time and if anybody has the resources to do that, the mega corporations do. They always get what they want, one way or another. Gentle persuasion or out and out terrorism. Governments are losing their grip around these monsters who dictate policy, poised to become both judge and executioner. Once the drying cycle is through, I step out, suit up and hit the town.

I run my shit differently as you must have already gathered by now. And if you want me to function at my peak - and that dear friends are a beautiful thing to behold, I need to be back on form. Maria's memory deserves no less. My mind is shredded, and that is a given and returning to a state of calm, I know is gonna be a lifetime struggle, but I can function. Meditation will help, but a cold, primitive focus was icing through me that I'd never experienced before. A rage that was distorting that easy-going self-image I had of myself from the inside and was snarling all the way from my gut to the light of day. I was wound tighter than a street hooker in a rented fur, and you know the streets can be a bitch. I need to be loose as a goose and ready to take shit on when it confronts me. I can't let the hollowness creeping through me win. I can't let the void that I'm fighting to keep at bay suck me in because I'd be done. And I ain't going out like a punk, dawg. Fuck that. The tears could flow, and the grief could double me up like an uppercut to the guts, but I would do what I had to do.

The Pink Lotus is one of London's secret treasures shared only with my closest homies. Madam Butterfly wouldn't appreciate too many rough ass niggas traipsing round Notting Hill trying to find her. Three naked girls work my six-foot-three-inch frame. Petite little things from Thailand, small in stature, very pretty with powerful soft hands. I always tip well in appreciation of their intriguing Eastern bedroom tricks and in return they alone pamper me. Phen has my head neck and shoulders, Fran, my chest and dangly bits and Saku my legs and feet. Tenderly they manipulate muscle tissue that had become tense and unresponsive after its recent trauma. I drift into total relaxation as they rub their oiled and naked bodies all over me. I start to stir too, always a good sign. The incense stick burns. String music hums in the background. The lights are low, and I drift for what feels like a long moment successfully navigating the unconscious dark rapids leading to the re-enactment of Maria's murder. I know I'm close to full charge then my bubble of relaxation goes Pop!

Suddenly I'm snapped back into wakefulness! My nerves explode as if two-forty volts have just been pushed up my ass. I roll off the bed and fall to my knees, taking the girls with me, my twenty: twenty successfully gaining my attention and pulling my focus into sharp perspective. I snap straight into my boxers pose and wait for shit to get real. My vision is heightened by fear, and now I see the men who've entered the room without a sound. Three, tall, identical, silhouettes, their hands clasped in front of them, reflective sunglasses hiding their true expressions. I guess them to be Chinese. Lead dude wears his red Mohican with impeccable style, one step ahead of his tough looking, neatly groomed charges.

I shuffle back, adjusting my stance like I'm in the ring. The ladies have long gone, rightly sensing that this confrontation is a 'dick thang'. I'm poised, fists up, dick swinging, racking my brains about why they're here, hoping that if they want to tussle, it'll be with fists and not the titanium carbide meat cleavers they've made infamous in settling beef.

'What can I do you for, homies?'

They glare at me.

'English not your first language. I can dig that. Let me say this slowly. What the fuck do you want?' I flex my shoulders, but they make no threatening moves towards me. Maybe they can rock my ass in their own sweet time. I wink at the guy in the black Christian Lacroix suit. The muscles around his eyes twitch uncomfortably. Little does he know I'm figuring to take him out first before working the other two guys with my fists and with the aid of that copper Buddha on my right. I probably won't get past the first man without a weapon, but hell I'm an optimist.

The icebreaker comes from the guy with a dragon tattooed on his neck and a face that seemed to be forged from wrought iron. 'Mr. Chen wishes to have an audience with you Mr. Campbell.' He snorts. Damn. Perfect English. These boys are local talent and haven't been shipped in from Hong Kong or mainland China, after all.

'Mr. Chen, huh.' I say, as if I know this nigga from around the way. 'Who the fuck is Mr. Chen and what does he want with me?'

They ignore my question and motion to the outside. The Triad aren't the most talkative of gangbangers they approach business and conflict with a directness that was comforting. If they wanted my nuts in a fortune cookie, they would have tried with no fanfare or remorse. Even my twenty-twenty considered the threat level acceptable as it overcame their initial arrival.

So, I dress in super quick time and gesture to the door, 'age before beauty,' reluctantly forming the meat of the sandwich between two heavy set Chinamen with expressionless faces. I step out into the damp night wondering what all this has got to do with me. Guess I'll know soon enough.

I sit at the back of a Jaguar sandwiched between the two Happy Mondays, the third one our chauffeur for the night. My mind churns with a million questions, but I resist trying to work them out. I'm in the mood to be spoon fed some answers for a change. After twenty minutes of speedy driving, we stop, and I'm led inside an Italian Bistro in Paddington. Fear becomes anticipation although I'm not sure why. The restaurant is dimly lit with round tables covered in chequered blue cloth and adorned with lighted candles. Very cozy. I make a note to check this place out with Maria, and suddenly I'm hurting all over again, and I feel as if life has suddenly lost its gleam. A cold fury wells up inside me. I want to focus on the job at hand not go gallivanting at the beck and call of every villain in town, but my intuition was telling me to chill there was something significant to this, so I roll with it. Funny,

I'd imagined these guys would be eating at a Chinese Restaurant, somewhere in Soho. It seemed like I'm wrong on all counts.

I approach Mr. Chen who's as well dressed as his cohorts, a white napkin down the front of his shirt, slurping on tomato coated spaghetti. His hair is pulled back into a ponytail, Manchu style, reminding me of Alexander Fu Sheng from the old Shaw Brother movies. Chen is smooth faced and handsome but carrying an aura of world-weariness and concealed cunning. He's battled hardened, but his scars only show in his leonine eyes. I estimated his age to be in his mid-thirties and even as his attention was engrossed in enjoying his meal; he exuded a quiet intensity. He swallows a mouthful of food and sips from a glass of red wine, motioning me to sit so I take a load off, not sure where to put my hands; on the table, in my lap, behind my head? Fuck it. I lay them on the table. He's obviously enjoying his meal, but his intense stare as his eyes meet mine, tells me he's not happy.

'Nice place,' I try to make conversation although those aren't exactly the words I want to say. 'Listen G,' I try again, 'I don't know you or how you found me, but you've caught me at a really bad time.'

'Adonis Campbell,' he said without looking up his voice modulating to comfortable timbre that was laced with steel and flavoured with a Hong Kong accent.

I nod and chew on my lip.

'Timing is everything Mr. Campbell and the bad time you refer to could get considerably worst.'

I'm already on edge and threats from this Fu Manchu motherfucker aren't helping. I stand, the screech of wood on floorboard a fitting introduction to the soundtrack of my departure.

'Maria was my sister and I want to know who killed her.' Chen drops the bombshell.

I swallow ponderously suppressing the shock of his announcement with the chutzpah of a poker shark. Now he's got my attention I start thinking. How the fuck does he know? Does he blame me for what's happened? I slump back into my chair any plans for pretence falling away with my initial plan of action. 'How did you find out and how do I know that you are who you say you are dawg?'

Chen takes another sip from his wine. 'Look into my eyes Mr. Campbell and tell me if I look like someone, who cares about your questions?'

I'm on my feet again, walking, but with the distinct feeling, they don't want me to go, yet. A hand that feels like ten pounds of pulverized granite slaps down on my shoulder trying to sit me back down. I grimace as he pinches the nerve in my neck and numbness envelopes one side of me. Once upon a time I'd be impressed with that bullshit, and he'd have had me at a disadvantage, but my threshold for pain has risen immeasurably since those days.

I kiss my teeth and reach for his fingers. Without even looking I twist, and the pressure eases. Next, he gets the full attention of the back of my fists as I windmill to face him. His head whips away ejecting globules of saliva, the blow twisting his upper torso violently the way his face goes, but he's still with me. I'm on him before he can adjust and the left hook connects to his jaw toppling him but my right puts that sucker on his knees. One more thunderous right plants his ass into the floorboards and blood drips from his busted lip. I turn to see if there are any more takers but nobody had moved from their positions.

Chen eyes me with intense scrutiny nodded as if he was gauging my reaction to threat and how I managed it. I fling him a look of scorn and in return receive a look of sorrow borne out of that pitiful hollow vibe that surrounds him. 'English born Chinese,' he says. 'No respect for the disciplines of the past and the old ways.' His criticism isn't enough to shame me into thinking I didn't whup his homies ass fair and square. 'We need to find her killers, Mr. Campbell.'

'We mo' fucker?' My voice sounded unfamiliar to my ears, vacant and listless as if my emotional batteries had run low. 'Whatever I do, I do alone.'

'What makes you think you can handle this alone Mr. Campbell? And why do you think I'm giving you a choice.'

'Listen, man; you do what you got to do and just leave me the fuck out of it.'

'Maria talked about you, talked about your son with such fondness. I pictured you differently, thought you would be the one to make what they did to her right, make it personal, a man of honour.'

The poignancy of his statement stings my eyes and shoots my heart with the molten lead of grief. I let him keep on coz my throat is dry and unresponsive.

'She was my only sister,' his voice lowered, the raw edges of anger self-evident. The youngest of our family. Try to imagine how I will tell the elders, how I will explain her murder.' Everything about this man screams a contained force of righteous indignation. I just wasn't sure if it was motivated by love or tradition.

'How come during the four years I've known Maria she never once talked about you?'

'How much did you know about Maria yourself?' He counters and I know he was right. Maria's life was a pleasant mystery, her death a gut-wrenching puzzle.

'What do you expect from me if you have all the answers?' I figure it's a reasonable question.

'She kept many secrets from her family. You were the exception.'

'Who are you fuckers?' My tone tells him I'll only accept a straight answer.

Chen removes his napkin from around his neck and stands up presenting me with his full, imposing stature.

He flaps the crumbs off a spotless napkin before folding it with annoying accuracy. He places the neat, fabric square beside his plate. 'We are the Dragon Syndicate,' He ends his pronouncement with a satisfying nod.

My smartass quips slam to a halt and my stomach twists into knots at his confirmation of what I feared most. I know just who these guys are and just what they can do. Electronic extortion, robbery, contracts and prostitution. Very few crime organizations can compete with their viciousness and efficiency. Stateside we called them the Tongs, here they are the Triad and outside of the 'Spear of the Nation' they were some hardcore niggas.

'Okay your credentials are hardcore, what do you need me for.'

'I have let down my sister before Mr. Campbell,' he murmured. 'I failed her. Not supporting the passion, she felt for things not associated with what was expected of her. Maria was taught independence and when she exercised that independence the family turned their back on her. I reacted like my father believing her destiny was only with the family. My sister left to live her life in isolation from us.'

Chen stood rigid, his eyes closed for a moment then slowly opening again he stares at me.

'She was family Mr. Campbell and I loved her. No matter what the elders thought of her decisions I understood her I just wasn't strong enough to admit it. When my business interests demanded my permanent presence in London, it was as if it had been ordained. I made certain

Maria was under regular surveillance not because of her safety but because I could maintain some contact with her albeit secretly. I failed her, disgraced her, now she is dead, and I want to know why.

'No shit.' I say. 'I'm in the dark as much as you man. I'm hurting as much as you.'

'You're holding back, Mr. Campbell.' Chen is impassive. He's still totally in control. I want him to think that nothing else matters but finding her killers, don't want him to guess at the turmoil within me that could cloud my judgment.

'What the fuck do you want from me, man? My woman is dead, and I know nothing about who or why! I'm fucked up inside, and you want more. I have no more to give!' I'm playing the anguish card to its fullness, but he's not taking the bait.

'We all have more to offer.' Chen is unruffled.' We only need to reach deep into our souls and coax it out. I'm a skilled practitioner of that.'

I go for full frontal. 'Threatening me ain't going to achieve shit dawg. Kill me and what you think I know dies with me. I'm done here man, see yah.' I get up, and this time I'm unhindered as I approach the doorway.

'They won't stop until you're dead too,' Chen calls out to me.

They who motherfucker? I mutter to myself. But I'm putting on a brave face. I know I'm in a whole new league of shit, here. I step outside into the muggy night and hail a cab heading for the Docklands.

8.

WILD RODEO

THE COMPU-CAB DRIVER DRUMS HIS FINGERS on the half-moon steering wheel as if the extra credits I'd paid him to wait aren't enough compensation. I had just visited Digital's crib in Hampstead. I had the security codes so I could access it in situations like this. The Tudor home was dark and empty. Not that he expected anything else. His crib was as secure as Fort Knox, but I had to be sure. Right about now I wished that I was on better terms with his bitch of an estranged wife; maybe she had some answers. But that line of inquiry could wait this was much more important. I shake my head with a combination of numb acceptance and shock. My focus was now on a crime scene unfolding before my eyes. Jesus H Christ. I'm lost for words and that's some rare shit for me.

This was surreal.

The Depot and what remained of the scarred and smouldering entrance loomed in front of me. 'Crime Scene Do Not Cross' Yellow laser beams enclosed the crime scene excluding all but Met investigators and CSI specialists. Three squad cars and two Met1 floaters are parked out front, their blue lights lazily revolving. Four armed Met-1 officers provide the muscle, lounging around craving action when the action had already passed. I'm no expert, but this looks like it was a military type assault. There's heavy damage to buildings, trains blown off tracks and hover vehicles discarded. What the fuck happened?

My humble conclusion? Some connected motherfuckers with military grade weapons tried to shake down Sixty-Nine, pulling out all the stops, no expense spared. Numbness takes me over again. A sledgehammer smash into my rib-cage where my heart used to be, and I'm light headed. I fight against the panic that is clawing at me and threatening to drown me. I cling to the one thing that keeps me grounded - the image of my son, shifting my overwhelmed senses from loss and heartache to the joy of a future with him. It works. Soon I feel the ground under my feet again, my focus and balance return but, unfortunately so do the questions.

I can't contact Digital, and I've tried all means at my disposal including a few secure lines designed for such emergencies. Now the attack on Steel Erection Headquarters could only lead him to believe his business partner was dead or abducted. I don't know why I feel it is connected, but I grapple with a name that Digital had mentioned to me a few days ago. A female CEO of a scientific consultation firm. I'd conjured up a wacky mind association technique to help me recall her, should I need to. Delicate features, thick blonde hair and atop her head with huge Minotaur style horns, snorting indignantly like a raging bull. The devil, Ms. Lorraine Van Horne.

Three hours later I'm standing about a hundred meters from the foyer of my crib, Crystal Towers, inspecting the joint. Don't ask me what I'm looking for because I don't know but I expect anything after all that has happened. Everything is everything, here. The usual suspects are bedded down as always at this time. Mr. Lambetta's Ferrari, Mrs. Granges's vintage roller and the other families with their understated Renaults and Ford SUV's. The launch pads for the floaters set to the back of the parking lot are fully occupied with the Bentleys, Rolls Royce's and Mercedes Marques from the three CEO's and five millionaire entrepreneurs who share my Real Estate space. Nothing seems out of place. No flapping Police cordons or laser barriers, no shattered glass or chalked impressions of fallen victims.

I walk past the abstract art piece that looks like a concrete fruit loop. I'm able to see inside as the glass adjusts to my presence. Why am I tripping about security? Out of the many constructs sprouting up like metal weeds across London's landscape Digital chose these luxury flats primarily for safety. They're equipped with a formidable catalog of counter-terrorist and geological measures to protect occupants against the uncertainties of modern living. But they hadn't made allowances for surreptitious, covert attacks.

Old Smithy, the concierge, is behind his desk as always. I relax - well a little anyway - at the sameness of everything while still looking for the twist in the scorpion's tale. Trust me; it's timed like this I appreciate Digital's almost pathological paranoia.

The door slides open, and I take two steps in, looking around nervously as I approach the front desk. Smithy's already sensed my presence but looks up and smiles as if surprised to see me. 'Mr. Campbell, how are you, sir?

I study his wrinkled face and white whiskers trying to figure from his grey eyes if there was anything's amiss but his jovial smile welcomes me as always.

'I'm good,' I say after a while. 'Anything exciting happening?'

Smithy chuckles.

'I don't think I could stand the excitement at my age, Mr. Campbell. I prefer the comfort of certainty it's safer.'

'True. I'm due a rest myself after last night.' Don't go there, dawg, I reprimand myself, the instinctive reaction to confide in someone is strong.

Smithy smiles again showing me his full set of teeth. 'Rest is for when I retire until then....' His words trail away. 'Still it was good of them to give me the morning off yesterday, really considerate like.'

Morning off? A slight tingle at the base of my head leaves me spooked wandering what the significance was if any. I discount it but give myself kudos' for thinking conspiracy at every corner.

'Is there anything else I can do for you, Mr. Campbell?'

I consider his question seriously as if he can help a man soon to be on Met1's most wanted list and already a target for professional assassins. It's funny, but I'm not laughing.

'Yeah, just take it easy, you here?' I walk away.

'Mr. Campbell!' Smithy calls out. 'I almost forgot, this came for you this morning via Royal Mail.'

'Royal Mail? You shitting me, Smithy.'

'No,' he grins. 'It was even delivered by a post man.'

'Damn.' I take the small padded envelope from him checking the name and checking the seal. Digital. No expense spared. Smithy waves at me and I dash to catch the elevator.

In moments, I'm inside, and I sit back in my leather couch trying to connect with my crib. I'm empty inside like nothing has any significance. The sparkle and gloss in my life had been wiped clean. Every aspect of my life, every nook and cranny are affected and the longing for resolution clouding my judgment like a hangover. I bounce to my feet and pace the length of the room. Already I've sorted a fresh change of clothes and packed my Louis Vitton overnight bag. I plan to be on the next Red Eye to Manchester to catch up with Popeye at our meeting place as we'd arranged, but before that, I had to gather my thoughts and formulate something that resembles a plan. My pacing gathers urgency as I prepare to leave.

I'm not sure how or when I pick it up but when I stand still to catch my bearings I'm gazing into a Holo Display picture of my first born. Face to face with another version of my-self in the picture frame I wonder about the past decisions I've made. One thing's for sure. My timing stinks. Don't you think I know there are more immediate considerations than wondering how my actions have affected my son? But I'm compelled to continue my self-analysis. Just like the ancient warriors from Africa had to make their hearts right before they went into battle and died.

Money is what's always driven me, but after gaining the independence, I always dreamed of I ask myself, where is the next great challenge? Vintage Adonis Campbell to think my next great adventure would be a complicated Scenario that would test me on all levels. Instead,

I'm trying to solve a murder, maybe two and trying to return to my son with my balls and sanity intact. All the while wandering; what will he think of his old man? What has he done to make this world a better place apart from something as superficial as pleasuring powerful women?

My destiny is much bigger; I can feel it. I just hope that Adonis Junior won't be reading about it in my obituary.

The subtle aroma of Maria's perfume suffuses my apartment. Images of her strutting naked down the hall float in front of me. This is harder than I could have ever imagined. I'm the proverbial man's man who should have been able to adapt to the reality of loss. Maria may have seemed blasé about her feelings for me, but you can't make love to the same person for years without them having an impact on your life and your heart. The potency of my feelings takes me by surprise. Every time I disappear in a haze of panic, I'm confronted by this weakness, reminding me just how vulnerable I am.

What yuh gonna do turf bwoy?

Whatever I gotta.

My dawg Digital must have been using a crystal ball because he had contingency plans in place which could only be made by a man expecting disaster. Or maybe he felt his past was bound to catch up with him, and he was just thorough. He was a hard man to figure, but I trusted his judgment without question.

Digital wasn't a paranoid genius; he was a prophetic genius. Security surrounding the Sixty-Nine operation had to be virgin tight. A year before the sex trade became legal in England, Scotland and Wales his business was blowing up underground. My man had been approached twice by the Yakuza to buy him out. They weren't stupid; they knew we'd have a runaway success when the operation was given a dose of governmental respectability. My brothers from the east didn't like to hear the word, 'No.' Try to picture a man who already didn't trust his own shadow reacting to the threat of a deadly crime organization. Predictably Sixty-Nine went on lock down.

Client checks became more stringent, and from then on, I had to permanently wear my quarter of a million credits image scrambler disguised as my platinum dog tags. Because of the emission of exotic sub atomic particle from the star metal that's within it, I can't be photographed digitally, or my voice recorded. Unless you're a gifted artist, you can forget about having any record of me. I'm the invisible man baby, unfortunately, it's not the case for the rest of the Sixty-Nine family.

This game is no kindergarten operation. It still carries old twentieth-century undercurrents of illegality and crime. The wrong type of competition could take us out of business permanently. Digital didn't intend for that to happen and neither did I.

I open the envelope and extract a small card with a Dummies installation guide, an instruction manual explaining a rerouting program and a high-density micro disc. I immediately knew where this was going. Be careful what you wish for, partner, you wanted more responsibility outside of the field, you got it. Till such time that I knew what was happening, Sixty-Nine was under my control. But this was not how shit was supposed to pan out. Digital could have easily sent me this stuff through the net, but instead, he decided on sending it to me through a government snail mail service that most people thought of as dead and was so expensive to use it might as well be. I guessed that was the point. No one would think of intercepting a message sent that way.

The lights came on as I enter my library and slide the disc into my PC, I hadn't planned to hang around for it to complete, but I'm alerted by Digital's aristocratic tones. I snake my head back into my library. On the wafer screen stood an avatar of Digital with his hands behind his back as he did in the real world, tapping its feet impatiently obviously waiting for me. I came back in and sat down and only then did the avatar bring his hands from behind his back and nod at me. My boy did not look happy.

9.

ELECTRIC CHAIR

MANCHESTER CITY OPENS MAGNIFICENTLY TO ME as the Virgin flyer reaches the apex of the elevated tracks, showing me a city bathed in the diffused rays of a blood orange sun. But before I could appreciate the morning's natural vista and the growing modern architecture that hung onto its northern identity we plunged into Piccadilly station, the train's magnetic dampers bringing us to a smooth stop. I almost smile at the memory of the scenarios we've constructed here. Not forgetting some of the characters we came across and especially the bulldog tenacity of a detective Inspector Ambrose Patterson who was a pain in the ass for some time but with diplomacy and smarts, we dealt with most things.

As the memories ebb, the pain of loss returns and leaves me with the cold fear that by the time is threatening to leave me as an empty shell, a soulless creature masquerading as a man, just like the many bums roaming the L-Town streets. I honestly don't know how much more of this I can take. I go over Digital's message again, wishing to God I'd never listened to it in the first place. Every word is stamped into my mind.

Adonis, by the time you receive this, I could be dead or worst, and our team destroyed. The worst-case scenario is you never receive this, and it was all for nothing but if you are listening to this then you are alive, and there is hope. Forgive my naivety; there's so much at stake I'd fooled myself into thinking this day would never come. And I know your mind must be brim full of questions. Some I can enlighten you on, others I cannot yet but in time, God willing you will understand.

I've tried to work out the best way to help you through this difficult time and have placed a few emergency protocols in place. By now you know unknown forces are hunting us and consequently, your focus must be on evasion and survival, in the meantime, Sixty-Nine will be on full automation for the next thirty days. Bookings, Client Care, Client Acquisition, Profiling, Scenario Construction, Marketing - everything will be dealt with offsite. Unfortunately, I can only cancel client scenarios for two days before your booking's resume. One word of advice, Adonis. If you insist on constructing the scenarios yourself, keep them simple and always consider yourself under threat.

The responsibility of upholding the Sixty-Nine brand will be your job. I can only hope I've prepared you adequately for what's about to come.

You have arrived at this dangerous juncture in your life because of me. All because of me. I never asked you if you wanted to take this journey with me, but I led you down the path nonetheless. You are special Adonis; there is no doubt about that. But I've used your uniqueness without your knowledge ever since we began to work together. It was the real reason our relationship began in the first place. Your kind of genetic makeup is found in one in a hundred million people, and here you are, delivered by providence. The technology I developed allows me to program cells using a language that your body and your body alone can interpret and act on. What I have done to you was inexcusable, but it was done for a greater good. Maria always said when the right time came you would understand, she understood and believed in what I was doing. We have experimented, augmented and subtly monitored your physiology after programming it with some exceptional modifications. Did you think that being free from the most minor of illnesses was a coincidence? Your strength, agility, and prowess in the bedroom are not mere luck. You are special and in your cellular makeup lays the potential to save millions. For this, you are a target, dead or alive.

Sixty-Nine was established for you as recompense for what we've put you through for what you are about to go through. As

I've said, this was my way to test and prepare you. Now please listen to me very carefully:

Leave your flat immediately and move to less conspicuous digs, perhaps one of your empty properties. No one, except a member of our team, must know where you're staying; the risk is far too great. Do you remember the invitation I gave you, for the industry ball at Nexus HQ downtown? It is imperative that you attend. Your future depends on it. The threat on your life only ends when you introduce yourself to Professor Reed Richards.

There's not much more I can tell you other than stay connected as a team and a family. Remember how I said I wanted to make a difference after Claire's death? Finally, I have, through you, my friend, thank you.

Look after my Godson.

It was great.

God speed, Adonis.

I don't know how long I'd sat there after the message was done, my mind adrift. I had squirmed through Digitals avatar pacing the computer screen nervously like the real flesh and blood, the simulacrum staring into my eyes as if it had emotion outside of what was programmed into it. I reflect on this shit for a mo. All this time I've been looking for clarity and I thought I found it, but my touchstone and passion – 69 – was not what I had imagined it to be. All this time they'd been testing me, preparing me and for what? For being played like a bitch? I'm special. Bullshit. Digital played me and right about now I don't feel special.

I cast my mind back, sifting through an unreliable memory for something that was said, some suspicious action that would explain all of this but nothing presents itself, I realize but don't yet accept that somehow, it's all related to Maria's death and possibly Digital's too. The old man was working off the premise that the team had been iced, but I was about to link up with what could be the only surviving member of the 69 family. When I find Popeye, I'd have some semblance of normality, and together I knew we could work this out because whoever wanted us dead was in line for some cold ass revenge. Revelations aside you fuck with 69, and I will make it my personal vocation in life to tear you a new one.

I rent a car as soon and head into Manchester Central. I make my way into the inner circle satisfied with my nifty ground hugger, glad that I've beaten the early morning traffic. I had nightmares of being wedged between some ram packed driverless buses and some gear grinding ancient trucks, grid-locked and late for my meet. At the next red light, floating just above eye level, I check out my surroundings. Parents are on the school run; delivery trucks manoeuvre around parked cars and businesses prepare to open.

In two two's, I'm parking the unit about ten minutes away from the five star Carlton Towers and making my way to the rendezvous point. The environs change dramatically from council run territory to land owned by the ever-powerful corporations. Manicured grass, spotless pathways that could have been cleaned by a manic compulsive with a toothbrush and state of the art advertising space. I approach the triple towers, ignoring the travellator bringing guests to its innards, like a factory conveyor belt. I'm amazed at how many people are milling around so early in the morning. I'm optimistic at the thought of seeing my homey, Popeye.

The last thought is barely complete before I've stopped in my tracks. My twenty-twenty grates at my nerves and suddenly I'm hit with the realization that this was one of the specialties I had taken for granted not knowing it was programmed into my physiology. An early warning system that had always prepared me for shit. I had developed a repertoire of responses to differing warnings that I have stored away in my consciousness and this. I haven't had this type of reaction for a long time. I stand still and make a three-sixty turn until the possible threat comes into view. It has to be the road hugger BMW coming from the hotel car park. My heart pounds and my energy levels elevate as I move without knowing exactly why.

Wait a goddamn minute!

That couldn't be who I think that is? Nah. The passenger side window is down, and I see thick manicured fingers playfully drummer on the glass, a lily-white complexion of an albino and a big ass sovereign ring on the index finger. Air rushes through my lungs in huge gulps as I prepare to rumble but I stop myself from running after it and instead watch as the car speeds away, my fight instincts sink back to standby.

I lose interest in the disappearing vehicle and pick up the pace towards the Carlton Towers, the gnawing sensation of my twenty-twenty in my gut is uncomfortable, try as I might to repress it. The revolving doors to the hotel foyer match my speed of approach and automatically synchronize their revolutions to my movements. I step into crystal, chrome and leather. My cheese bottom loafers squelch on the marble tile. I throw a cursory glance at unknown faces either side of me, my ears accepting the easy going classical music with environmental controls on medium, just how I like it. Down a flight of steps straight ahead through the wrap-a-around glass window and then I'm into the car park. I spot the surveillance van. 69's roving eyes and ears. Popeye's baby. When I want to fuck with him I call it a van, but it's an SUV Limousine, decked out in leather and suede, thickly carpeted and stuffed full of cutting edge surveillance equipment. Independent rear suspension, armour plated and rigged with stealth capabilities. I check my timepiece. I'm ten minutes early. The big man must be inside snoozing. There's no way he'd miss our rendezvous. Popeye would be bubbling over with questions, but he'd have to help answer mine first.

My instincts are still unhappy.

I reach for the sliding door only an arm's length away and my twenty-twenty bristles as if the threat is immediate. I back up, responding to the tension in my muscles, my former joy at seeing Popeye draining away. I go into another three-sixty shuffle, but the new threat moves into my space with a calculated swiftness blocking my way into the car park.

'I would think long and hard before I went out there, Mr. Campbell.'

My head shakes almost without me realizing it.

'Come again, nigga?'

Chen stands in my shadow, left hand in his pocket, right hand swinging at his side clutching a pair of binoculars. He's laughing silently at me like I'm some incompetent clown with no idea what time it is. The question is in my eyes.

'How did he find me?'

Since last we met, less than six hours ago, he'd changed into a fresh Armani suit and tie, figured out I was in danger and appeared out of thin air to save me from myself. Smug, self-righteous and annoying motherfucker. Despite my humming twenty-twenty I realize that my man is no more a threat to me than the concierge. Something else is creeping me intuition out, made worse by his cryptic warning. Still pissed, I stare hard into his eyes.

'Homeboy this has gone beyond a joke! What the fuck do you want from me, man?'

'Let me see,' he counters. 'I've just saved your life, haven't I?

'What the fuck are you talking about man?' I say to him, and he just ignores me and says.

'When will you wake up to the fact that we need each other?'

Hombre is just too on point, too convenient. No wonder I'm suspicious.

'If you want to help me Chen you can start by getting out of my way.'

'You have trust issues, don't you Mr. Campbell?'

'And you have a hearing problem, motherfucker.'

'Be that as it may, if you make your rendezvous with your colleague you will be dead.'

He knew about Popeye.

'Is that a threat?'

Chen hands me the matt black Omni-Viewer. 'The black van.' He states the obvious. 'Take a long hard look.'

'No shit,' I focus on the modified SUV, the image enhanced by the intuitive software in the optics pinpointing what I'm looking for with laser-like precision. I stiffen, and my early warning system goes crazy. An injection of cold fear pumps into my spine sending me into near panic. My hands shake and it takes immense concentration for me to steady them.

'Shit, no, this ain't happening!'

The departure of the BMW earlier suddenly holds chilling significance. Yellow Nigga.

How the fuck did they know?

Popeye is in the driver's seat, beaten bloody, his mouth stuffed with a rag. His swollen lips loose, his eyes puffy and dribbling but he's not dead, not yet. My homie is struggling to keep his head up. Drugged, I guessed. I couldn't stand around and do nothing. Fuck my own safety and Chen's advice for that matter.

'Today is not a good day to die, Mr. Campbell.' Chen reads my mind.

'We all have to die sometime, dawg.'

Nobody else is around the SUV. Chen's right, it's a trap, but I just can't leave him there. My mind spins even as I contemplate what lies before me. Walk away from this and Six-ty-Nine survives, be a hero, get a cap in your ass and all that hard work will be for nothing. Guilt nibbles away at my insides. This is some hardcore shit, urging me to act rashly when I know I need to remain calm.

Over the last few hours, my friendship with Popeye has gained a new significance. He was the last of a lucrative business, my passion and my extended family. A tenuous symbol of what was left of my life when all around me had gone to hell in a Lamborghini. Our fortunes are intertwined. I had no choice, but to save him or at least die trying. I brush past Chen, fire blazing in my eyes, his unspoken words echoing in my head. It's a trap. Like a good choir boy, I'm gonna save the fucking day.

I stay low and keep moving, winding my way through the maze of cars, glancing up occasionally to catch my bearings while checking for anything of concern. It's deathly quiet until an automated maintenance vehicle bursts onto the car lot. It skirts around the perimeter puncturing the air with its whirring sound. I freeze giving into my paranoia, only relaxing when the vehicle keeps moving between the rows of cars on its way to some housekeeping emergency.

My twenty-twenty is constant, sending out strong Ju-Ju vibes moments before things kick off and keeping quiet when I'm knee deep in it. Right now, it's silent. My swagger is shot to shit, I'm hyper-ventilating, and I'm still trying to keep moving. I tell myself I can't be a hero without my focus, but that shit has no effect on me.

I'm about four cars away from the SUV. The persistent hum of the maintenance vehicle gets louder. I'd thought it was leaving but it scuttled back towards me. I strain, to hear how close it is, my head to one side, spitting distance, I guess. I try to put one foot in front of the other, but I'm stuck in stasis.

'Ain't moving dawg, comprende.' My survival instincts scream at me and freeze my muscles. I kneel. My ears are flat against my skull listening for its progress. Surely the automaton had gone past Popeye's SUV by now? An eerie silence soaks into me, through my pores, deep into my skin, right into my bones. I'm still crouching, my senses numb, my mind hazy unable to make head or tail or this shit.

A high-pitched squeal suddenly shatters the quiet followed by a rush of air. My nervous system goes on lockdown courtesy of my twenty-twenty and I'm flung to the floor landing firmly on my ass. A ferocious roar surrounds me and lifts the SUV high into the air. It seems to move in slow motion, rolling onto its side before disintegrating into a flaming fireball.

Shrapnel radiates outwards like a deadly hailstorm of metal, heat, and sound. I curl up, my arms protecting my head, my ass and balls exposed. I'm engulfed in a black hole, all thought and action sucked into its darkness. My last thoughts are that I wish I'd listened to Digital, to Chen even, but it's way too late for that shit.

Way too late.

10.

SLIDER

'COFFEE, MR CAMPBELL?' THE VOICE SOUNDED AS IF it was coming from the end of a dark tunnel, the words echo off damp walls before reaching my ears. I look up and see the blurry outline of a stewardess, cup in hand, Miniature Espresso machine steaming. My V-Comm buzzes in my waist. Absent-mindedly I place the caller in a virtual queue without checking their identity.

I shake my head, and the stewardess attempts to leave, but I hang on to her hand, nearly falling off my chair. Regaining my balance, I treat her to a watered-down version of the Adonis charm. 'This may sound stupid but, where am I?'

She openly appraises me, focussing on my torn shirt and the rock-hard pecks nudging through it. 'You're on the Virgin Flyer to London Paddington, first class sir.' Her smile makes me feel brighter inside.

'Bear with me. Did you see me get on board by any chance?'

If the stewardess is surprised by the question, she doesn't show it.

'No sir but a Chinese gentleman requested I look after you.'

'And you've done a straight up job.' I look at her badge, noticing how well she fits into her short skirt. 'Debra, come back and shoot the breeze with me. If you have a moment...' My eyes massage her thighs and soak in her muscular flanks. She smiles, blushes and excuses herself quickly.

I've been on my ass for too long. I stand up and check myself for damage. My bruises and bumps are making themselves known by the small explosions of pain I feel when I move. I squeeze my eyes shut again wishing away an almighty headache. Popeye's murder forces itself to the forefront of my thoughts. Death had whispered in my ear again. Stay out of my way cocksucker, or you're next.

I collapse into my seat, my head in my hands, tears rolling from my eyes. First Digital, then Maria and now the big man. I'm overwhelmed by what has happened and struggle to come to terms with the reality. I'm drowning in a sea of deep dark despondency, and my lifelines are being dragged away from me at every juncture. A malicious current is pulling me down to the depths that I know I can't return from if I succumb. What if I just take my money, disappear to the Caribbean and leave this shit behind? Forget it all in my chalet in Negril or better still my island crib in Dubai. The intensity of the thought shocks me; the guilty excitement is thrown into the mix of these emotions to wreak havoc on an already fragile psyche. Maybe in my past life in Hallelujah Land, I would have acted on the idea without a second thought.

That was the time I was dragging my ass through the grime with all the other lowlifes in Los Angeles. Now like a caterpillar that has gone through a transformation I was a butterfly. I had immerged better and smarter. I have a family, a purpose even though I've never felt so alone and frightened in my whole goddamn life. I've no idea where to go or what to do next. Maybe a transformation to a better person is not what I need right now but a reversion to my past as a grimy nigga, with swagger and a thug mentality.

I look around, restless and that's when I notice the large brown envelope on my laptop on the seat next to me. Chen, I think. The oriental motherfucker's nowhere around, but he's still got my attention. Reluctantly I open it. There's a slip of paper with Chen's direct line scrawled on it, skin tone Bio-chip, old world photographs and a

Newsweek Nano magazine. I pick up the periodical. The memory card is three months old, and the power cells that charge the opti-plastic sheet are running low. The featured page has a jerky video clip of a press conference taking place in a swanky hotel somewhere in London. The headline scrolls across the top: Expansion plans welcomed by stockholders of Nexus, the most Innovative Pharmaceutical company in the World. Nex-us? Expansion?

I wrack my brains wondering why that name seems so familiar. I don't have any stock investments with them; it's more like I've experienced them in other ways. Whatever it is I just can't put my finger on it. Then something else catches my attention. Surprise, surprise Ms. Lorraine Van Horne, that same bitch who gave me the heeby-jeeby's at Digital's crib, the one who arranged the scenario that took Maria's life. My friendly neighborhood CEO is fronting before the paparazzi. But guess what, she's not the chief executive of an accounting firm as Digital was led to believe, she's leading this Nexus outfit!

The announcement is made by a professional looking and silky-toned spokeswoman, Carla Parsons. I'm all for confident women. Women on top in the bedroom and boardroom. The ones that ooze intelligence and sexiness by the tone of their voice or the look in their eye and the reassuring swing of their hips. This sister has made a good impression on me. Piercing gray eyes, long stocking legs, full bodied dark hair that bounces naturally with each step as she approaches the rostrum and let's not forget a thirty-three-inch chest.

How could I forget that?

The sound bites and the text inform me that the corporation is heavily into pharmacology, pumping millions into human improvement drugs that haven't yet seen the light of day. They're also being investigated by the monopolies and mergers commission. Aside from the fine figure of Ms. Parsons something else catches my eye and has my heart racing.

Yellow Nigga.

An imposing figure just outside the camera shot, suited as he was the last time we met, standing next to his mistress, wired up and fucking warped out. I scroll the stills of about ten Nexus executives and their stats concluding that they're all one big happy family conspiring to eliminate Sixty-Nine from the face of the earth.

But where do I fit in? What is it about me that required the senseless murder of my family? What threat could an erotic entertainment company pose to an international Drugs conglomerate that had money from the floor to the ceiling?

I was beginning to see that Chen was leading me, even though I'd consistently resisted his sound advice. He knew more about Maria and possible about Sixty-Nine than he was letting on. What the hell did he need my raggedy ass for then? The pieces were coming together but not nearly fast enough.

L-town is just before me, but the familiar feeling of longing has been replaced with an emptiness that won't go away until either this is behind me or I'm dead.

As an afterthought, I pick up the Biochip, obviously doctored for my purpose and squeeze it to the back of my hand. The widget sizzles and then secretes an enzyme that bonds painlessly with my skin. I read the name, Maria Chen and the details of her crib etched into the silicon superstructure. Another nudge in the right direction and no better place to start digging.

'What will it take to get you out of my fucking life Adonis?'

'Unrestricted access to my son would be a start,' I say to the woman I used to love but who I now refer to as the Battersea bitch.

'You have as much chance of that happening as me giving you some ass!'

What else did I expect from Yvette? A little understanding would have gone a long way. Sure, I wasn't exactly a glowing example of patience myself, but I had a good reason.

'Fuck you,' I spit. 'But I guess I made that mistake already, didn't I.'

Do I need to go on? I'm sure you get the drift of our argument. Yvette, the mother of my son, cozy in her little world, a haven of stability that excluded me. And here I am, reduced to obvious vulnerability cos I'm desperate to hear my son's voice until the Battersea bitch hangs up on me.

I reign in my world of hurt with a sigh. Just take it easy, I tell myself, this is only round one. But right now, I had other things to hold my focus. She I can deal with at my leisure, cos I've had plenty of practice.

But this. This required focus.

I'm close to where Maria lived when she wasn't hanging out at mine. It's a nerve-wracking thought. The Compu-cab drops me off early so I can walk, think and calm my ass down before I get to her crib. I stand out in this kind of neighborhood. My Versace two-piece is crumpled, a few damp patches are drying out from under my armpits, and my white T's are passable, but don't get too close. I'm functioning but in no fit state to entertain. The stink of fear crystallizes on my skin. A remote mainframe is on my shoulder, and I'm swinging another case trying to pass for a very world-weary engineer.

I've known Maria for nearly four years, yet this neighbourhood is one of the last places I'd expected her to live in. She'd always struck me as a voguish Manhattan loft, kind of person. Or at the worst a high-rise luxury apartment, but this right here, was L-town old money; Millionaires who liked to maintain a generational presence in one area for many decades, who could trace their ancestry back hundreds of years in these self-same properties. The fringes were occupied by the trendy, sometimes ghetto fabulous breed of entrepreneurs who were striving to build their own history. Flamboyant and eager, there was nothing low profile about this part of town. This was the suave new Bishops Gate and, maybe for once in London's class obsessed history; it represented multicultural Britain.

It's late evening and the last rays of sunlight squeeze through the architecture leaving hues of orange-red smearing the brickwork. The biochip gives me access into a miniature courtyard shared by the classy residential homes in this exclusive row. No need for a human presence here, this spread bristled with the best surveillance equipment money and applied science can buy. If not for outlawed technology embedded in my necklace and earring I would already be the subject of numerous digital recordings that could be used as extenuating evidence against me.

Number 17 looms ahead. I'm half expecting Met-1 to have a scene of crime beacons circling the front of her crib, hoping against hope that they'd used their vast resources and found Maria's body along with whoever had killed her. But the reality is that the authorities will realize that something's up when a concerned colleague reports her missing. By then I could be up to my neck in kaka or dead.

I have strong doubts about what I do next. The weight of something far more serious than I understand rests on my shoulders. My bold as brass, hard as balls confidence is severely diminished. But I can't let the effect of Maria and Popeye's murders paralyze me. I decide to ignore the fear lodged in my craw and find the motherfuckers who did this. As usual, I'm alone. Chen had saved my ass, proving that I needed him and now he was allowing me into his sister's world. But I'm still asking myself, why me when he had all the connections and the manpower?

I push open the wrought iron gate, mount the steps and wait for the unobtrusive security measures to scan me. The Biochip heats up slightly, I look around and crank the Victorian style door handle. It gives so I've been identified as a friend and the door hydraulics kick in swinging it open. I tense, aware that I'm about to enter a previously forbidden place, Maria Chen's head. Heavy curtains filter out most of the evening sun. Thankfully my presence doesn't activate the lighting, alerting the neighbors. Shadows gather pace just as fast as the setting sun sinks low. With no torch, I work quickly before the faint streams of sunlight totally disappear. But I'm still careful; I can't let these murdering cocksuckers off the hook because of a lack of thoroughness.

The mail that is on the floor, I stuff what I think is relevant into my shoulder bag the rest I leave beside a chrome bucket filled with umbrellas. Spiral stairs are directly in front of me, an elaborate kitchen to my right, and an extensive lounge to my left. Erotic sculptures cast lustful shadows on the walls; canvases of Victorian voyeurs are half-hidden in the gloom. None of the downstairs room's reveal anything of interest, confirming how organized she was, or how meticulous her maid is. If I've learned anything from my years as a confidence trickster, gigolo, and thief in LA, it's that the bedroom always holds the secrets. I take the stairs two at a time, trying hard to shrug off an overriding feeling that I'm just not welcome here.

What is it about Sixty-Nine that made everyone involved in its success protect their private life so fiercely? I've known my shorty from time, but I knew nothing about her. From the beginning of our relationship the ground rules were laid down. I was always an open book, but Maria always said that what was private in her life would remain that way. I never knew exactly what she meant and didn't think it was important enough to pry. Now our agreement is null and void because she's dead and I want to know everything.

I move quickly opening doors until I'm standing on the threshold of her bedroom. I smell her favorite perfume. The one that so complimented her natural bodily essence, her unique scent that told me that she was aroused or she was ready to party. Images swim in my mind; Maria is applying her make-up. Maria nude, with her legs crossed, her back to me, her long black hair imbued with a dark sheen, the Chinese symbol of prosperity tattooed at the nape of her spine. I blink as my eyes blur and the beautiful, sensuous apparition disappears with another piece of my soul.

Maria's personal space is sparsely but luxuriously furnished. From the bed to the light fixtures, everything shows class. I venture into her ensuite bathroom and switch the lights on. Pristine. I'd think twice before taking a piss. Back in the room, I eye the contents on top of the antique bureau. Nothing there except a copy of the Bhagavad-gita not what I'd expect but yow, what's new? It's like I don't exist! Nothing I've seen so far gives the slightest indication that I, or any other man for that matter, was ever a part of her life. That shit cuts me to the core. Was this all a front? Had I been played like a ten dollar 'ho'?

I plow through drawers and cabinets, recognizing lingerie, bras and panties that I had coaxed her out of on many occasions. A lump in my throat, I take extra care not to disrupt the orderly formation of her clothes, an inconsequential act that makes me feel marginally less than scum. Across the room is a set of sliding doors which conceal a walkthrough closet with an impressive selection of designer threads enclosed in monogrammed plastic dust covers, hung on racks around an automatic track. At ankle level are slots filled with an equally impressive collection of Jimmy Choo's and a few Manolo Blahnik boots. Along the top walls are shelves stacked with hat boxes and document boxes, a sliding ladder conveniently fitted to help with retrieval. I swing on it like an eager monkey, rifling through filing boxes, swiping photographs, more letters and anything else to help unravel this puzzle. With as much hard copy and optical discs that I can easily carry, I jump down from the ladder, noticing for the first time the safe, well camouflaged and embedded in the wall. Checking out the contents is a mouth-watering prospect but one which I won't satisfy. I was never into safe breaking, always thought that was for the truly professional, career criminal who'd studied under the didactic gaze of some OG dying of multiple gunshot wounds. I rub my fingers over the surface wondering if Chen could deal with this, wondering if I should even ask him.

Suddenly I feel a subtle gust of warm air that makes the hairs on the back of my neck stand to attention and roots me to the spot. I jump up, exit the closet through the automatic doors, switch off the lights and, on my hands and knees, head for the landing hoping to dodge the unseen threat. Voices drift up from downstairs, close to where I left my bags. I figure my ass is grass. The scene below me is dark, but surprisingly I can make out what's happening with complete clarity. My love of carrots or another of Digital's modifications.

Three armed men, a guy hefting a tool bag and an older, clearly frightened woman stand in the rectangle of diminishing light cast by the half-open door. I guess they're a part of the same unit that wants Sixty-Nine dead. Yellow niggas posse. I'm carrying around a block of hate for this murdering motherfucker, like a drug induced hard-on. I won't settle until I hang his head out to dry on a spike. They're here to either clean-up or get information. I hug the rails and listen intently to the conversation, call me paranoid, but I'm expecting to hear my name mentioned any minute.

'Fuck,' one man says.

That's not even my middle name, I think.

'Where's the lights, bitch?'

They sneer at the older woman. There's tense silence be-fore she speaks, her voice trembling with fear. 'Lights.' The automation system is obviously programmed for her voice too. The magnificent crystal chandelier set centrally in the ceiling overlooking the downstairs reception area slowly gains intensity, chasing away the oppressive shadows and bringing what should remain hidden out in the open for all to see.

Namely my black ass.

I shoot backward into the master bedroom revving my mind into a frenzy, hoping my next move can save me. The bedroom is open plan, so hiding places are virtually none existent. Then, the obviousness of the solution brings a smile to my face. If I was a kid skipping from Ma where would I be? Where was the place my first pubescent fantasies unfolded in my head? Underneath the bed playa! It's not the safest place, but it had to do.

Funny but it all began in a place just like this. At seven years old and under the tuition of my older cousin, I was tonguing and fingering all the little honeys in the neighbourhood. My boudoir was under Ma Campbell's four poster bed. Intimate, secure and roomy enough to fulfil my preadolescent lusting. Damn, it must be some psychosomatic shit, because I can feel the scar at the back of my head throbbing from my last and final romance with the underside of Mamas bed.

At twelve I knew all the theoretical mechanics of sex, but what cousin Tosh failed to tell me was what happened when a young cat like me busted a nut for the first time. Trisha an older woman of seventeen had heard about my skills, or rather my tool size. I invited her over and was into her panties before she could ask me length and width. But Trisha flipped the script on me because as good as I was with my tongue, that honey wanted cock. I played the big man, blessed, or cursed, with a size of dick that God should have given to someone more adept at its use. My first orgasm scared the shit out of me. I felt the ejaculation readying to explode and screaming like a little pussy, I pulled out, jumped up and knocked my fucking self out cold on the wooden slats! Thankfully Tosh had the presence of mind to get me my ass into neutral territory sticking with the story that I tripped and hit my head.

It was Fubar, man.

My old lady was worried, my boys were unable to keep straight faces, a hottie was telling the world you're not as hardcore as you make out and a mild contusion as a reminder. The jokes, all at my expense, lasted for months and they stung too. What goes around comes around, though, and here I am again, afraid and getting horny under the bed. But now the stakes are so much higher than pussy. Lives are at stake. This older woman's and mine.

All five thugs come straight into Maria's bedroom obviously following the directions of their terrified hostage. I lie still trying to identify the players by their shoes.

'So, this is where she keeps all her personal stuff right?' Timberland asks, pushing the woman down onto the bed. I feel her shaking her head. Timberland does this tapping thing with his feet when he talks.

'The safe?' A Spanish loafer with an arrogant, nasal tone, probably the leader.

'In there,' the old lady says.

The man in work boots and a boiler suit goes into his canvas bag rattling with tools. This woman has to be Maria's maid. Maria was a lot of things, but certainly not domesticated. Her crib is spotless, and the only way anyone could know her house so intimately was by cleaning this sucker week after week.

'Is there anything else we need to know, any surprises you've conveniently forgotten?'

These guys have spot-on intelligence, covering all bases with worrying efficiency.

'No,' Mammy answers, too eagerly. 'Nothing more.'

'Why don't I believe you?' Spanish loafer's teases?

I'm beginning to really dislike this dude.

'An attractive woman like your mistress, with no partner. No traceable family, just business associates and you? That strikes me as strange, the actions of a woman who has something to hide, maybe?'

'I've told you everything I know. You brought me here and threatened my family I just want to know where Ms. Chen is and I want to go home.' Mammy's voice breaks, anguish and uncertainty in her answer.

'I wish it was so simple,' Spanish is relishing his power over this woman. 'But I just feel you're not being honest with me and I'm a good judge of character.' This cocksucker is full of himself.

'What more do you want from me?' The maid pleads. 'I've shown you all I know. I'm just a cook and cleaner. Ms. Chen treats me well, and I respect her enough not to pry into her personal life.'

'How many years have you worked for Ms. Chen?'

'Three.' She hesitates a moment too long.

'All that time you heard nothing, saw nothing.'?

The shake of her head is enough to make the bed vibrate.

'Bullshit!' Spanish commands everyone's attention. 'Lis-ten up!' He's on the verge of losing his temper. 'While the Doctor works his magic on the safe we'll look around, see what we can find.'

'Okay.'

'Cool.'

'Bring the lying slag with us, yeah?'

'Yeah.'

Spanish loafer, Air Jordan, Timberland and the maid in sandals depart the room.

In the gloom, I think of escape and payback and not necessarily in that order. I force myself to be patient and take my chances as soon as an opportunity arises. The Doctor in the neighboring closet gets on with his job while I lie in the shadows watching and waiting.

I have incredibly strong fingers and arms. Three minutes have elapsed, and I'm hanging from the banister by one hand. The drop to the floor is about twenty-five feet, but my main worry is the chain smoking motherfucker coming my way. I feel the burn from my fingers right through to my upper arms, but I have another two minutes' discomfort before I let go. Punk above me lights up and inhales with a grateful sigh.

It seemed like a good idea at the time. While they were rummaging through the upstairs rooms, the Doctor is trying to open the safe, I head downstairs, get my shit and disappear. But I picked up unexpected company as I was making my way along the balcony just before the grand sweeping stairs. Air Jordan coughed and was traipsing my way. I'd silently spun back, scurried in the opposite direction and vaulted over the wooden balustrades.

Air Jordon, joker smoker that he was, takes his time, enjoying the feel of the nicotine free menthol fumes bathing his lungs from his E-Cig. God, I wish he'd leave. It's gotta be five minutes since I've been hanging here, my limbs screaming for mercy, and I'm not sure how much longer I can do this for.

'Orlando, where the fuck are you?' Someone calls from downstairs. Air Jordan curses then walks off but not without making his presence felt. He sighs and then breaks wind. I grit my teeth and shake my head in disgust, letting go, free-falling all twenty-five mo' fucking feet. As I plummet to the marble floor, a weird sense of well-being overcomes me. I should be dead, but I'm not. You guessed it; I'm in slo-mo, aware of each fractured second, the constant of gravity all around me until time resumes its hectic charge. Son-of-a-bitch.

I land on my feet, my piston-like thighs absorbing the massive shock without a hint of complaint from my ankles. I roll away from my point of impact, checking quickly in case curious eyes are looking over the balcony. When I come up from my crouching position, I realize that for a normal dude I should have at least fractured my ankle, patella, and fibula but apart from an all-over tingle, I'm okay. How can I be fine? With this amount of nervous energy in my muscles and adrenaline coursing through my veins, I could take two energy rounds and not feel the effects till later. I'm alone now. It seems like a good time to head for the front door. I glance at the upper reaches of the building just to make sure. My stuff is untouched in the hallway beside the umbrellas. All I need to do is to pick up my kit and leave. I reflect on this. On what I've gained from this experience, asking myself what exactly do I have? Some letters and a feeling that there's so much more to Maria than meets the eye.

    I reach for the door knob, but I just can't bring myself to leave. This egotistic self-preservation shit just isn't me, and I'm not about to let circumstances bring me down to that level again. My family has been ripped viciously from me. If I'd only had the opportunity to stop it, I would have given my life. My next decision could be suicidal, but I'd rather face death than slink away like a coward. I had to find out what was so important inside that safe and I had to help Maria's maid get home safely, and finally, if possible, I'd somehow give these wanksters some heavy-duty mo' fucking payback. My brain cells are charged, constructing some devious shit to keep them entertained. I back away cautiously into the shadows allowing my mind to drift to a place of no stress, just peace and some nasty Machiavellian schemes hatching in the virgin soil of my mind like fungus.

One moment there's light in the bedroom upstairs and the kitchen, the next ... darkness. I'm the sly fucker who's caused the blackout and, as sure as my hood is the Docklands, I'm the inky figure darting up the stairs as the protests erupt. The principal routes are burned into my mind as I feel my way to the main bedroom giving my eyes time to adjust to the darkness. For the first few minutes or so the thugs are in a state of confusion allowing me, the man with the plan, unhindered access. I'm trusting in the doctor's reaction to my presence, and he doesn't let me down. Two minutes after I'd taken off downstairs, I reappear behind him looking as if I've been dipped in molten midnight. He's just rummaged through his tool bag and is about to switch on his flashlight - the only man who I knew who would come prepared for this eventuality. Such a pity the safe was still intact.

'Tsk!, tsk, tsk'. I give him my best Isaac Hayes impersonation. 'Ten minutes and zero results. Man, you're one wack safe-breaking motherfucker.'

The voice is unfamiliar to him, so he turns wildly on his knees, his eyes white in the darkness and I swiftly send him to sleep with a looping right hook. The force of the blow raises him off his ass as if for a second he's excited to see me, then he slumps sideways. I stand over him readying myself to go, but I stop in my tracks. A thought grabs me by the collar demanding my attention. I look down at the safe and shake my head in disbelief.

Naw, too easy, I tell myself, but I'm always the one to test providence. I reach down to crank the handle and press the disengage button. Son-of-a.......! It opens. I grab everything I can and stuff it into my shoulder bag. I pat the unconscious Doctor's bald head and hustle out the room towards the commotion.

Ten steps along the upper balcony someone stumbles out of the room to my right. My eyes are wide open taking in as much ambient light as is available, enabling me to see them clearly while they can't see my black ass at all. I sweep low, like I'm about to hurl a discus towards the ceiling. I spin on the balls of my toes; my open palm follows a trajectory that skims close to the floor boards then takes flight smashing into the thug's throat. His Adam's apple sinks into his trachea with a moist crunch, the gag reflex making him splutter like a busted spigot. His momentum somersaults him into a disjointed bundle that slams against the wall. The commotion alerts his dawgs who come running.

'Doctor? Doctor!' The calls, which come from a lower level, go unanswered. 'Orlando! Where are you, man?

Stop fucking around.' Still, the caller receives no response from the unconscious Dr. Orlando.

I hug the balustrades hoping that Spanish Loafers will be as rash as his homie. He's not running the show for nothing; he was even dumber than his boy ever could be. Baby boy knew something was fucked up and allowed fear take hold before rational thought. The retard lets his Gatt do the talking for him in the darkness, surprising even me for sheer stupidity. The first energy blast lights up the place like a lightning storm. For a split-second, I see them as clear as day. Spanish Loafers is taking point and just behind him, Timberland hanging onto the maid with his weapon drawn. For a split second, they see me looking like a man-sized fox caught in the headlights of an approaching car and to my right Air Jordan messed up against the wall. A second later darkness embraces me. Spanish Loafers rips off another ear-splitting scream and jerks his finger over the Gatt's trigger, aiming at where he saw me last.

Too late homeboy. He's only succeeded in blasting a baby size hole through the wooden banister. And in the meantime, I've already tackled Timberland slamming him into the wall in the process. He releases the maid as his weapon goes off. It was so close I can smell my singed eye-brows. In that heartbeat of twilight, I see Spanish loafer trying to figure out where I am. His confusion at the sight of me and Timberland tussling, apparent until once again the scene fades to black. Using all my strength, I effortlessly carry Timberland towards him. He thinks he's got the bead on me, his finger is wrapping around the trigger and in anticipation he's expecting an energy round to incinerate my ass but I've got my game face on.

Spanish comes out blazin', intent on smoking me. He pops off two rounds in rapid succession, and they both smack into Timberland's torso. The force of the concussion slows my pace but I keep coming. The look on Spanish's face is priceless as he realizes he's just killed his partner and I'm heading his way like a silent loco. His grimace says he can't pop off another round because I was in his personal space so Spanish swings at me with the Plasma rifle. I go low his move was ridiculously telegraphed, I read it without effort and strike him hard in his solar plexus. He pinwheels trying to maintain his balance but is unable to. Completely disorientated he slams into the railing and tips over. The night devours him, and his screams continue even after the sickening thud on the marble floor below.

'That's what your punk ass gets when you fuck with the wrong nigga, nigga.' My burst of machismo spent, I'm ready to bounce. If it's at all possible, it feels like my night vision is getting better.

The maid sits beside one of the major door jams that run across the balcony every ten feet or so, sobbing and shaking. She's not the only one. I whisper to her. 'Ma, we need to go.'

She doesn't seem to hear me, so I move closer and touch her shoulder.

She looks up at me as if all hope has departed.

'We have to leave now Ma, you got to trust me.'

'I do Adonis,' she says, leaning against me as if seeking refuge from the horrors she's just witnessed. 'I do.'

11.

G-SPOT

THE SHARE VALUE IN THE EROTIC GOODS MANUFACTURER Steel Erection Ltd finally fell by 25% for the first time in five years after it succumbed to the worst two weeks in its history. The Research and Development centre in Middlesex was destroyed in an unprovoked para-military attack. Unconfirmed reports state that in the same incident its charismatic CEO has been possibly abducted or killed. Theories abound that the assault came from terrorists of the Christian far right or Islamic extremists. Analysts had expected share values to tumble dramatically; however, shareholder confidence remains buoyant. But no-one can say for sure how much longer. Sources say that a Senior Detective in Met 1 is the leak behind confidential information that what began as a kidnapping investigation may now become a murder hunt.

'Professor James Marsden has popularly been recognized as inventing 90% of the company's range of best-selling products', said economic analyst Ewan Carr from Paddick Moore Financial Institute. 'If the news of his demise is true then the loss of this creative dynamo will create an innovation vacuum that could destroy or, at the very least, have a dire effect on the market's confidence in Steel Erection's future performance. That forecast has yet to become a reality, but the question remains, for how long?'

Damn. I watch the Business News fade into an animated Entertainment page, fold the Nano-sheet in half for convenience and glance casually at the video streaming clip on the page of Ghetto Confusion band playing to a stadium of thirty thousand adoring kids in Nottingham. The shareholder's meeting is being convened in the foreground and a chill of fear spears into my guts. Something about this situation makes me uncomfortable. Things are not as they should be and it ain't just paranoia. I have a conditioned nose for trouble, and when it alerts me, I don't second guess it for a reason. I'm aware that what I had worked so hard in achieving this shit could all come tumbling down. A claustrophobic cloud of despondency shrouds me since I received the e-mail requesting major shareholders to attend this emergency meeting. It was like

I knew I was about to be ambushed but I still turned up to the mugging.

I adjust the Li-Fi headphone in my ear and look at the heavy hitters and executive suits seated in the Imperial Room of the Hilton Exquisite Hotel, Park Lane. I'm relaxed as I can be, absorbing everything being said by the Chairman mucho punto - Steven Hudson. I've met this mo fucker maybe twice at Central London HQ. He's in his mid-forties with a thick head of black hair, a snappy dresser, hiding a concealed viciousness behind Cecil Gee threads. He has a thing for designer spectacles too. I was damn sure he'd had laser treatment, spectacles were for the poorer classes in the zones who could never afford corrective surgery, but he liked the look. He must have thought that this would endear him to the scum classes, but this playa fell well short of the mark as a humanitarian. His fake ass couldn't fool my bull-shit detector, and I told him straight up the first time we met. His professional experience wasn't in question, though, Digital himself had head hunted him, but from company reports I'd read, this boy was ambitious, making critical decisions that were at odds with Digital's world view. But instead of considering it as a challenge to his authority Digital classed it as single-mindedness and some exemplary character trait, but I wasn't so sure. Digital going AWOL would prove an opportunity he could not ignore. I joined the dots, and this gathering did not bode well.

'Can you turn that down, please?'

A nudge on the shoulder jolts me out of my thoughts. The article I'm listening to fades to accommodate the ambient sound of the kid leaning over me. Slowly I face what I choose to think is some pretentious looking junior exec mistakenly guessing he's dealing with some zone punk who got lucky. I remove my earphones and glare at him.

'What the fuck is your problem, dawg?' I growl. I stared at him and watched the blood drain from his face.

'Yu-you're distracting me, and I'm sure some of us came here to learn what significant changes are going to be made to our portfolios.'

I check the Infotablet on his lap for at-a-glance information of who he is and what investment exposure he's experiencing. I chuckle humourlessly.

'Check you out, peckerwood Norman! All you're holding down is a measly two percent share value while I'm rocking a fifteen percent share in this mo fucker! Look at me, I'm chillin! Which of us do you think has more to lose by missing out on what the dickwad chairman has to say?'

I speak in low tones from the back of my throat, and he quickly understands that the rules of gentle society don't apply to hood-rats like me. He looks to the podium for relief and remains focused. I let it ride cos he did say please; I just didn't like his tone; the one that implied that I wasn't legal and that my credits were somehow less valuable than his. I get uptight when jumped up corporate pussies try to test my credentials. Thanks to Digital not only am I familiar with the inner working of a shareholders meeting and everything investment related, but I was given a share option of fifteen percent from Digital's majority shareholdings. I was speechless when he presented it to me after three years, but now I could appreciate the method in his madness.

I wish the proceedings would gather some speed but the Chairs take their own ponderous time until a resolution on the Report and Accounts is put to the meeting and a poll finally declared that it's passed. I sit through the Remuneration Report, the Election/re-election of Directors, the Re-appointment of Auditors, the remuneration of auditors and then finally, Special Business. Through a kind of veiled optimism, the room senses something momentous is coming. The hum of excitement spreads through the elite collection of shareholders. Paparazzi and Journalists edge closer to the stage. News channels and business monthlies jockey for prime positions near the podium leading me to believe they knew something I didn't. I resolve to keep my eyes and ears open this time. I glance at Peckerwood beside me. He nibbles on the quick of his finger, his crossed legs shaking in anticipation. Steven Hudson enters the stage to a round of applause, and my whole body tightens up 'cos beside him steps up Lorraine Van Horne. She's accompanied by a small security detail parading as assistants rigged up with Li-FI headgear and Info tablets. They sit with Van Horne be-tween them. The CEO of Steel Erection walks across the stage to the podium. I'm tripping big time. I squeeze the liquid plasma so tightly it distorts the screen of my Infotablet until the audio begins to garble.

'Good to see you all,' Hudson's syrupy voice seems hollow, a distant announcement that quickly loses significance amidst a tidal wave of anxiety.

I check to make sure my surprise is only manifesting internally. Suddenly I want to leave before I do something out of character, destroy my advantage of surprise and fuck up my chances of resolving this shit. I shuffle back in my seat, a possible eruption of disquiet bubbling in my gut, my face twists with that same sense of creeping discomfort.

Calm the hell down, man, I murmur as images and memories of Maria, Popeye and Digital surface in mind already overwrought with pain, threatening to vent my emotions in some crazy act of violence.

Be sensible dawg. We need strategy kid, not an over-reaction. I wonder if anyone else is watching my schizoid struggle. I ease off, pull back, just relax. Slowly my need to vent diminishes. The pulsing at the back of my head subsides, and I let Steven Hudson's words seep through.

'It's with a heavy heart,' he begins confidently. 'And with profound sadness that I announce that Scotland Yard has concluded that James Marsden's disappearance has produced no meaningful leads, no demands from the abductors, nothing within the initial two-week hot period of investigation. The statistical likelihood of solving his kidnapping or murder has diminished dramatically. Of course, the case will continue just as vigorously onto the next phase, but the chances of a happy resolution are slim'.

He paused.

'Unfortunately, the business machinations of our industry do not allow us the luxury of time, and it's my job to convince you, our shareholders, that even after everything we have suffered, we are still in a commanding position. We are not in a vulnerable position, but we could have been if we didn't act in time. I'm pleased to say your investments and our well-known name and our collaboration with Nexus Corporation. Now, please consult your Infopads, ladies, and gentlemen, as we will transfer the relevant files to your units.'

Everyone looks to their Infopads eagerly while I look to the stage, monitoring Van Horne's reaction to all this shit. She flashes that thin smile of hers, cool like a cryojock strap, secretly conveying that she's got it all under control, leaving the nervous, expectant fidgeting to her lackeys. My reflection from my Infotablet shows the angst in my face, but I'm keeping it together. The Steel Erection three-dimensional symbol floats away, and the files are made available. Peckerwood beside me skirts around the real meat of the issue, a purist obviously, reading the company's Mission Statement, its Vision, and Values and getting a hard on from the message from the Chairwoman. It makes depressing reading as now I know where this bitch and her cohort Steve Hudson are going with this shit. Now I understood the possible motive for what has been happening to me. I'm losing focus again. A red veil of anger is tinting my perspective, but I try to side-line it with some tangential thought, smothering the emotion until this kamikaze vibe passed. I start playing out a scenario in my head. What if I was just a hotshot city man in it to win it? A sophisticated investor like me would be interested to see how our operation fits in with the leading developer of life enhancing biotech and prescription medicine for humans. What conflicts would I expect in its operation and, crucially, is this a takeover, amalgamation, combination, consolidation or even an absorption? Digital's business can't match the global reach of a giant like Nexus under any circumstances. What the fuck do they want with Steel Erection or, from what Digital had implied, what did those niggas want with me? I'm thinking every single one of those sons-of-bitches on the platform is involved with the murder of my family and I'm sitting here tripping. Keeping up with the shifting screens proves ever more difficult as I grow numb letting the rage take its course without restraint. Hudson takes to the microphone again.

'Take your time to analyze the figures in detail, but the main points of interest are; number one: Ensuring that the Nexus Corporation realizes the phenomenal market potential of our business and number two: Enabling Nexus Corporation to see our present tragedy as an opportunity to joins us and legitimize who we are.'

He rubs his finger around the rim of one of his glasses and peers out to the shareholders from above the lens, probably expecting resistance but receiving none.

He goes on. 'Nexus is one of the oldest and most respected PharmoBioTech corporations in the world. Established in the 1840's it has a history of world-changing innovation and a unique philosophy to risk-taking that has placed them at the forefront of human well-being and advancement at every decade. Now they want to help us to bring about the renaissance in the most basic need of humankind, namely, sex. Imagine a world where your experience of sex is enhanced safely and immeasurably by a combination of drugs and technology. Our forecasted accounts should prove to you how successful our amalgamation could be. Share prices up by at least forty-five percent, plus a year on year bonus in the thousands!'

His virulent grin infects everybody except me cos I'm immune to bullshit.

Enough was enough.

I stand, shuffle out of my seat to the aisle and stride forward, approaching the platform with the effortless swagger of a man not worried about a thang but inside

I'm on a razor's edge. I'm passing rows of people thinking about how to spend their money, thoughts of Digital, the original CEO, who had brought them this far, already forgotten. The traitorous motherfuckers watch my progress already interpreting my intent with curious looks and whispers. The camera crew always anticipating a major story had been disappointed so far until my black ass turned up. A young buck from the financial Satellite Station sniffs out my approach ahead of the more jaded hacks. His camera swings my way. I ain't worried 'cos I know he's recording thin air. I continue walking until I'm about fifty meters from the podium, every eye is on me including Hudson's. I'm an oddity. A smooth dude with the obvious means to be here, but with deeply pressing shit on his mind that's compelled me to leave my seat.

The camera man squints at me as if he can discern what I'm about by looking directly at my approach with an unaided eye. I stop, and he refocuses with the aid of his camera. I switch shit on them and address the Eck - Zeck's way be-fore they're ready to take questions. Not the done thing but Fuck em!

'This is bullshit, man!' I spit at him. 'Digital put his trust in you to do the right thing and you ain't doing nothing but abuse that trust! You're selling him out dawg! You know it and I know it.'

If Hudson could have reached over and patted me on the back with his condescending wry smile, he would have. Instead, he continues with his practiced rhetoric.

'No sir, this isn't bullshit, this is business. Despite the tragic circumstances, we're still running an operation, I've got a challenging and sometimes unappreciated job, but my duty is to keep this company buoyant at whatever cost, even if it alienates supporters of Marsden......'

'Dr. Marsden to you bitch!' I flare up in hot-tempered anger before finding my stride again. 'You're talking about the man who single-handedly established all this right here. The man who gave your punk ass a job.'

'You're losing your temper, Mr...?'

'I'm chilled Steven, don't get it twisted. I'm just passionate. Can't you tell?' Calling him by his first name throws him. I move closer to the stage; I can see the security types on stage starting to get antsy.

He's been struggling with my identity from the time I addressed him. But he can't bring up a visual of me on his smart podium. I know he's trying because his eyes flit about the plasma screen embedded in the rostrum, fix on me for fleeting seconds, then fly back to the screen as his fingers manipulate the icons, his eyebrows knitting together in frustration. He's at a disadvantage. I save him the trouble and step even closer.

'Adonis Campbell. Your equipment having a problem Id-ing me dawg?'

'It would seem that way.' he says evenly.

'Don't worry you're not the only one who has problems pinning me down.'

'Mr. Campbell,' he continues freshly armed with my name. 'I'm sure you're experienced in attending previous shareholder meetings. You strike me as someone with a broad and varied, maybe even elaborate portfolio across many companies. We follow the rules here; it helps us focus on the important aspects of our business. I'm sure you can appreciate that?'

'Sure I can.' I respond as though he's getting through to me. 'But what I don't appreciate is when some dude thinks they can take me and my money for a ride without being challenged.'

I've now got everyone's attention including the resident Po-Po. There are four of them stationed in the meeting room, and in the short time, it takes me to get within forty meters of the stage I graduate to public enemy number one. Guess they thought that the evening would pass off uneventfully in the entertainment stakes except for maybe helping some loaded heiress with her pedigree Chihuahua. Two of them hustle in my direction.

'Mr. Campbell, I've outlined my conditions and that is the end of it.' His fingers move craftily over the touch screen again. The significance of his actions is not lost on me.

'You got my motives all bent out of shape Stevie baby. These motherfuckers right here,' I point to the seated share-holders, 'will vote for anything you present to them as long as they make substantial chips from the deal. How much stock options did you get from Nexus to sell Digital down the river?'

He stares at me. Whatever he's feeling it is locked away so tightly I don't have a hope of seeing it.

'This conversation is over Mr. Campbell. Either you take a seat while these proceedings are completed with no further interruptions or you will be escorted out of the building.'

I fire what I guess will be my final verbal salvo before the Po-Po dive on my ass. 'You took a contract out on Digital head, didn't you? Or did you just watch your murder buddies at Nexus take care of bizniz?

Steven Hudson goes to speak but swallows his words instead. His rage is imperceptible, but I still sense it. Madam Van Horne and her entourage don't even try to disguise their anger. The security cadre closes in on her as if I'm firing bullets and not verbal shots. I stand my ground waiting for a response I know isn't gonna come. Amidst the news crew's frenzied attention, I sense the first member of the security detachment position himself beside me. I turn to the approaching security guard with the most non-threatening body language I can muster and read the confusion in his face. He was just out of his teens, a young Asian kid with kind eyes, a small mouth, and lacking in build. Not the physical profile you'd expect for this kind of work but I warm to his courage.

'I'm going to have to ask you to leave or take a seat, Mr. Campbell.' He says shit scared.

'Okay, I'm cool. Whatever you say.' I raise my hands in a show of over the top submission and motion with my right hand for him to lead the way. He shouldn't have because if I was a shyster and intended to hurt him, I could have, but he leads anyway, and I follow him from behind in good faith.

That's when my twenty-twenty pimp slaps me upside the head stopping me in my tracks. As soon as I realize that shit is about to pop off a hand falls heavily on my shoulder. It takes all of my willpower not to react.

I don't have to turn around to know that some rent-a-cop has just joined the party probably thinking that he's apprehending some low-life zone thug. I shrug his hand off my clavicle and turn to face him. In the background, Steven Hudson's smile broadens. The brother in the neat Khaki and blue security uniform tries laying his hand on me again as if he hasn't got my hint. I block his arm flinging it out of the way, sending him three steps back and off balance in one sweeping movement.

Judging from his determined grimace and the brace of his chest, somehow, I don't think Slick Rick had expected what just happened. The thought pissed him off although he tried not to show it. Unfortunately, his instant dislike for me or the hidden agenda, he's stroking like a hard on, clouded his better judgment.

Surprise, surprise, wankster reaches for the Shock Baton on his hip. I shake my head. He slaps leather and fires up thirty thousand volts' charge on the prod in a practiced movement just as my fists go up and I step away bobbing and weaving. I smell the sharpness of ozone between us and I'm not about to add the aroma of my burnt flesh to the melange.

The motherfucker has one chance, and you know what? Yeah, that's right he squanders it. The diagonal swipe across my chest comes straight from the shoulder and if it had connected my ass would generate enough light to illuminate Wembley Stadium. But for that fractured second it takes him to engage his higher brain functions, I've already fallen backward, the Shock Baton sizzling dangerously above me. I use my arm to piston myself to a standing position just as he completes his failed attempt.

We're talking seconds but my fight heightened senses to make this dude seem as if he's moving through a wind tunnel. I step back, my looping right fist catching him at the back of the head. I've been the pacifist long enough; now I'm applying the Queensberry rules to his punk ass. He stumbles face down from the sucker punch. I walk over him and kick the Shock Baton out of his hand. Then I step back again allowing him to get to his feet. The dude's not thinking straight; he could have stayed down but thought he could take me.

Big mistake.

For a full minute, I take out my aggravation on him. He can't take his eyes off my footwork because when I'm in the zone, I'm pretty man; I'm a force of nature. I've got him and the shareholders who've backed up to give me space, mesmerized. My jabs rain down on him with speed he can't possibly react to. He's utterly bemused like he wants to congratulate me for whooping his sorry ass. A body shot clinches the deal, and he drops to his knees in supplication, face bloodied, eye swollen. I glare at him suspiciously. He stays on his knees and I back off, my hands at my side showing that I'm done.

Backup Po-Po arrives as all this is happening and I remember the Asian kid who was leading me out of temptation when I was attacked. I had my back to him all this time, and he hadn't moved throughout this one-sided beating. I guess that plain fear had cemented him to the spot. The remaining security guards give up trying to get their colleague off his knees. They knew I was involved but didn't know what had occurred. Not that any of that shit makes a difference. They already have shock Batons at the ready, guilty until proven innocent. I snap back into battle mode ready for their best.

'I'd put those away,' the Asian kid says to them, his voice carrying with uncharacteristic force. 'Vic attacked Mr. Campbell as I was escorting him out.'

Tweedle Dee and Tweedle Dum look at each other quizzically.

'I think we'd better give Mr. Campbell our sincerest apologies and hope we don't get sued for grievous bodily harm.'

The Asian kid said.

My grin is a broad one.

'Apology accepted,' I say and mosey on out of Dodge City.

12.

KATTY

I'VE BEEN THINKING ABOUT LITTLE MAN A LOT these last hectic days. Our tenuous father and son link had me anxious so when our weekly webcam chat came around nothing would interfere with that, no matter how badly the storm raged around me.

    I'm in Jess's crib sat in her rec room, online and for the first time waiting for him to log-on. He's usually all ready and waiting for me, his Moms making sure our time together is precisely one hour and not a second more.

His cute face as animated and upbeat as ever soon materializes on my wafer-thin screen. Everything that's recently been chipping away at my sanity dissolves immediately.

'Dad!' He says brightly.

'Waddup little man?'

'Fine.'

'What you been up to since the last time we rapped?'

I'm so eager to see him that it takes me a while to casually scrutinize his image, seeing how he's grown or changed since the last time we talked, and that's when I notice the damage. My last question answers itself. He had bruising on his face and a small swelling on his lip. A minor ruck? Schools have their rules and hierarchy like any other society. And to know where you fit in you must accept what you're given or stamp your authority and take your place. He ain't no punk. And Adonis junior has learned to look after himself. I know he won't start nuthin, but that lil man staring back at me will end sumthing if you persist. Still, I can't shake the paternal instinct of wanting to protect him from the hurts of growing up.

We talk about everything except the obvious, if he doesn't think it's important to discuss with his old man, it's not important. I should have known it wouldn't be left at that. The Battersea bitch, Yvette, my baby mama, muscles in, taking up a chunk of our precious time.

'We need to talk,' she says flatly.

'You got me,' I say.

'Your son is acting up. Talking back, throwing tantrums and getting into fights at school. I'm not putting up with that kind of behavior, Adonis. I've spoken to him about it on numerous occasions. He won't listen to me or my partner; maybe you can talk some sense into him.'

Suddenly it's convenient for me to help solve a problem in her household. Even asking for help from me is tantamount to her admitting defeat and that must be eating her alive. My son. Problems at home, not listening to my partner. Who gives a shit if he's listening to her partner? I thought she'd be telling me about conflicts at school, how he got his bruises.

I know Yvette wouldn't lay a finger on him, that's not her way. I would slap him, maybe rough him up a little, but certainly not bruise him. A picture forms in my head of disharmony in their home, an unknown nigga trying to be the top dog, my little man caught in the middle. In simple terms, shit had got chronic.

'What did he do?' I ask.

The Bitch turns to the little man and says: 'You tell your father.'

Before I can call her back, she's gone. Father and son face each other in silence.

I'm in the shower when I hear my Digi-Scroll chime, and my heart misses a beat. My mind is on Adonis Junior and my little tussle at Maria's Crib. The most important person in that situation, Ms. Brown, will be able to relax once she knows she'll be looked after. Another good deed was done. My mind snaps back to the present.

Business, I whisper to myself and try to align my thoughts to what my tasks are for the day as water massages, splashes, and tingles my ass to cleanliness. Some ghetto cat said: 'When you're a big dawg, sitting on big credits, you gotta pay the cost to be the boss?'

After half an hour, I pull the shower curtain back and step out. I love the feel of plain water on my skin. My shower is pressurized, hot and steaming, not some dry ion shower crap that charges up your balls then blasts the dirt off your ass. What's sexy about that? I step out onto the heated floor my body glistening from the spray. I feel like a clone freshly created from a nurturing tank at the peak of physical perfection. A different man from who I was four days ago.

It's good my imagination is still intact, and I nod at the fine figure of a thug staring back in all my glory. I make no apologies for loving myself, 'cos if I don't which other motherfucker will? The bathroom reacts to my presence and dries me with gusts of warm air. I walk over to the warm scented dresser just as the door opens. My reaction is immediate. I step back deftly and lock into a T-stance. I'm loose and ready, my fists and body set to deliver and receive some pain.

Jessica steps through.

I let out a long stream of anxious breath.

'Hey!'

'Hey,' she says.

My Angel has been busy, and I haven't seen her for a few days, but as always, she looks a dream.

It's funny because I know y'all think I'm superficial but what I missed about her the most was our conversations. Straight up. This girl could be a councilor or life coach. And when all this is over I'm going to suggest it. When I say, she was hot, I mean it because she helped drag my sorry ass out of despondency. Beauty and intelligence like hers are always in demand, even on the lap dancing circuit. On top of that, she had the most important thing a thug of any description would want, a good heart. I was still hurting from Maria – always would, but she was a sweet salve to any wound. Oh, did I mention her strength of will? Peeps are seeing me butt naked, but she's like, so? I ain't bragging or boasting, but not many women can keep it together like that. I've had reactions that range from; Oh, my God, to prayers of thanks, to tears of joy. Jessica was cool.

I draw her close, the sexual energy between us crackling.

'Where you been?' I ask, 'trying to ignore me won't work.'

She smiles.

'I can't ignore someone I don't see.'

'Fair play, it won't be like this forever, though.'
'I hope not, but I'm worried about you.'
'It's all cool,' I say.
She shakes her head.
'I know you can't tell me what this is all about but I wish I could do more to help.'
'Baby, baby, you've done more than anyone could under the circumstances. I'm gonna have to thank you properly later, but for now, I just want you and the little one safe.'
'Why shouldn't we be?'
'No reason,' I lie through my goddamn teeth. 'But I need to be sure. Call me paranoid.'
'You're one of the coolest paranoids I know, but it's good to hear you care.'
'I care, baby. Are you careful?' I ask.
'Yes.'
I can't bring myself to lie to her; I prefer to be cryptic.
'I don't want you worrying about anything, yah hear? When I needed someone the most, you were there to straighten my ass out. You gave me room to explain shit to you in my own time with no pressure. I gotta thank you, baby.'
'You'd do the same for me?'
'Straight up.' I answer.
She nods and places her forehead on my chest.
'Streets have taught me to be careful,' I say. 'Even when things look cool I keep my shit focussed. Just follow my directions, and we'll be fine.'

'Is it that you're just concerned for our welfare out in the wicked streets, nothing to do with what you're involved with?'

There's a pregnant pause before I speak again.

'Let's just say I'm all over this. You have nothing to worry about, and that's my word. That's the only thing that's real about this baby, all I have left to give.'

Jessica smiles and grabs the length and breadth that had up to that point was swinging between my legs like a gentleman. But the thug in me takes precedence, and I swell up immediately to fill her warm hands. She runs her fingers over the shaft as if to make sure her eyes aren't deceiving her, her inability to circle the bamboo confirms this is the real deal. I feel her warm breath on my neck. Jessica arches her back and carefully lifts her skirt, placing me between her legs. I feel the warmth of her thighs, the smooth silkiness of her panties, and the fleshy impression of the kitty as she gyrates that coochy over my dick effortlessly. She kisses my neck then slowly pulls away. 'When this is all over, maybe we can spend some quality time together.'

'Is that a promise or a threat?'

'A promise.' Then she's through the door only her perfume left lingering in the air and that fine ass sashaying with her.

I roll out the nano-sheet, from my mobile scroll and it lights up. Using gesture and verbal commands, I navigate my way through the program to the secure Sixty-Nine site. Entering is less straight forward, as I prick my finger for a blood sample – DNA authentication - then peer into a receptacle for my eye to be scanned by subatomic particles making a random cone and rods count. Convinced that I am who I say I am, I'm allowed to move through the layers easily, feeling more reason to be thankful for Digital's foresight. This operation is completely automated except for my vital contribution. Digital had worked hard at making this a turn-key run bizniz meaning a company virgin like me could run it at a moment's notice. He obviously knew something I didn't and was preparing for a time like this. From marketing, which was mainly word of mouth, to client profiles: criminal, psych and medical. Even gifts sent out to patrons on their birthdays and at Christmas was handled automatically, and the parent company invoiced. Then there was the army of players from the PI's and actors to stunt men and women, brought into the scenarios as and when Digital and now, I required their services. I just had to pray it held together. No disputes, no resignations just until I got out of this clinch.

New business, I say to the screen, the icon tinkles then opens. The vital statistics of five confirmed clients are now at my fingertips. Luckily for me, four of them are regulars, but a new one is expecting a tailor-made scenario in a week's time. I'm wary because I'm still being hunted. I use my judgment to decide whether this is kosher or not. I immediately refer the file to our Dirt Digging program designed to peer into an individual's personal history and dredge out any unsavory facts. Only when my gut says yeah and all the checks come back favorably do I even start thinking of creating a scenario. In the meantime, I look to see if this person has any ties to Nexus. I run a search to see if anything obvious comes up.

Pro's wouldn't leave an obvious trail, but to satisfy my curiosity and then let technology do its thang. I bring up a 3-D model of the client watching it rotate in cyberspace and construct some ideas based on her sexual preferences, just in case she is clean. In five years of full operation once a client has been confirmed with us the scenario always took place, no matter what outside circumstances dictated. Sixty-Nine could be depended on to deliver, and that was a given, a constant in regards to Digital's laws. Satisfaction is guaranteed. I wasn't going to be the one to fuck with bizniz tradition. I promised to hold Digital's principles high no matter what because those self-same principles were now mine.

Then suddenly it dawns on me that I haven't fully explored all the information I had at my disposal. Events have overtaken me to such a degree that obvious shit just didn't seem so obvious anymore.

'Address book.'

I direct my voice to the Hitachi scroll, and it bleeps in response. A large file comes to the forefront of the nano-sheet and announces its presence with an astonishing million gigabyte content. I browse through it. 'Man,' I mumble. So many familiar faces'.

Some I'd forgotten, some I'd neglected. People who had played a part in some kick ass scenarios never to be seen again. Teachers, trainers, doctors, some I'd taken their details figuring I'd be in contact but never did. One name stands out from the rest. Madame Zorva. One of a few people that I should have contacted to give me some direction in all this but didn't.

It's funny because before this shit happened, I had thought of her. And as always, any thought of the woman who taught me true poise and sex appeal was always a pleasant one. The last time we met had been six months ago, something I tried to do regularly, see how she was, stay current, talk shop. Over the years our relationship had changed from student to friend, it was her relationship with Digital that was the important factor. He had the hots for her even when he was still married, and I know he sampled the poontang many times on the down low. Outside of his Sixty-Nine family, Digital trusted very few, and Zorva was a part of that select group. I needed to talk to her. My stomach swears indignantly, reminding me I'm running on empty. I heed the call of my raging metabolism and let the ideas for a fresh new scenario bath the old brain synapses.

13.

POOLSIDE

BEFORE GOOD FOOD WASTE MEK BELLY BUSS. Ma Campbell used to utter that Jamaican proverb shit in times of scarcity. I look up only when I'm done eating and that all-over glow of satisfaction warms me from my head to toe. My internal engines roar at maximum giving me the clarity I need for any future conflict. I leave the table that now resembles a neatly arranged battlefield of chicken bones, salad, fruit, pasta, hard dough bread and two pitchers of fruit juice. I have a voracious appetite and a metabolism to compensate. It hasn't always been like that and from all indications I'm in better condition now than I've ever been in my life. Is this the new and improved prototype that Digital was talking about?

After feasting on this lavish spread, my Angel's crib feels even more like home. Jessica's was the second call I'd made from Central London after I'd two-way Chen about the slight dilemma I'd found myself in. At least Playboy had arranged for Ms. Brown and her family to be relocated until this shit blew over.

The more I put my neck on the line the more I appreciate my eastern thug allies and their resources. I fully intend to make sure that no innocents I encounter would suffer a loss as I had because of my carelessness. Maria had been secretive for a good reason, one which I hadn't figured out yet, but I knew for sure that she cared about me. She'd confided in Mrs. Brown and, as much as that makes me feel good, it also brings home her loss like a sledgehammer to my heart.

I walk over to the window and part the curtain with my finger. Chen is parked below in his Bentley, waiting patiently to discover what I've dug up and my conclusions about what I've found. I look around the small apartment and yow! I'm scared all over again. Not for me this time but for my Angel. She's asked no questions, just been there for me, no idea where I'm coming from but still resolutely trusting, even though she doesn't truly know me. What if just being around her means I've consigned Jessica and her baby to a similar fate as the Sixty-Nine crew? I haven't even met her daughter. Because of Jessica's shifts, she stays with her grandma. But she's another link that some vindictive cuss could use to their advantage. I swear on my mother's grave that I won't let it come to that.

I've already taken enough liberties with Jessica's kindness so leaving her kitchen untidy would be wack, so I get busy with the Fairy liquid and sponge.

The warm water and bubbles relax me. Soon I'm ready to break shit down in my head in an unhurried kind of way. I analyze everything, examining the facts logically removing the emotion that threatens to well up in me. It's been almost five days, and the mysteries are increasing. I'm single-handedly keeping Sixty-Nine afloat, servicing any incoming contracts that might have been sealed just before or just after Digitals disappearance. I was also faced with untangling the real person behind the woman I cared for, the woman I had been making love to for years. Maria Chen was a professor of Biochemistry. Five years ago, I was introduced to Digital, having known her two months prior. It's like six degrees of separation and all that shit. I had met her while being a paid guinea pig at a medical trial; never quite knew what she was doing there but we hit it off immediately. Thinking about it now, it was only after our friendship that all the pieces of my life started to fall into place.

But why after studying for eight long years does a person dump their lifetime passion for the risqué venture of the sex trade. Okay this business has its challenges and a powerful intellect like Maria's could bring to bear some of her creative gifts, but sex will most certainly never garner respectability credits. Ms. Chen was classed as a new age, Madam. She may not have had a string of high-class girls offering their services but what she did still take a keen understanding of human nature, as well as organizational skills second only to a marketing pro. My China Doll ran ten swinger's clubs across the country with a waiting list of couples that resembled the voter's list for a small rural district. Top class venues, Michelin-starred chefs, membership fee in the multiple thousands, you do the math baby. Sure, the money was fantastic, but the motivation just didn't add up, and I'm the kind of nigger who likes it straight. One plus one equals two.

Then it dawns on me. I've never actually been to any of these swinger's parties. Did they even exist? Everything I know about her I've been told, or I figured out.

Sonofabitch! What if I could get some answers there?

I put my floss on and head for the streets to see what the Dragons will make of it all.

We're rapping on the move. I'm almost convinced that Chen has a doppelganger stashed away for emergencies, believe dat. He's either an insomniac and can stay awake for days on end like me, or he's got a clone. Over the last forty-eight hours my man has changed his threads five times replacing each outfit with some fly shit every time. Nothing excites this mo' fucker except his passion for clothes. My boy is full of surprises. Who knew?

I stretch out in the supple leather seats, more comfortable now around my Chinese thug and strangely, I'm not afraid to admit, he's proving to be the kind of moral support I need to get through this. I never thought being a team player could ever become a handicap but as I consider my situation I question my ability to function on my lonesome. Fear doesn't become me, but I'll have to deal with it still. Chen is re-enacting the Tao of calm, either for my benefit or his own. Our conversation ends abruptly, and I leave him to his cogitations while I absorb the landscape streaking by.

Streatham is a memory. We've made our way through the sophisticated bustle of Brixton along Kennington road, approaching Old Father Thames, the river is a calming hue of crimson, the bridge awash with blue light. We cross Waterloo Bridge; I cast my eyes downriver the spectacular light show airbrushing away the drab gray buildings and the brushed steel and glass hyper structures along the riverside.

L-Town has shown me a new sinister side. The makeup is off and the virginal façade exposed as a goddamn lie, but that's the appeal of the woman laid out before me with her legs spread wide and the aroma of her juices repulsive. No more mystery, no more sex appeal just the stark reality that there were more layers to this bitch than I realized. But it was all love. This was the real London, a place I know at a gut level from my experiences but never needed to confront it before now. I'm not sure where we're going, but hundreds of questions run through my mind.

'Yow, Chen, explain something to me.' I say.

His eyes gain intensity as he gathers focus. 'If I can, Mr. Campbell.'

'How come you found out about the connection between Sixty-Nine and this Nexus company so quickly? That must have been some badass detective work, amigo.'

His calculating eyes question why I'm bugging but still show patience despite my brashness.

'Did you read any of the letters you picked up from Maria's home?'

I nod knowing exactly what he's going to say.

'Time didn't permit a detailed analysis. I just thought it was weird people still used letters. And then I was recouping from the damage inflicted by some grimy niggas trying to take me out at your sistas crib. But I'm aight, thanks for asking.'

His shrug was almost imperceptible.

'My sister was a professor of Biochemistry; her title is Doctor Maria Chen.'

I nod again in acknowledgment. 'And I guess with this Nexus outfit; you have some idea how they fit into the equation?'

Chen flutters his fingers and places them purposely on his lap.

'Before Maria disappeared seven years ago, Nexus was the company she was working for. One of the few high fliers whose career was about to take off. Then suddenly she changed course.'

'Why?' I ask.

He shakes his head and looks at me as if I'm a dumb shit with the intellectual capacity of a mayfly.'

'Hey,' I continue in my defense. 'That was way before my time with her. Fill a brother in.'

Reluctantly he lets his words form allowing me the benefit of their meaning. I have an urge to tell him to kiss my ass.

'All I know is she felt stifled at the company. She wanted to do much more than she could and finally decided to go her own way. Nexus wasn't happy about her sudden departure because they had spent money developing her talent too. I surmised that she might have wanted to set up a research facility, but when she turned to the sex industry, I was perplexed. I was simply hoping the company name would ring some bells for you and it did.'

I slump back, needing time for all this to sink in. And surprisingly it does, with crystal clarity. I start to believe now that my supposed uniqueness was a deciding factor for two scientific heavyweights to drop what they're doing to come fuck with me. My breathing heightens. Now I'm excited, but I keep that titbit to myself.

'When they dipped me six years ago from the US, I was penniless, badly in need of food and shelter. I got involved in drugs tests among other things. I only did that scary shit a couple of times because it was so well paid. It's just dawned on me that one of the companies running the tests was possibly Nexus and that's where I met Maria. Maybe our meeting wasn't pure chance, after all, maybe she knew of me from my drug trials at Nexus, turning on the charms for an end, an angle. She could have engineered our meeting. Think about it. Me, Nexus and Maria, all connected.'

'When I find out why, I'll be closer to knowing who.' He said matter-o-factly.

'So, where we heading?' I ask.

'Our first port of call is a police informant in Soho who could have some relevant information for us. Gaining some-thing useful unlike your attempts so far.'

Goddamit, I think. Does he do that on purpose or was it his mission in life to rub me up the wrong way?

'Aight,' I shrug off the ice from his comment. 'But I don't know anything outside of what I've told you. Maria was my girl, and she believed in me from day one. There was nothing unusual about us. We loved, and we lived. How am I gonna find the grimy ass bastards who killed her, if she's still a mystery to me.'

Chen tugs on the sleeves of his pinstripe. 'That's the reason why we're here, to unravel the mystery. Anyway, she must have had a good reason for holding the truth from you?'

I didn't like his tone

'Yeah,' I spat. She had a reason all right. With Maria, it was love and fear, straight up. She was protecting me. She wanted her man safe. But what's your fucking story in all this, outside of that family honour bullshit?'

'My story is my concern; our story is something entirely different. I don't trust you. Your people have a problem with discipline and control. If I didn't think for one moment that you were essential to solving this riddle, we wouldn't be talking. Our relationship was conceived on an uneasy footing from the start, we both need each other. The less you know about me, the better for you.'

'My people, mo' fucker?' I reply like a seriously delayed echo. 'My people are helping to ease that five-spice mixing; Chicken fried rice, wok ass conscience of yours. I'm not the one who turned on her. I had her back dawg. Your bitch ass is as clueless about her life as I am. Don't try to play a playa, playa.'

Chen shakes his head. 'You're forgiven for not having the genetic advantage of being Chinese. Saying that I do believe that you truly loved my sister and that shared motivating force of anger will keep us going until we've reached a satisfactory conclusion. When it's done, we are done.'

'You self-righteous cocksucker! That's fine by me.'

'Perfect.' Chen said.

'Punk ass,' I mumble.

'Until then I decide what is relevant.'

'In your dreams playa, I do what I got to do and you can't tell me shit.'

The finality of my statement leaves no room for negotiation. I grab my balls, making it perfectly clear how I feel about him. Swallowing my pride is not easy but I manage it with a smile. It's funny how far I've come then it becomes hilarious. I crease up in the aromatic leather in the back seat laughing my head off with Chen wondering if I've just plain lost my mind.

14.

MISSIONARY POSITION

IF THERE WERE A TRUE TWENTY-FOUR-SEVEN KIND of place in L-Town, Soho would be it. Utilizing Chen's intricate knowledge of the area and his contacts, I follow him down Old Compton Street, onto Dean Street, and along some alleyway. I felt better amongst the crowds we meet on the fringes of Gerrard Street, but here it's dark, moist and quiet. The night is getting chillier, the frigid edges of rain in the air. The place feels enclosed, every sound was amplified in the gloom. It's devoid of any life at all, and strongly reminiscent of some Victorian slaughterhouse at closing time with an oppressive smell of slick condensation and affluence.

I listen even more keenly to my internal defense system checking that my guides are ahead of me where I can clearly see their punk asses. Buildings issue puffs of steam at ankle level. The only giveaway that business is taking place and that these spaces are occupied are the parked hover bikes and bicycles chained and leaning idly on the walls. I'm thinking wild goose chase until Chen stops and knocks at what looks like another stretch of darkened wall. I can't see anything but a nondescript wall with graffiti scrawled over it. Then I see the illuminated edges of a door frame. The illusion of a wall dissolves away like the entrance to some fantasy never-never land.

Son-of-a-bitch.

Only big or criminal business can afford stealth technology of this caliber, and my vote is on criminal. Chen waits for me to catch up before he steps through. Alexander Fu Sheng's double follows, and I follow him. I'm not usually easily impressed, but this is some class joint right here. Gambling, food and live music. I expect Chen to stop at a table, but he nods to a few high rollers and keeps on walking. We're now through into what would have been a large traditional beer garden if it wasn't hidden away and undercover. Flora and fauna aren't all hydroponics in nature; the grass has that synthetic texture, but the atmospheric controls make you feel as if you're outdoors on a cool summer evening. The Chinaman stops. His eyes fixed on the human-shaped shadow under a flowering apple tree up ahead.

'I'll be five minutes.' He said.

His henchman nods and stays put.

I move into the shadows getting as close to the conversation as possible. I sit on a picnic table with my back to them hoping I can pick up some interesting shit that I can use. Fortunately for me my enhanced hearing, makes the conversation clear, so I lean back, get comfortable and let them enlighten me.

Ten minutes' tops are all it takes to convince me that I know what's going down. I maintain my cool with difficulty. The Met-1 detective had sold Chen a Holo-clip of one of the assailants leaving the hotel Maria was murdered in on foot. I guess that he's the same detective who broke the bad news to Chen and his family in the first place. He'd somehow gained access to the surveillance footage and the greedy mo' fucker now wanted to be paid for giving us the privilege of viewing the disk and Identifying the killers. He's demanding enough paper credits to retire and send his kids and his grandkids to private school. This fool is tripping.

I turn just in time to see the undisguised pain in Chen's eyes, and I turn away immediately with shame. The disgrace of having his sister's burnt body held at the morgue like some common criminal and not being able to go through the Chinese traditions of burial must be tearing a traditionalist like him apart. It was tearing a thug like me apart too. I watched the reflection as he shook the hand of this extortionate snitch, their small talk done, as the detective leaves empty handed.

'I'm sorry Chen,' The detective shrugs. 'But business is business.'

Every departing step he takes is a stab of grief to my gut.

Chen walks away without a word of protest, or even with the slumped shoulders of a man defeated. I can't put my disappointment into words. The pussy was just walking away, and so was the Five-O, nice and easy. Can you believe that? Disappearing into the night with the confident gait of a man who had options. Ready to sell his wares to the highest bidder, knowing he'll get what he asks for even if it's not from Chen. Totally unconcerned about a case with the tortured body of an entrepreneurial Chinese woman known to be Chen's sister. Not giving a fuck about trace blood matches to hired guns known to Met-1 and the stench of a conspiracy being played out. His slow cowboy sway said that he didn't give a damn about the previous occasions when Chen paid him for information. No matter that his paymaster's sister had been murdered when all is said and done, he was all about the credits.

I look at Chen, my eyes telegraphing my anger. He looks at me impassively. I look back to Detective Wolsey who's fading into the gloom, then shoot a look in Chen's direction, our eyes meet again, my intensity and disappointment transverses the distance between us. The Chinaman signals the end of our emotional exchange by turning away from me. He continues walking to his homeboy, who's been waiting patiently.

'Kiss my ass!' I toss my words at the detective's diminishing shadow. 'Yow, Five-O!' I call.

The Detective's darkened image stretches along the ground morphing back into human form as if a playback button has been pressed from a hidden editing suite. His approach is cautious, but there's a twinkle of certainty in his eye, aided by the halogen lights and much more sway to his swagger.

This cocksucker needs something special, and like a genie my subconscious threw up a doozy. The lexicographers at Collins Dictionary are gonna love my ass because I've just coined a new business term for their legendary publication; G-Neg or for the mentally lame amongst you 'Guerrilla Negotiations.' It's a bit raw having just been conceived out of this shit but with some clarification and general usage who the fuck knows? It could become common usage.

Detective Wolsey looks over my shoulder expecting Chen, but there's no sight of him. He looks me up and down unsure what to make of me.

'Mr. Chen?' He grins at his own hilarity.

'He's asked me to make you an offer,' I respond.

His grin broadens. 'You're a bit dark to be Chinese, aren't you son?'

'A freak of nature.' I quip.

'Look, what I said to Mr. Chen, I'll say to you. I don't make offers. The figure I gave him, is the only figure I'll accept.'

My expression is that of contemplation. 'Have you ever heard of G-Neg dawg?'

He shakes his head, his exasperation mounting.

'Striking a deal on the street is not too different from striking a deal in the boardroom. It's just that you're dealing with OG's in the hood, Pimps on the strip, each with their own take on how to transact business. G-Neg just levels the playing field and forces an understanding of the parties involved. A common ground. Nah mean?'

The bent copper nods his head encouraging me to continue.

'It's like this. You hook me up with whatever information I need and take what Chen was offering you, or I take the information, and you get diddly squat.'

His lips pull back over his gleaming teeth like a smile from a ventriloquist bot. 'Is this Chen's way of strong arming me? Using some snot nosed kid, he dug up from Brixton to do his wet works for him?'

'This shit has got nothing to do with Chen; he was walking away, remember?'

'And you junior had better do the fucking same.' His tone was a mixture of threat and uncertainty. That tells me gentlemanly conduct had just gone through the window. The DI knows he's amongst some raw, totally unpredictable niggas. But as I write the rules in my own game in my head I share my five G-Neg commandments with his back, keeping in step with his retreat.

'Number one. Research your shit before you come to the table. Number two. Take nothing at face value.' Number three. Never come without backup because whether you're Five-O or Feds your ass can still get smoked.'

DI Wolsey stopped in his tracks my implied threat maybe a cause for concern but I keep going, still preaching to his shoulder blades.

'Number four. Never have your bargaining chip on your tired ass self, that's just plain fucking stupid. Keep up with the time's mo' fucker. You've heard of NFC - Near Field Communication or close-proximity data transmission? It's some old-school shit that was replaced many decades ago. But what a lot of people don't know, it's still viable.'

Wolsey turns around his eyes blazing and only then realizing I'm two arms lengths away from him.

'And last but no means least, never, never, never try to pass off your skills on street treachery to a G-Neg aficionado cos you will get your ass beat down.

For an older guy, he is quick on the draw, but I'm much quicker. He must have imagined lighting up the young buck with a nerve scrambling thirty-thousand-volt charge would be a piece of cake. But I eat up the space between us with knee trembling speed and the double pimp slap catches the DI unawares and gawping. Wolsey rocks back and tries to gain his composure reaching for his heater again, but I'm on his ass pulling his jacket down over his arms, making it impossible for him to reach for his weapon. His struggling is comical making him look like an inept escape artist. I put him out of his misery with a feigned left then a sweet right hook. The greedy son-of-a-bitch bounces once before crashing into a garbage atomizer slamming his head into it. I'm poised to whip his Anglo ass like Kunta, but he stays down. Typical Five-O, bringing a gun to a fist fight.

Nice suit, though.

I probe his inside pocket and emerge with a memory strip packaged in gold leaf. I knew when I interrogated its contents it would have the password to a secure site and server with the pictures from the hotel cameras. I gently slide it into my Sean John oversize jeans and kneel beside him and whisper in his ear.

'Moma say knock you out, motherfucker.' Quoting LL Cool J's flow feels damn good.

I'm in the back of the luxury road hugger, heading to God knows where. Chen gives me the silent treatment. My V- Comm buzzes. Someone wants my attention. I answer without looking at the readout.

'Yippy yah yea!' My swagger returning after the brief adrenaline rush.

'Lizard,' comes the baritone reply as his fly ass features swim into focus.

'Whaddup nigga! Didn't think I'd hear from you again, son.' I try to play it cool but my relief at seeing another of my extended family who was alive and concerned for my welfare as almost overwhelming.

Lizard's chuckle softens his eyes. His face is taut with smooth skin that makes it impossible to guess his age which I should know but always forget. 'Hey! Your psych and voice stress stats were off the hook. I figure you in deep, choir boy. Tell me it's not so?'

'I wish I could cuz, but it's fucked up.'

'Damn, nephew; I saw the pictures of your boss's place on the network. His crib was some kinda fucked up.'

'That Amigo is only the goddamn tip of the iceberg.'

Lizard's lips pull into a grimace as he shakes his head. 'I'm sorry I wasn't here for you man, but I've been away in LA. My Gulf Stream jet touched down at London City airport twenty-four hours ago. But the information you talked about? I think I got something.'

I remember the time immediately after Maria's murder and the vague, frantic calls to people I classed as peers, peeps, and family, the questions, the favors, but more memorably the cold shoulders I got in response. Just like cream, the true blood finally floats to the top.

'Swing by the Playhouse later tonight, this shit is time sensitive,' Lizard warns, 'I'm shooting all night, and you know how we throw it down,' he brightened up. 'Fun, drinks and hot pussy!'

'Aight!' I say. 'Meet you at the spot, dawg.'

My conversation over I refocus on Chen who's intently watching the History channel with his earphones on. More upbeat than a minute earlier, I remotely turn the volume down and face him.

'How'd you like an OG getting shit done? Taking care of bizniz.'

'I didn't.' Chen spat. 'You've just cost me a valuable con-tact whereas if you'd allowed me to handle it, I would have retrieved the information and still have my inform-ant intact. Every Friday night he shops for Chinese food in Soho, considers himself a dab hand in the kitchen. Then he's with one of my girls in the House of Light on Jermaine Street. Between the supermarket and my seduc-tress, he'd have had his pocket picked and been none the wiser. That meeting was simply a ruse to make sure he'd brought the disc with him.'

Damn! This nigga was slick, and I was a comparative peewee when it came to Machiavellian shit. As much as it pained my black ass to admit it, he could teach me a thing or two about channelling your anger. He's just as devas-tated as I am over this but he's holding it down better than I ever can. I try to salvage some self-respect.

'You hold the thieving Anglo's hands, and we get the in-formation in three hours. I beat him down and get it in five minutes.'

Chen shakes his head knowing he's not getting through to me.

'Give me the secure web address.' The Chinaman stretches out his hand impatiently wriggling his fingers.

I pass him the memory strip, resisting the urge to crack another smart-ass quip.

He unfurls the gold leaf protecting it and watches it being sucked into the cars onboard CPU, bringing up the screen as he does so. The voice recognition system finds and opens the site before the echo of his voice diminishes. We stare without comment at the footage. Detective Wolsey was kind enough to provide a helpful commentary like he'd already figured that I didn't need to know who killed Maria because I'd met the cocksuckers up front and personal. But I was anxious to know more about who had sent them and why? We skip from the main road to car parks one, two, three and four. Then we focus on a Lexus sedan. The license plate is obvious, but I ignore it because in today's world plates can be forged by ten-year-olds. But even the most nondescript of car's is unique. If you pay attention.

Chen straightens his tie. His shit is focussed too. We're in luck, and we know it. Most establishments have straight-forward optical cameras that handle surveillance, but five-star real estate always go that extra mile, rocking the multi-spectral joints. If they had you in their sights, they could go from IR, UHF Exhaust analysis, and mass spectrometry to statistical profiling. New or old cars are unique, and we've got its fingerprint right in front of us confirming what I already knew, but Chen must be a hundred percent certain before he starts taking cat's out. I hope these boys hadn't had any dealings with Five-O in the last week because if they'd been stopped for speeding or even a parking offence, Chen would be on their ass.

I see now just how much of a contribution I'm making to this investigation. Nada. I feel impotent, and for the first time, I understand how exposed the sisters feel after going through emotional shit from some swaggering, unscrupulous nigger taking advantage of the situation because he knows his chances for some Nescafe kitty have risen exponentially. I can relate, man.

Chen has all the answers, the sense of purpose, while I'm hanging on for some brilliant lead like a poor mutt expecting leftovers. Lizard's call has given me a chance to prove my significance and up my game. I make my apologies to my host and ask him to drop me off at a Compucab station; I have an appointment to keep.

15.

MAMBO

'COME THROUGH DAWG, COME THROUGH.' Daddy Lizard, pimp extraordinaire, is nothing like his reptilian moniker. He's slim in stature with tight muscles stretched over his frame. He has a handsome but unmarked face for someone who revels in the stories of his tough upbringing in the New York projects. He wears his age very well for a man in his mid-fifties who'd never had augmented surgery to keep him young. Lizard attributed his youthfulness to what he called pussy over the border - which in street parlance meant young women just over the legal age of consent.

He ushers me into a vast sound stage with rap prodigies Sign of the Times thumping through speakers in the ceiling and walls with an accompanying party in full swing in the indoor pool. I soon forget the throng of B-listers, penny pieces and wannabe's crowding the entrance as I approach the action. The place is filled to the rafters with the ghetto fabulous crowd. Cristal, Armitage cognac, and Hypnotic being the drinks of choice. Gucci, Prada and Versace rock on every svelte form. G-Unit, Sean John, Roca Wear and Akademiks drape casually on the thugs. Ruby-platinum bling, sable collars on throw-back baseball jackets, Platinum and Astro Diamonds for designer V-Comms and Oakley smart shades. It's pouring down outside, but no one in here gives a damn; there's enough OG, star and playa power in here to keep everyone hot and sweaty. If ever a party was off the hook this was it!

True to Lizard's style, the honey's outnumber the ballers, and the Cristal flows with uninhibited ease. He moves through the joint with difficulty. Sugars in bikinis and impossibly high heels, some fully clothed, some topless, a few completely naked except for high heels but all appearing from out of the dancing, to hug and kiss him with genuine love. I'm getting some hungry stares too and the instinctive urge to do what I've come to know as Stop and Search with some of these fine dime pieces is strong, but I hold it down, that's not what I'm here for.

Lizard touches fists and pumps arms until finally, we walk into an area cordoned off with light beams and protected from the bangin' bass by sound bafflers. Privacy is a luxury for a man in his position. Two huge motherfuckers flank the entrance instead of the traditional velvet rope. We're in a cocoon of calm, uncluttered with two lounge chairs, a bar with two stools, a split screen monitor showing the video of the music and a myriad of CCTV camera angles. The film shoot he'd mentioned earlier, with a set designed in the style of a plush Victorian bedroom, has been relegated to an almost insignificant part of the floor space, the actors and crew huddled around as if providing protection from an ever-encroaching party. All of this could have been my destiny if I hadn't agreed to work with Maria instead of taking Lizards generous offer.

This party is typical of his type of soirees, anything and everything goes. My man has worked hard to achieve the elusive combination of mixing business with pleasure and creating a global empire in the process. The Playhouse is the HQ of Lizards multifaceted erotic entertainment empire in Europe. He's one of the few people who, in his earlier days, had the cajones to successfully float a brothel on the stock market. He'd dedicated his life to the ethos of party and sex. You couldn't mention the porn business without Daddy Lizard's name cropping up.

'What you drinking, cuz?' Lizard asked.

'Carrot juice.'

Lizard nods.

I ask.

'Smokes?'

'Only the best dawg, a Cuban Partagas?'

My face lights up.

'Staines!' Lizard hollas into his Wi-Fi headgear, and an immaculately dressed gentleman with similar equipment outside of the bubble comes alive. He looks like a friendly uncle, a wise twinkle in his eyes, distinguished appearance with a pure old school fashion sense.

'Sir,' the man answers, his voice as syrupy as a shot of ten-year-old Crofts.

'A carrot juice for my compadre,' Lizard says, 'and my usual. Oh, and the best Cuban we got.'

'Yes, sir.' He leaves.

We sit down and get comfortable.

'You got me thinking after your message Adonis. I don't scare easy, homie, but you had me, nervous man. Telling me about the consulting outfit somehow involved with your shortie's killers and that name, Lorraine Van Horne? My orgy parties are fully booked for a year, so I checked your data cloud.'

I nod, his tale drawing me closer.

'I have a list of all the companies we deal with and their profiles. Ran a search on that bitch's name too. Her company ain't into consulting! She's all about drug development, and they're holding three parties with us this year, starting tomorrow, that's why I had to holla back.' He's silent for a moment letting the information sink in. 'So, what yuh gonna do?'

My head is reeling with the serendipitous break that had fallen into my lap, and I wasn't about to taint the opportunity with any vibes of doubt. I contain my excitement.

'I want in.'

'I was afraid you were gonna say that dawg.'

'Problem?'

'Damn right there's a problem. Nexus security is asshole tight. These mo' fuckers security and med screened the whole entourage for the night and made me sign some non-disclosure shit to say the performers in the contract will be the performers on the night.'

'Let's do a switcheroo on their executive asses. We all look alike to them anyway, right?'

Lizard chuckles.

Our refreshment arrives. Staines nods and I take my carrot juice off the silver tray. Lizard unwraps his multicoloured rocket lolly like it was Ruby-Platinum noticed water. Staines lights up my stoogie, and I exhale dense aromatic smoke with a hiss.

'That's only part of the problem, dawg,' Lizard continues. He pauses to catch a bead of strawberry juice running down his thumb, and I'm reminded why the girls gave him the moniker Lizard. My boy has a tongue like a tree sloth, long, thick and almost prehensile. He's gifted. A slight sway of my glass urges him on. 'Griffin is involved, and you know that mo' fucker likes to stand out from the crowd. He's made sure he'll be the only high profile entertainer performing tomorrow night. He calls that shit personal impact. Lucky fo' him, he's good at what he does but he ain't you.' Lizard points and I follow his diamond circled index finger to the wanksta we're discussing.

'Let me deal with him.' Griffin is Playhouse Entertainment's most celebrated Gigolo, a cottage industry all by himself. Reveling in a celebrity lifestyle. Fan clubs, a clothing line, film parts and even an autobiography but still the nigger's hating on me 'cos he knows me and Lizard are tight, sharing a friendship that extends beyond business, something that he'd never get to do.

I think about how best to disarm him. I'll just have to make him an offer he can't refuse. First, I check out what he's wearing. Emporio Armani. How come nobody told this dragged up motherfucker he ought to be wearing Giorgio Armani, not its illegitimate second cousin? Fake ass. But give him his props his clothes fit perfectly. I try to maintain that hater's mentality, letting it slot into place as I walk out of the enclosure over to where he's encircled by a throng of female groupies.

The following night the country manor looms ahead, vast and imposing. It's at times like this I appreciate how much credits my man Lizard has at his disposal. Four similar set-ups like this across the country and money ain't a thang for him. I picture the original owners of this aristocratic pile having made their wealth from slavery, wallowing in the blood of our forefathers not giving a fuck about consequence. In the twenty-second century, the place is owned by the ancestor of a slave. It's simply divine cause and effect. Damn that's some deep shit for this time in the morning but to my way of thinking it rang true. I walk up the gravel driveway with the other entertainers leaving the two tour buses parked up in the shadow of the extensive car park. We are the second wave, here to tear that mother up! Alpha team is already getting the party started. We approach a phalanx of Nexus security, manning the stately homes massive swing doors, set up with a Biometric security post, which checks our identities as we pass through. I'm nervous 'cos I know it could all end right here. With the best intentions in the goddamn world, Lizard is only human, and he can make mistakes.

Checking a brother's face these days means jack. Retinal scans, fingerprinting, voice analysis even minute verification of DNA profile is standard procedure with these hard-assed security types. Me posing as Griffin is no easy task, but Daddy Lizard is no ordinary multi-millionaire. The pimp broke it down to me like this: He wanted to make two additions to the number of performers in the troupe and had their details digitally transferred to the Nexus mainframe with what he called an Anansi program. Nestled away in the other packets of data and disguised by some intricately designed machine code this baby hits their system and will overwrite Griffins details with mine. Five hours after they access the file it will auto-delete, and I'd be back to being anonymous and comfortable. Just five hours to make shit happen or my ride home becomes a pumpkin.

Apprehension creeps up on my slick ass as I get closer. The dudes in crisp Tuxedos and black overcoats are professionals; the checks are done quickly and efficiently. Some nervous small talk from me and my Retinal scan is done and dusted; Lizard has come through for me yet again. I mix with the troupe as we're guided to the changing rooms at the back of this luxurious crib, everyone weighed down with outfits, sex toys and body paint. The excitement ripples through me, and I keep reminding myself that this is business, not pleasure.

The corridor is long and dark. I can just about make out grand paintings of the former owners and their ancestors along the walls. It could all be stage managed, but then again, I know Lizard's flair for the dramatic and I also know his admiration for history. No matter what, he'd restore it to its former glory with some hood flourishes. So, I'll stick with the theory that it's all effect.

I walk up to the ring of light like a prize pugilist ready for a world title fight. Slamming bass replaces the roar of the baying crowd as I approach an archway of radiance in the distance. I'm here and Griffin's not. And to think I wasn't sure if I could convince him that this was too important to be railroaded by some trumped up gigolo. He enjoyed the fact that I was asking for a favour. I expected that punk to milk it for all it was worth, but over these last few days I've become a jaded son-of-a-bitch, my tolerance for bullshit considerably lessened since Maria's death. The question I asked him was simple and to the point: 'You help me, or I take up Lizard's offer and come work for him. See how you like some competition.' Very shortly after that, we had a deal. Anyway, he couldn't carry off this look with as much ghetto poise as me. Damn if I wasn't better at being Griffin than Griffin himself.

Some sexy and cool shit is what's needed to raise the game tonight, and I'm looking and feeling good. I haven't worked out in a week, but I'm still tight. My eye-popping body definition intact, my muscles contracting and relaxing with powerful ease, an impressive network of veins transporting much-needed nutrients to tissues like I'm a human IC board. I'm masked adding to the mystery and appeal, wearing a Slinky silver chain mail shirt, like a crusader out of his armour, my platinum scrambler around my neck seemingly chosen for the ensemble and not the other way around. Down below I'm sporting leathers with the crotch missing, replaced instead with a bulging codpiece that houses my prize-winning manhood, length, and breadth. I'm about to get this party started and see what secrets I can pry from willing or unwilling lips alike. I look forward to the challenge.

16.

Ballerina

MY FIRST PORT OF CALL AFTER THE SHOW IS THE BAR; luckily, they have chilled carrot juice on tap. With a glass in one hand, I trawl the open areas, dance, engage in small talk and decline some very tempting offers all the time keeping my eyes peeled. Lizard had given me the layout of the mansion the night before. Handy for when I wanna get somewhere quickly, not so good when you have nothing to show for it. Staying unattached all evening is a recipe for suspicion and I'm being watched, so even though I'm determined not to waste this night on some stray Coochy, I need to show interest in someone, or I'll be fucked.

The rules of the game are simple. The guests can freely sample the pleasures of any of the theme rooms, from the S & M torture chambers, Cybersex pods, Cybernetic Aids room to the Golden Showers fountain. The rest of the troupe, apart from the pole dancers, will act as glorified hosts and hostesses.

I'm desperately, looking at faces praying for someone of importance to jump out and demand my attention but seems like this time I've struck out. Maybe top management won't be at a party thrown just for their minions? Pity, the real insider shit would only be known by people at the very top, right? I look at this from a different elevation, and straight away the possibilities are wide open. The answer could still be among the unfamiliar faces of middle management but how do I find out without drawing attention to myself? My tongue probes last the remnants of ice in my glass before I circle the joint again. I don't get very far before someone demands my attention, eyeing me with such intensity I can feel the heat flow from them to me. Casually I scan the room, nodding my head as my scalp tingles. Germaine, the bisexual PA, comes my way even after he's been politely told to chill the fuck out, but interestingly he's not the disturbance in the force. A group who had impaired my view break up and a dark-skinned nymph smiles at me with bee-stung lips. Her character tonight is the hooker with a heart. She's wearing a fuck me dress with cock sucking red lipstick for emphasis, a nice touch. Recognition and a wave of relief plant's my ass to the spot. Aisha Townsend. Her name trips off my tongue without effort. She was one of the few photographs that stood out and not just for her beauty, but because she was a PA to one of the department heads when I was researching Nexus. One of the three that had been included in the photo-shots which Chen had at his disposal.

Her radiant smile is interrupted abruptly as my booty is fondled by strong, insistent fingers. I turn with an amused smile on my lips to face Germaine, the dude who won't take no for a goddamn answer. He's fronting because of our current circumstances. In the hood, he'd end up as road kill, but in Rome, you do what the fuck the Romans do.

'I have a room ready,' he coos sweetly.

I don't pay attention to his advances. In the distance, some dude walks over to Aisha. I'm curious to see how she'll react. I'm also wondering how such a fine woman could be alone in the first place. His body language is confident but not overbearing while her signals are shielded. He leans in and whispers close to her ear. I smile as I enjoy seeing the classic cock block and the brother reeling out of control to crash and burn. He goes to mine booty gold in some other part of the party, and I come straight to the point with Germaine. My smile remains super glued in place, hiding a raging sneer. My shit is focused, my delivery pitch perfect.

'I'm flattered, Germaine, but I'm straight and unadventurous.' And if you bother me again kid, I'm going to plant your sorry ass into the floorboards.

'You don't look unadventurous to me,' he can't resist pushing, 'and anyway, we all have gay tendencies. Look at me,' he grins. 'You, my big dicked friend, just need a bit of coaxing from someone who knows, someone who cares.' His eyes fix on my crotch.

I don't have time for this shit. Aisha's waiting. Bi-Guy is so full of himself that it's comical, but I appreciate his belief in himself.

Then he crosses the line.

Mo fucker reaches for my cod piece desperate to touch the prize. He looks surprised when I grab his fingers and twist. Bi-guy squeals like a punk as his index finger dislocates. His cry of pain is drowned out by the music and, as I'm still displaying my disarming smile, who knows what's going on between us? I kiss him on the forehead, applying pressure as his body folds and just let my elbow smash into his face as he goes down. Before he can topple backwards, I grab him by the scruff of the neck and heave his raggedy ass up. As far as I can tell our little rumba has gone unnoticed, so I hug him and dump him on a sofa in the corner, propping his head against the wall, the blood dripping from his nose. I look at the messed up still life composition I've created. I'm not satisfied. I tilt my head to one side, thinking, then I wipe his nose and unclip a sonic dildo attached to his waistband. I balance it between his lips and step back to admire my work. Very clumsy, tripping and falling on your own dick, homie. I call for medical assistance and disappear.

I'm scouting the guests, looking out for my target. When judging a woman's physical attributes, I zone in on the ass. I'm a booty man, straight up and with no apologies. It's the X-Factor that makes a woman unbearably attractive to me. No booty, no game and as they say; the bigger the cushion, the sweeter the pushin. Don't get me wrong the legs, breasts, eyes, lips, height are all important but when everything, else is right the decision is swung by the ass. Then you can get to the soul and the personality. If that all checks out then, you are in Nirvana playboy. Aisha has it all. It was a pity I had to be coming at her with some hood subterfuge, but there was no other way to get the ball rolling. I had to present myself unapologetically and seduce her to a time frame. Don Juan could do it; Casanova could do it, and I'm sure as hell gonna do it too. But like those historical OG's, I'm using not just guile, charisma and technique but science. I had to disarm my target and approach the kitty from the back door if you know what I'm saying.

I stand behind her; a slow jam imbues my work with the sexiness it demands. She's got a jade dragon tattooed on her supple shoulder, the upper part of her flowing dress drops precariously between her butt cheeks, held on only by string straps. She wears Platinum loop earrings and a twisted lock of black hair rests on her back. I reach over and adjust her ponytail my pinky glances the smooth skin of her back.

She turns like a ballerina, and I'm in front of her like some thugged out prima donna, my whole body screaming, you're the one baby! I turn on my famous hundred-watt smile. Her's takes longer to materialize but when it does appear it's worth the wait. Women moan about how they hate men who talk to their breasts and how the art of eye contact is dead. Shit, sisters are no different from us cats. Check this; the brothers used to be more blatant in the expression of their feelings, but these new age women make no apologies for where they're coming from, and they can be just as hardcore. She's still appraising me unapologetically, and I let her without a care in the world, confident in my own skin.

Aisha oozes sophisticated ghetto. She's sharp-tongued, extremely intelligent and mouth wateringly sexy. I sip sparingly on her image wanting this picture to linger, and it's sweetness to last.

'Is there anything in particular that you're looking for?' The spell is broken by her husky voice.

'Your fingers,' I say without the slightest hesitation, but in the tone of a puzzled man.

'My fingers? Why?' Her face is unsure.

'I'll let you in on a secret. I like strong women, I like how you carry yourself, but then you are an executive in a Fortune 500 company, poise is important right?'

She doesn't correct me, so Aisha is ambitious, not willing to let me in on the fact that she's a PA. 'Have I been under your watchful eye?' She asks.

'You're to blame for that.' I gesture at her outfit. She smiles but keeps it together. 'I was drawn.'

'To my lovely fingers?' she responds.

I smile acting as if I don't notice her checking out my package again. 'At first, I thought no ring, so she's not married, gave myself a little score on my list.'

'You have a list too?'

'Hmm.' I continue anxiously to keep the momentum building between us. 'But then I took a closer look, could see the impression of a married band circling your wedding finger. So I figure it's recently come off. Repairs? Divorce? Infidelity? Not that it matters,' I add quickly, 'but I just wanna know where you're coming from.'

This time her laugh is reserved but not excessively so. She leans towards me, and I reciprocate, we're mirroring some classic body language textbook shit. The doors of opportunity have just been flung open.

'You seem like a confident man. No hang-ups about your body, obviously. Can you please a woman without taking her to bed, though?'

'Try me and see.' I say.

'Will you dance for me then?'

For sure, my eyes say, but I soon realize it's not an invitation but a challenge.

We retire to the chill-out-room after an hour of getting to know each other. Our conversation strays away from the usual taboo subjects of religion, politics, money and former boyfriends. I up my level of rapport so I give a little. I have the advantage of saying anything I want to cos there's no way she can check me out, visually or electronically, Remember my state of the art cloaking device?

I know enough about her to gauge whether she's telling me the truth about herself and the company. It's also made easier for the guests knowing that all of Lizard's people are secrecy chipped so nobody could let slip any trade secrets or call any names to the electronic papers after they've left the safe confines of the mansion. As far as she's concerned, I'm a listening ear with no consequences and no repercussions. But still, she's holding back.

'Strip for me?' She asks an undercurrent of challenge in her words.

Aisha had been married, as I'd figured and it had lasted no more than six months. She'd had a string of wankster boyfriends after that, none of who could satisfy her on any level.

She was an old-fashioned girl, married to her job and smart enough to not mix love and lust. She didn't even own a vibrator bot. My question is what the fuck was she doing here? The only answer seemed to be Nexus. The more I hear about these cats, the more I know I'm into some corporate conspiracy shit that previously I've only ever read about.

Aisha had come clean explaining that being here would turbo boost her chances of promotion. They were flexing like some Millennium cult binding their top people to them through extortion and blackmail. Tools they'd use to keep niggas in check. Now she was in a dilemma about sleeping with someone she wasn't attracted to for the sake of her career. Shit, I'm her step up the corporate ladder, her Knight in shining armor all rolled into one.

So I strip for her.

I've mastered this to such a degree it no longer looks like stripping. I throw them off guard with what I'm saying, stimulating their minds with words, painting a picture of what is to come and exciting the most unappreciated sex organ – the brain. Then suddenly you're staring at me in my full glory. Damn!

Normally after this, they're on their knees salivating for a touch of the package. I sensed Aisha would be different. I was just in my leather thongs, my chain mail shirt on the floor beside me, and so were my leather pants. Her right eyelid twitches in my direction for a mere second, the only part of her body not under her iron will then she quickly reins it back in. I feel a rush of fear and excitement coz I knew this sister would be no pushover, so I attempt to drop kick the trepidation and try to savor the challenge.

Normally I'm in control, normally my woman and friends aren't dead, normally professional dancers don't get aroused, we do the arousing. But now the lines have blurred or more like they've been fucking erased. A new set of standards has come into play.

I can't fall off my throne, can't have you thinking I've gone soft.

So, I turn up the heat.

At first, her resolve remained intact, but her piercing hazel eyes were losing focus. Soon we're feeling each other, and it's like some deep connection shit, and I'm dancing my way into her soul.

My body gyrates over every part of her breaking down her barriers one by one. Her nipples push against the fabric of her dress, the dark circles them clearly visible. I kneel, a reverent genuflection, and place her feet on my lap. They are small and perfectly formed, no calluses, no corns. Beautiful. Patiently I undo the Grecian sandals strung around her calves then massage her pleasure points. trailing my thumb along the bundle of nerves at the balls of her feet. Her reaction could be a fluke because it doesn't always work, but she seems to have felt the electric shock of the corresponding tingling sensation in her clitoris. Gently I pull her to a standing position, she hasn't yet come down from her clitoral shock, and her knees are still weak, but I don't care, knowing it will heighten the pleasure even more.

'Don't move,' I whisper in her ear as I slip to the floor and slide between her legs, lightly breathing hot breath on the inside of her thighs. I can smell the aroma of her arousal, and I'm tempted to let my tongue probe, but her moaning tells me she's not gonna simmer for much longer. It's time to play by the Adonis rules. She's glowing as she lifts her dress, no pretense now, she's letting me see how she feels. Her fingers probe and find the moistness between her legs. I grab her hand and lick her sticky fingers before lifting both arms above her head. I slide down her body, her nipples as hard as cherry pips. She sighs softly. I stop at her stomach, feeling the heat, the muscles of her abdomen tightening with anticipation. I kiss her navel with a slurp and felt her entire body quake. Suddenly I feel her hands at the back of my neck, forcing my face through the barrier of her dress, hoping my tongue can pierce the fabric of her panties. The music ends, and she's breathing heavily, stretched out on the leather sofa like a lioness resting from the kill. I step closer and kiss her on the lips. Her cinnamon taste increases the blood flow to my favorite extremity. I'm ready to saddle up on that fine ass there and then but I resist, pulling back before displaying my master stroke. I walk away. Yeah playa, you heard me. I walk away.

Seconds pass before a sweet sound tickles my ear. 'Where do you think you're going?'

I turn around, and I'm blinded by her flashing brown eyes.

'Drinks,' I say innocently.

'Drinks can wait, Mister. I can't.'

I smile and sweep her up into my arms, knowing that the next sound I hear will be the sound of her singing sweetly like a canary as she surrenders her ass to me.

17.

FRENCH KISSING

THE COACH DRIVER WANTS TO DROP ME HOME me but first I've got to get this all clear in my head. The crew is hyped, and I'm buzzing still, but I need to come down from it all. I'm not enervated from the bedroom work that I've just put in because unlike so tired ass niggas who talk the talk, I was taught how to have a total body orgasm without ejaculation – or the loss of vital energy as my Chinese teacher said – and I'm still good to go. Even after Aisha orgasmed thrice and fell asleep. Yeah, dawg, you heard me correct, it does mean three times in old English. Still, I don't have the luxury of sleep like my peeps, I've gotta file what I've been told, see if the new information changes anything, possibly allowing me up front and personal access to the bastards who killed my family.

Trying to reconcile solving this mystery with using my talents in the bedroom arts is hard. I've just been with an utterly fantastic woman, who under different circumstances I'd be returning to on a weekly basis to work that pussy till it sang, but she was simply a means to an end, a tool for revenge.

The coach drops me off in bustling West London. I'm hanging around at this all-night shopping center in Shepherd's Bush waiting to give Chen the skinny on my night's findings. Let him break this shit down using his cold, analytical mind. Two heads are better than one, right?

It may seem like I'm tripping but if I want to relax I go lingerie shopping. And no, motherfucker, it's not for me. When I was with Maria, I bought nearly all her underwear, including the most provocative pieces in her wardrobe because that's what I wanted to see her in. Nine times out of ten I'm the only man in these types of places, outside of brothers who have been threatened with celibacy if they don't step up their game. The colors, the music, the smell and the figures to match the skimpy creations, yow, I'm in my zone, man! Plus, I get crazy love from the female staff. This is when my subconscious works best. Strange I know but if shit works, I won't question it.

It's four forty in the morning, and I'm not the only XY chromosome in the joint. Two young women stand at the cashier's desk waiting to pay. Near them are two guys.

Straight away my twenty: twenty confirms that something's not quite right with this picture. These ugly son-of-a-bitches are sweating me unobtrusively. They must have tracked me from the country house. They may even be figuring my name is Griffin, a self-obsessed wankster that I wasn't. Hate to admit it, even to myself, but now I'm concerned.

Chill homeboy, I tell myself. Force of habit. I check out my surroundings again.

Two sisters at the counter with a cashier, a blonde near the exit checking out a lacy number, the two gorillas acting like transvestites concerned about the size of their drawers, a customer service rep tidying shelves. My head whips to the back entrance and right on cue one of the heavies edges his way over, ready to cut me off. These mo' fuckers are figuring out my moves before I make them. Well, bring it on. I'm thinking brave thoughts, but my fronting doesn't last long as I glimpse a big ass cannon swinging from under the arm of one of the heavies as he leans over to check a floral thong ensemble. Shit.

My speed and agility takes them by surprise as I make a b-line for the cashier's post leaving the pearl stringed panties I was scrutinizing almost suspended in mid-air. My rapid haste had me at the sliding doors, in an interrupted heartbeat, leg outstretched ready to depart like a real life Speedy Gonzales. Arrogance is a bitch because

I'm about to give these kooks the finger when my balls jangle. Instinctively I turn on my heels, and my legs do what to an untrained eye seemed like a ghetto curtsy, but that move deflected the blow from the nightstick that bounces off my clavicle instead of fatally connecting with the back of my neck.

Goddamn it!

A rush of pain explodes inside me, and I go down. The nightstick whistles down on my back again, as I'm crawling on all fours, I catch sight of my assailant. The blonde bitch with the silicone implants and I'm not talking about her breasts either, is beating me like I'd just stood her up on a first date. Worse still this freak of nature with her false ass jiggling behind her is obviously immune to my alluring animal attraction. Shit, she may even be holding that against me.

I tense every muscle causing the blows to be less effective but still painful in the tight confines. The ferocity amped up, and she yelped like a puppy being molested by the big dog next door – such was her pleasure as she exacted her punishment on my black ass. I was in a tight ball moving around as best as I could and making myself hard to pin down. I vow to swiftly dispatch her ass if she goes anywhere above my neck and my fears manifest almost immediately. She swings for the skull, but I see it coming and stop my struggling suddenly. The baton bounces off the prefab flooring harmlessly.

In the confined space, I twist around sweeping her legs from under her. The blonde takes to the air like a carefully orchestrated ballet move, but with a lot less grace. Her Barbie doll head shatters the glass first, followed by her messed up artificial ass which splatters all over the entrance.

I use the momentum of my swinging legs to regain my standing position and realize at that point I gotta keep moving - no time for goodbyes. A glance over my right shoulder confirms my fears. I've got company close behind. Extremely athletic men are barrelling their way through aisles of lingerie and clawing the air towards me violent intent gleaming in their eyes. I bust my way to the outside, stomping on the unconscious assassin bitch and her messed up Glute surgery. The fresh air is cool and sweet, and I suck it into my lungs and hit the stairs at a run, arms pumping only slowing down to negotiate yet more stairs. I'm fast, but still, the mo' fuckers are on me, matching my desperation gasp for gasp. I slow down and cuss.

A computer controlled traffic light halts my escape. Godammit!

Might as well just face them and put up my dukes and let them charbroil my ass with some plasma rounds. What do I do? Traffic hurtles in both directions at a relentless pace at this juncture. Lane Tech controls the juggernauts hauling cargo on the arterial route, manned by drivers who have nothing more to do but monitor their load and who have limited control over the vehicles transit. I'm pacing the area just off the curb, looking at the traffic and shaking my head in disbelief. I look back, half expecting them to be right behind me. Instead, they've slowed their pace knowing there's nowhere for pedestrians to go while the lights are favouring the motorists. Their big grins mean they know cornered prey when they see it. I spy the bitch with the nightstick hobbling up in the rear, her hair matted with blood, a look in her eyes that would scare a prog junky off their next hit. The pedestrian crossing glows, a sign that it's recognized my presence. Still, it'll take at least ten minutes for a red signal to appear, and the gorillas are less than a full minute away from creaming my ass.

Crazy thoughts rush through my head. Should I rush them? Call Chen? Give up? Fuck that. I check out the heavy loaders and land huggers speeding past, compare that with a possible cap in my ass. My sight alternates between the traffic and the cocky saunter of the gorillas. Back to the traffic. Then again to the heavies. A sudden and unexplained sense of certainty overcomes me. I've felt it before, and it cocoons me in an umbra of calm and invincibility, injecting me with a brand of optimism that was like lightening in a bottle. I wait for the weird shit to follow as it inevitably does.

I step over the barrier aware of the frantic look of my pursuers as I prepare to commit suicide. Motor vehicles scream in front of me as I keep my eyes fixed on both juggernauts and private vehicles. Just waiting, gauging my chances. Then... I step into the maelstrom.

When Chen finally picks me up, I've stopped shaking. The buzz of whatever it is I did back there is all that remains. I sit quietly in the seat in front of him as we drive off. He's dressed in a double-breasted gold and black pinstripe suit. No, sign that he's been awake for the last forty-eight hours, except for his sad eyes.

'I've got some bad news for you,' he looks at me keenly. 'Although I imagine you may have already found out that a contract has been taken out on your head.'

'Why ain't I surprised?'

Chen ignores my sarcasm.

'I didn't concern myself with your safety before. I knew you could take care of yourself but... I may have to review that.'

'You worried about me, dawg.'

'What did you find out from the mansion?' He asks obviously in no mood for my dark humour, but then his ass ain't just been beat down and nearly killed. I need the levity and go through what I found out from Aisha my way.

'More or less a confirmation of everything we imagined and worse. Still don't know the reasons why or who exactly, not even enough info to protect our asses on Friday night.' I match his sober mood and give him a straight forward factual answer.

'In Chinese business circles, any failure of your company is the CEO's failure. Ms. Lorraine Van Horne is going to answer to me for my sister's murder, and she will take responsibility' Chen sinks back into his chair shrouded by a veil of silence. I need some down time too so I can get my shit together. I ask the driver to swing by the Docklands telling the Triad Boss that we'll hook up later. Chen does that frown and nod shit before uttering something totally unexpected.

'Be careful.

18.

FELLATIO

GODAMMIT! I LEAN ON THE CHROME doorframe leading to my crib and shake my head. Smithy touches me on the shoulders in consolation and departs. I walk into the chaos and feel the door close shut behind me. Every nerve is on edge as I expect the unexpected. But I'm alone, reassured by my concierge that they were disturbed before they could do more damage; or were they? Now he waits for Met-1 to turn up and I've got to deal with the messed-up Feng Shui of my fortress of solitude.

God damn!

Why am I even surprised? Maybe it's the fact that this development is supposed to be intruder proof, chosen so residents could have peace of mind. Or maybe it's the realization that these dudes are not playing tick tack toe with my black ass.

I rummage through the debris. In the bedroom, lounge, utility room and bathroom, paintings are slung from walls, books scattered around the floor, info-discs smashed and hurled to the four corners, crystal figurines broken, furniture overturned. Weirdly my library and gym are intact. I sigh gratefully and jump over the shit in the hall, breaking left for my room of carnal knowledge. My precious books are still regimentally in place and spotless. My computer is in low power consumption mode and wiped clean without a doubt. Digital's disk from earlier had worked its magic remotely linking me to his hidden mainframe and backing up my contents. I just gotta reboot my laptop then I'll be back in business.

Damn! I pause for a minute as the enormity of this shit slowly creeps up on me. Just as I'm about to start feeling sorry for myself the memories of Maria, Popeye and Digital pull me back. They deserve and demand respect and the only way for that to happen is for me to take a grip on my emotions.

I've no time for moody introspection; the killers had come here looking for something they could use to find me. I stretch out in my Waldorf chair; any doubts that I was dealing with some hardcore niggas laid to rest. I spin the full three sixty, scanning the room carefully. Something's missing. I stand and run my fingers over the works of Don Juan, Machiavelli, and Casanova. That's when I notice the space. A small 2-D photo of Adonis junior usually on a shelf just above and beyond my screen is gone replaced by a .655 hollow point plasma round ominously sitting on its butt.

These cocky mo' fuckers wanted my attention, and now they've got it. Although the word attention is probably too mild a word. My nervous system is firing its synapses like I'm about to go into overload. They were playing me. Leaving clues to confuse and frighten. Ordering me to do shit, knowing I couldn't refuse. Yeah, they had me frightened but not confused. I was as clear as a shot of hundred-year-old Vodka. I leave my library like you lit my ass on fire. In my bedroom, I stuff clean clothes and some other necessary little pieces into my leather Dolce bag. Now, this shit is getting personal.

A bad, bad idea.

I leave my tower block at a run, and I'm in my car revving the engine in under ten minutes. I risk getting a thousand credits fine and my license suspended for disabling Traffic Tech restraints that allow me to break the speed limit at will but I don't give a fuck. I've been frantically trying to get in touch with the Battersea bitch but, hey, you try and program your way through a temporarily blocked line. It ain't easy and I just know the games she's playing right now. My name comes up on the smart V-Comm, and she ignores me, unaware this shit is a life and death situation.

My next call is Chen. I explain everything that's happened. He shares his plans to mobilize himself and his troops over to the Dirty South for backup. I don't bother to comment that I'll be there way before him, dealing with the situation on my own. Driving my Aston Martin isn't the most sensible thing to do, but it's faster and more reliable than any form of public transport.

Yawning, I disengage the autopilot, feeling the familiar tug of resistance as the on board computer hands back control to me. I send up an Eye-in-the Sky Drone from my boot and let it do its thing. I plot a course along the endless stream of the road ahead, the cat's eyes imbedded in the tarmac phasing from safe white to pulsing red, signaling an accident or at the very least upcoming congestion. Shit! Not now. I slam the steering wheel with the heel of my hands.

'Talk to me 'puter.' I scold the Artificial intelligence unit. My windscreen glows pale blue in response to a feed from my drone. The VR route finder flashes a string of data that confirms my fears. A map dislodged from the central tableau of facts and figures hovers before my eyes, highlighting the congested roads and offering alternate routes to my baby mama's crib. Once again, I ignore the expense of traveling on the suggested 'A' roads, my overriding concern is simply to get there.

The cockpit is quiet except for engine vibrations. No vintage Hip-Hop or Reggae tracks playing as was expected, just the eerie luminescence of the VR animating my bald head, highlighting the images of my frantic thoughts. I picture little man, happy and well. A vision at odds with the churning in my heart at the theft of his picture and the macabre possibilities of that. I rub my hands over my face, closing my eyes for a second, trying to block out thoughts of being too late. Time to put the pedal to the metal.

Streatham High Road is uncharacteristically busy, but eventually, a break appears in the line of oncoming traffic, and I turn into Angles Road. I'm calmer now as I approach the unknown situation. At this stage of the game, I'm praying that something greater than me will keep the remainder of the family I have left in one piece. I have no idea of the details, just a constant, uncomfortable and instinctive nagging from my intuition. Shit is about to go down, and I plan to be in exactly the right place when it does. My confidence is sky high. I'm riding on a wave of positivity with a brand-new set of belief systems telling me I'm at my peak, the best I will ever be! Whatever kind of Dr. Frankenstein procedure Digital had used to enhance me had some freaky side-effects on my thoughts.

I swing the Aston into a neighboring estate, less than five minutes away from where I need to be. I'm telling myself that nothing is as it seems, everything has a sinister and evil intent and that's the way I'm wired. No-one's gonna catch me stumbling into a bad situation without serious forethought.

I touch the paintwork on the door of my whip and watch it discolour around my five fingers as it goes into phase one secure. My drone returns like a bird of prey and locks into place in the booth, humming as it shuts down. I laugh silently picturing some cocky turf boy seeing my whip and figuring this was his lucky day, never dreaming that some real sinister Tech lurked under the hood of my ride.

'Arm!' I growl. Armed! The synthetic voice of my Aston responds and I hear the comforting sounds of some advanced security shit prime for action.

I head up the road at a steady clip, discretion uppermost on my mind. I stop just before the fourth storey flat that my son shares with his mom. As a ploy of misdirection, I produce my car's starter card and turn toward the garages behind the building. I'm acting like an ordinary Joe going about his business. I see Yvette's car, parked up back. It's cold from lack of use; I go weak with relief.

Looking up to the fourth-floor gauging how far I need to climb, I step back, run up and explode into the air. The leap is impressive, super human if I'm honest and in moments I'm pulling myself up to the balcony of the first floor flat. A dozy-eyed Tom cat, the only witness to my extraordinary feat, licks his paws then his balls, evidently unimpressed. Probably thinking,

'yeah I can do that cuz with my eyes closed.'

I clamber from one protruding balcony to the next, effortlessly leaping the five feet between each floor. Eventually, I stop outside a curtained window. I could be wrong, but I think this is it. My heart is beating, but my breathing is steady. I call Yvette from my V-Comm. This time she's ready for me.

'What is your problem, Adonis? Do you want me to call the Met and say that you're harassing my son and me?'

Good to see you too baby, I'm thinking.

'Shut the fuck up and listen, for once in your goddamn life.' I reply. For once she's speechless. Guess my venom takes her by surprise. 'This is a life and death situation so. I'm on your balcony so let me the fuck in.' I rap on the window like I want to put my fist through it.

'Off.' I say to the V-Comm, and it collapses around my ear in its dormant state. 'Open up!' I holla at the full-length sheet of Tech Glass that's between my boy and me.

The glass becomes transparent, and I can see images behind the curtain. Somebody draws it back, and I'm face to face with Yvette's new boo. He's a big motherfucker in shorts, gripping a baseball bat and glaring at me. The N.A.H - Nigga at Home matches the profile of a post-Adonis-syndrome-boyfriend to a T. Pumped up macho asshole trying hard to fit the original but never quite cutting it. I should be flattered, but nothing makes a man feel more used and abused than your ex being fucked by an Adonis clone and your kid being influenced by him. Okay, I know Yvette would never hurt Junior, but a man around my son makes me anxious and angry.

I gesture at him to open the window, knowing he won't back down from the opportunity this presented. For one, he's got my reputation to live up to, two; he's probably looking for payback for what I've supposedly done to Yvette and three, he thinks that 'cos of his size he can whip my ass.

Reluctantly the balcony window slides open, and he steps back, giving me access but making it feel like he was stepping over an imaginary plate like he's waiting for the pitch. I step through planting my size elevens on their wooden floor. The apartment smells of cinnamon.

'What the fuck you doing on my balcony, man?' Baby boy asks and pauses to peer over my shoulder confirming what his feeble mind should have already known. 'How did you get up here, friend?' His tone was playing down the incredulous and amping up the vehemence.

'I climbed,' I drop it on his ass raw.

His grin slips as he realizes I'm not kidding. He grips the baseball bat and takes a step back. I take in my surroundings. Yvette felt that this was not a good idea from her protests, but I've already side-lined her voice to background static. She never did understand the workings of the male mind. No way could she comprehend that this was a once in a lifetime opportunity for the question of who deh man, to be answered. It's hard-wired into the male psyche from prehistory, and no manner of human advancements was going to rewrite that genetic imperative. I look over at Yvette standing under the archway leading from the lounge. Her eyes are frantic, but I'm cool insanity.

'We can all leave here together,' I say. 'Or I can take my son and fuck y'all.'

Baby boy emits a cynical laugh perfected by some of the best OG's in the business but coming from him resembles a pitiful cackle. I scowl, set my dick to conflict mode and wait.

'Do you tell a good story, friend?' He asks.

I clock him in silence. He slaps the baseball bat into his big hand and points it to the floor. He has the savage stare of a man savouring impending violence. I let the chump jerk off and address Yvette instead.

'Please believe me this is serious shit. If I ever asked you to trust me on anything in your life before let it be now. Forget about the bullshit, forget about our complicated history, I need you all to leave with me now.'

'Leave with you?' She's incredulous. 'Why on earth would I want to do that, Adonis?' She laughs. A mocking guffaw that says: you've just messed up again. You done broke the exclusion zone and now you're losing your goddamn mind.'

I glare at her. 'Because if you don't they'll be taking you and baby boy here out in body bags.'

The chump grins again, like whatever he thinks could be original or funny.

'If you ask me...' he snickers.

'I didn't mo' fucker.' I snap back.

Still baring his teeth, he continues.

'...you need to stop jacking up on street trash programs friend. Check into rehab or something. Use your credits for more productive shit.'

'You talk a good game homie but this is way above your head. Don't push it; I ain't in the mood.' The warning in my tone should have been enough.

'Bring it on, man, if you've got the stones.' He beckons to me making small circles with the bat.

Yvette bristles.

'Are you out of your mind?' She asks.

I focus on Yvette again.

'Do you really think I'd make this up?' I shout. 'My woman is dead, my friends are dead, and the rest of my family could be next.'

'Family?' Yvette scowled. 'You mean your son.'

'Does it matter? I'm here to save your life.'

'Or are you trying to play one of your stupid games to get back at Richard and me. I know you can't stand us being together but for the first time I'm happy, and I won't let you destroy that.'

She laughs again tempting me to go postal on her selfish ass. Ma Campbell never met Adonis junior in the flesh. She had a picture of him on her old-style dresser in Jamaica, asked for him, talked about him, was proud of him but died not knowing him. All because of this selfish, arrogant, vindictive bitch making it all about her as usual.

'How the hell can anyone take you seriously?' She counters, fear, anger, and disbelief in her words. 'You're wondering around, climbing buildings in the middle of the night, trying to frighten me with stories of murder. Does that sound like the actions of a sane man to you?'

Where do I start? How can I even begin to explain? I look straight at her but say nothing. Sixty-Nine was my family, and they are all dead. All I have left is little man, my only link with sanity. I'm not my deadbeat father. I will not abandon Junior no way, no how. Despite Yvette's emotional blackmail, I'm his pops, and I'll do whatever it takes to protect him.

She had spouted this same bullshit before she kicked me out some years back and I didn't stand my ground then. Right on cue, my subconscious plays devil's advocate. What if my fears are unfounded and I'm jumping off at the deep end? I let my intensity speak for itself and for a moment I think I'm getting through to her. Her eyes glaze over and mentally, she retreats deeper into herself, but her introspection doesn't last. Her defenses spring back up, and it's obvious that she's not going to be reasoned with. Yvette is still hurting and that is reason enough to distrust me and my motives.

'I ain't got the time for this shit, Yvette! I'm telling you this here is life and death.'

'Go!' Yvette says in almost a whisper. 'Just get out of my house.'

I shake my head in frustration. There is no way she's going to pack up and leave with me just on my word. And I have no intention of leaving here without little man, so we have a Mexican Standoff.

Just then, raising the stakes even higher, my little cowboy walks in. Adonis Junior rubs his eyes, stopping short of walking into the door frame by a hair's breadth. My boy sleeps with one eye open, and the other eye closed metaphorically speaking. In other words, he's a light sleeper like his old man. I want to laugh, but this is serious. The look on his face says 'Now you sorry assed mo' fuckers woke me up, where's the food at?'

Unnoticed by Yvette he takes in his surroundings. The big guy who makes his Ma scream, deeper baby at nights is swinging a baseball bat. Yvette stands in front of him, waves of tension rolling off her. Then, there's this handsome, dashing, debonair dude standing with his arms folded. Recognition lights up his face. I break into a big ole smile even though I know things are about to get ugly.

'Daddy!' He screams and hurtles my way. My reaction is instinctive; what else could it be? This is the first time in months we've been face to face. So, I forget that the Chump has my ass staked out and move to meet my son half way. Man-a-yard takes two steps back and swings the bat, the smile on his lips like that of a man who's fulfilled a dream. The Scandium alloy of the baseball bat impacts with a solid whack at the back of my leg, forcing me down on one knee like I'm being knighted for services in getting my ass whooped. A jagged streak of pain shoots up the right side of my body as I fling my head back and grit my teeth. His next swing almost splits my skull, his primary target I guess, but he misses and glances off my shoulder, sending me completely to the ground.

I've been caught unawares; my reaction time is slow because my focus was on Junior but even with my senses scrambled I'm still aware of Little man's fearful screams. Yvette is screaming too, but somehow, I don't think she's all that concerned about me. Chump smells blood, and he wants another shot.

But it ain't gonna happen.

Yvette shrieks at him to stop as I slide Junior off me and rise to my feet, ignoring tiny explosions of pain all over my body. Yvette rushes the Chump and tries to grab hold of the bat, but he flings her across the room rendering their relationship null and void from then on in. She lands in a heap, slightly winded and surprised, but okay. It's obvious that Baby Boy has a point to make, regardless of whether my son gets hurt in the process. The fool swings the bat, back and forth, left to right still trying to intimidate me. My patience has almost expired. He comes at me, swinging for my head, nearly losing his balance as the bat contacts with nothing but fresh air.

Fuck it; I think. It's time to get up close and personal.

I grab the bat with both hands, and we wrestle. His eyes tell me he thinks it's a done deal, he's got the advantage. That I'm still weak from the battering I took earlier. His complacency makes me happy 'cos it means I've got him exactly where I want him. He thinks he can match me strength for strength, but Baby Boy soon realizes he can't. The look on his face as I slowly pull him towards me is priceless. He's grunting. Sinews are taut and muscles flexing as Baby boy uses every ounce of strength in our little tug-of-war. He knows it's a losing battle when he's yanked off his feet and I head-butt him in mid-air. His neck snaps back, and he's on his ass, trying to shake away the fog thickening between his ears. I'm up in his face like cheap cologne as he hauls himself back to his feet. Baby Boy's eyes are rolling as I feint right and weave a little. He's recovering well, but I still catch him, with a jaw twisting right hook. I'm thinking that this shit is almost too easy, but Baby Boy takes the punch surprisingly well. I float left and sting his ass with three swift jabs. He swings at me again, and I get under him and work his ribs. He twists around with each blow trying to protect his insides. And that gives me the opportunity to come up under his chin with a hook, right on the button. For a split second, he's off the ground from the ferocity of the blow, his legs turn to jelly, but I hold him up by his neck and slam his limp carcass to the wall. My strength and power takes even me by surprise as the apartment shakes to its very foundations and I see Baby Boys perfectly formed impression in the plasterboard.

Have I just smoked his ass? Damn! Didn't know I was that strong or that angry.

I let him slid to the floor before I examine him. The Lights are out, and nobody's home, but the shallow rise and fall of his chest tells me he's still breathing. I brush myself off. Little junior's grinning at me. He's just seen a different side of his old man and he likes it. I raise my eyebrows, wordlessly calling him to me. He runs into my arms, and I hold him close oblivious to everything else; Yvette's sobs, Baby Boy's groans, the mashed-up furniture is strewn around their small lounge, the fallout from my beat down.

'Daddy...?' Junior begins, and I hold him closer, willing him to shush, cos I know what his questions are gonna be, but I can't give him an answer just yet. If he's quiet, I can be his hero for just a little longer.

'Look after your momma.' I say softly as I release him. He puts his arm around her. I watch them for a second as a familiar longing comes over me and I know we've got to get out of here.

19.

POWER OF PUSSY

THE CITYSCAPE SPEEDS BY THE darkened window of the Bentley. Chen clears his throat several times. It's no surprise he's having trouble getting through to me. I've got a lot on my mind.

'Could the message you received from Mr. Marsden been tampered with?'

The power and authority of his voice interrupt my selfish reverie. What he's just asked has never occurred to me, but I respect the way he views things. His unique take could literally save my ass. I had told him about Digital's message including the mysterious invitation to the Nexus ball. He'd just absorbed this new information without saying a word, the concealed excitement behind his dark eyes the only clue to his analysis of it all. Now, days later, he asks me the question. Flashes of past conversations fill my thoughts as I recall Digital constantly emphasizing my need to be there.

'Nah, I don't think so.' I finally answer. 'He'd been on at me about this thing for about two weeks, right up to when he disappeared. If they tampered with it, they didn't fuck with the message itself. It hasn't changed.'

Chen nods.

'We now know Nexus doesn't want you to attend. More reason why you should.'

'Sure, but how? I can't just pimp walk up to the foyer and produce my invitation. Even if I get in, I'm sure as hell ain't getting out.'

'There is always a way.' Chen says coolly.

'Spare me that Confucius shit man! We just don't have enough time on our side. Breaking into a building like that takes months of planning, and that's with the expertise and cash behind us.'

'I have a plan.' Chen drops his bomb with such calm I shut up immediately because I know he has a plan.

'...but we need to keep you alive long enough.' He continues.

Alive in the meantime my ass! I want to know what he means by 'having a plan.'

'Yeah......?' I coax.

He points his fingers under his chin. Sometimes I just wanna ram some urgency up his ass. Remind him were on western time now. Breaking into a five-minute meditation regime every time he needed to consider something was trying my patience.

'I sent a team to the building to observe and take readings. The building is fully automated, run by a neural network computer that can compensate for most weaknesses.'

'My ass is fucked,' I mutter to myself.

Chen ignores my pessimism.

'But the building's balance is unstable. Its Feng Shui is out of step.'

'Feng Shui? Nigga you tripping.' I knew from my prison studies about the Chinese art of 'wind and water,' I've used it myself. I just couldn't see how that would help our situation in the real world.

He educates my dumb ass.

'No building in the East Asian Pacific Rim, big or small is planned or constructed without considering the precepts of Feng Shui. We believe building structures need to harmonize with and benefit from the surrounding physical environment. If you want your business or your workspace to attract favorable conditions such as luck, prosperity or longevity, they must be enhanced by having balance. The architects who designed and built this smart building flaunted every Feng Shui rule. Consequently, since it opened five years ago, the Nexus building has had problems. That could be our way in.'

'How?' I'm asking incredulously.

About now I need something more substantial than that Ying Yang crap. Give me guns and bullets, or at the very least, brute force. Failing that I'll slay 'em with bad language and curses if I have to. But hell, anything's gotta be better than basing a plan around Feng Shui.

Chen shakes his head.

'I should listen to your advice, right?' I say after the prolonged silence that was frustrating the hell out of me.

'That would be a step in the right direction.' Chen says.

'Okay, bro. What do you want me to do?' For the first time in this conversation, our eyes meet.

'Take a back seat for a few days until the plan has been finalized.'

I sigh cos homeboy just doesn't get where I'm coming from. I never listened before, not about to start now. He thinks I'm him, into the softly, softly approach. After all the times, he's stepped in to save my ass, he should know me better by now.

'Don't even go there, man. I ain't taking a backseat to shit. As far as I'm concerned, Sixty-Nine will stay afloat until I can put a new team in place. It's business as usual.'

Chen shakes his head, again - he does that just to annoy me, I know it.

'Why are you still here Adonis? Why are you risking your life when you could abandon all this and retire somewhere with no extradition treaty?'

I close my eyes feeling them prickle with the heat of tears. Man's words have cut me to the core. A rage builds within causing my muscles to clench from the balls of my feet up to my neck. I want to explode on his punk ass for questioning my commitment again but how can I when he's used his resources to protect the family I have left, stretching the capacity of his organization at my request? Nah, I ain't mad at yah. I whisper under my breath.

'I don't think you heard me mo' fucker,' I say in a measured tone, loud enough, this time for him to hear. 'Part of my family is dead, kid. I want to know how and why. I'm in this shit storm to the bitter end, you feel me.'

Chen smiles.

'You've surpassed my expectations, Mr. Campbell.'

'You looked worried, Chen. Am I fucking up your preconceived ideas about me? Nothing good can come from the likes of me? Is that it? Well, fuck you. And let me say this real slow. I will do whatever it takes. You feel me? Whatever.'

Chen's smile broadens some more and I know it's from his heart. He places his ponytail along his right shoulder where it trails down to his chest. He strokes the plait of hair in contemplation and says nothing for a long time.

20.

JACK HAMMER

IT'S FIVE-TWENTY, THURSDAY MORNING. My pillow gently massages me awake glowing lightly. For a tech item that was supposed to rouse you gently from slumber – which it had to be fair, but it also dragged me from a nightmare and brought the subjects of my grief with it. Gloomy spectres of Maria, Popeye, and Digital stared down at me. Their eyes are like saucers, their skin bloodless, their bodies ethereal. I'm not sure if my expectations had manifested the rancorous smell of decomposition, but I automatically held my breath.

'I'm sorry.' I say over and over again. 'I let you down, I let my family down.'

But they ain't ascribing blame; those vacant eyes say they are lost and unable to find peace. That was my mission.

For a long, while their sadness washes over me like a dark, Dead Sea and for a moment I'm sharing the horror of unfulfilled dreams and incomplete lives snuffed out in their prime.

My cheeks are damp, and I'm sobbing like a bitch. They didn't deserve to die. They didn't deserve to be done like that.

The ferocity of my words chases me out of one reality and dumps me into another thinking these ghouls would be at my bedside. Gasping for air I look frantically for their presence again but this reality was free from apparitions and damn, I was relieved. Now that I'm properly awake I notice that I'm fully clothed. I lie still, not daring to move in case the panic attack building in my head and chest smothers me. I concentrate on my breathing. Softly in and softly out, holding each breath for a few seconds longer until the terror dissipates.

Slowly, carefully I stretch. First, my legs, then arms, bend my neck and flex my fingers. It's a painful process. My back, shoulders, and limbs are sore from the multiple beatings I received from the bitch at the mall and from baby boy at Yvette's crib. Luckily there's no swelling or bruising. I swing out of bed and smile wryly; 'Lucky's' probably the wrong word. I close my eyes, and everything comes rushing back with a sense of fear and wonderment.

For an instant, I'm back at the mall stuck with the life and death dilemma of crossing a busy freeway with three bounty hunters with burners ready to ice my ass just steps behind. My world moves in slow motion, courtesy of panic and my twenty: twenty. I step out ready to play a starring role in a 'thugged out ballet' of chaos or become inconsequential road kill. I decide on roadkill. And before I could talk myself out of it, I'm in the zone as I duck and roll, with startling dexterity, evading oncoming motorists with split-second precision. I didn't slow my pace and hurtling forward with a speed that frightened even me. A hover cyclist was the last person to see me flashing past him in mid-air as I dive and roll to safety on the other side of the traffic. We're both shocked by how close he came to crushing. Close enough that his sensors didn't have sufficient time to brake, close enough that I could see the whites of his eye and he could see the steely determination in mine. All he could do was a double take, nearly falling off his Yamaha, while I end up crouched in shock and wonder at what Digital had done to me. It may have looked cool, but trust me, it wasn't done for any dramatic effect.

I had taken a quick look over my shoulder to gauge the mayhem I've left behind and my blood chills. I knew the rest of the day's traffic reports would make for some weird reading as they clear up the wreckage. When shit happens, I find Jesus and I prayed no-one got hurt.

Shrugging off my reverie, I wonder over to the solitary window and pull back the curtain, bathing a small rectangle of room in streetlight. I'm at Jessica's crib in the spare room. The only place I could think of to chill. I lean my head against the glass, struggling to make sense of this craziness? A strong feeling in my nut sack was saying there was more death and mayhem to come. Maybe that's why I stare at the uninspiring view of the avenue below I notice a picture of activity uncharacteristic for the time of night.

One at a time, what looks like a woman and three men silently exit from both sides of a vehicle and converge on the same building, my building. They walk forward from the clinging shadows with a regimental ease of familiarity. A kind of group dynamic team's exhibit when they're focussed on a similar goal. Shit! I lean back against the wall, well out of sight. How long had they known I was at Jessica's place? Chen knew this game better than he knew himself. All the way from Yvette's place to Jessica's we'd checked for tails, digitally as well as visually, thanks to Chen's expert techie dudes. But the China man knew this would be a perfect place for an impromptu trap, so he left some of his soldiers with me. These Nexus dawgs must have checked Yvette's place realized we'd departed in a hurry and were now staking out the next best thing. It's started. The panic I'd felt earlier rises inside me. I pace my breathing.

A double knock at the front door echoes all the way back to the bedroom. I tense, my heart pounding in my chest. After a pause comes another knock. I wonder if the alert button on the main door is broken or maybe they've found another way to intimidate me. Whatever their thinking, it's working. I look around wondering how I'm gonna fight for my life, and win, in such a small, uncomfortable space. I'm talking out loud now, softly, being reassured by the sound of my own voice.

Blank your mind and calm your ass down.

More deep breathing helps, but it doesn't stop my mind flitting from one bad mental image to another. I can't just stand here waiting for the inevitable, but I've been told to stay out of this. And for a tough headed mo' fucker like me, that was hard.

I look through the window again. The streets are still quiet. I know that the punks I saw less than ten minutes ago, are at my door, posing as the Po-Po. I pick up a handgun Chen's given me, remembering our conversation.

'I hate guns' man,' had been my response as he'd handed me the cold shiny piece of ceramic steel.

'Just in case.' His tone told me he hadn't expected any resistance but still I persisted.

'Just in case of what, dawg?'

'Just in case I have made a fatal mistake and completely underestimated our enemy. Then your life and the life of your family will be in your own hands.'

'So I'll be on my own?' I'd asked already knowing the answer.

'You'll be on your own.' That one simple statement was worth more than a thousand words expressing the same thing. No sugar coating, no fuss from Chen. Just the bare facts son, as always.

I feel the weight of the plasma gun. Turn it over and around, familiarizing myself with its working. They're not gonna take me down easily; this is going to be a bitter victory or a complete ass fuck for them. I reach for the knob on the bedroom door, hesitating as the knocking starts again. No code, just a rhythmic pounding followed by a stern booming voice.

'This is Met-1, and we have reason to believe Mr. Adonis Campbell resides here. You have twenty seconds to open up.'

Not bad, covering their asses just in case eye witnesses come onto the scene after the carnage. I cock my ears and listen keenly.

Your move mo' fuckers.

First, there's silence then comes an almighty explosion. Immediately I hit the decks. The four-inch dense Plastik compound that constituted the front door buckles but doesn't crack from the sound wave spreading from the epicentre of the blast. Plasma rounds pop off amidst shouts of conflict and pain and screams and shrieks of hurt and dying. From my prone position, I see the areas beyond lighting up from the volley of super-heated pellets hurtling randomly from weapons. I had to get out of this bedroom. Staying here would be suicide.

I push the door and roll out, gun at the ready, the weapon humming for release in my hand. It's dark, but my eyes adjust quickly taking in the sad state of the main room. Jessica's lounge is fucked up. Her floor sprinkled with glass shards and blood. Two of Chen's men hold up one of their colleagues whose been hit. A bounty hunter has slumped over a chair, the remains of a gaping hole through his thoracic region completely cauterized by the intense heat. The others who I'd spotted from the window are nowhere to be seen, but I hear their shrill voices and covering fire as they retreat down the corridor. Two of Chen's soldiers take point in the corridor and only then am I confident that the shit storm has passed. I look around at the damage and cough at the smell of burnt flesh wafting from a few bodies. Then my attention comes to rest on a scene that could have been dragged from a classic Shaw Brothers production. An Anglo with his back to the wall and Sammy Wong has him pinned in place with the heel of his flat loafers - Wu Tang Clan style. The congealed mucus and blood gathered at the back of his throat, and a size nine against his oesophagus means his curses come out gurgled.

'Son-of-a-bitch we have a live one,' I murmur as I walk over to them. 'Lights!' The sodium spots rise to full intensity in mere moments, causing everyone in the room except me to blink. My eyes adjust automatically.

'Break his neck?' Sammy asks as if he's referring to a chicken picked for our evening meal. God knows I want to give him the nod. The first person I thought of to watch over Yvette and Junior had been Jessica. Her place had been the next stop after the altercation at my baby mother's crib. Sensei Chen wasn't happy with this one bit and convinced me to move them, again. He'd been right. I was losing count how much I owed this cat.

I shake my head and peer down at the man struggling for air 'Do I know you cracker?' I kneel beside him and look straight into his grey eyes, now dulled from pain and the looming eventually of death. Sammy Wong's heel is still pressing into his Adam's apple. The sucker's too pre-occupied with forcing air into his lungs to pay much attention to me but the memory comes back like I've been backhanded in the chops. The limo job, that's where I knew his ass from. The client, Fernanda Figueredo, Brazilian Commodity trader. This mo' fucker had been the chauffeur! I remember he'd strained to make me out in his mirror, wanted to see me in action for himself but I had frozen him out.

Now I was beginning to understand the depth of this conspiracy! I was being played from the word go even though I'd truly believed that I knew what it was all about. They must have tried to take me out on scenarios before, but Digital's security protocols saved my ass.

This cocksucker was one of maybe three men on their payroll who could finger me. If anyone knew about the inner working of these guys and why they wanted me dead, chauffeur boy would know.

Pinned to the wall by Chen's men, I come up to him close and personal.

'You wanted to do me like that, bitch? Didn't know I was connected, thought you could take me out like a two-bit hooker? Catch me if you can, I'm the gingerbread man.'

They let him slide to the floor, and by this, my anger is controlled. I assess the wreckage to Jessica's pad. My angel's home would be off limits until we knew what was going down.

A bitter sadness prickles my heart as once again I've made another friend's life that much more complicated and dangerous. My only solace is that at least Jessica's safe and alive. I look over to the injured China man, nursing a wound to his leg. 'Will he be okay?' I ask.

'Nothing our healers can't deal with,' the one I call Bolo, answers.

'And the dead dudes?' I ask.

'We take our own.' He said.

'Well do your thing and let's bounce before Five-O arrives and we gotta explain shit.'

Moments later everyone, including our captive, has departed to street level and I take one last look inside before I close the door and wipe it down for prints. I'm missing my little room already, and for that, I want to see this treacherous Cracker squeal.

21.

WILD STALLION

'HOW OLD IS THIS PLACE ANYWAY'? I ask as my eyes quickly adjust to the dimness.

'Almost seven hundred years old, dating back to the Ming dynasty. Shaw answers haughtily.

I do the maths in my head, not believing China had a presence in England just after the Black Death had wiped out nearly half of Europe.

'Brother, you sure 'bout that?' I ask him.

'Very.'

'Shit!' I say.

The Shaw brothers lead me into the guts of a building that looks, feels and smells like some subterranean chamber of an urban Shaolin temple. I remember that old Missy Elliot joint, 'Get your Freak on' and the location shoot for what they called videos back then. Same goddamn place, believe dat.

Don't ask me where I am because I'd been blindfolded all the way here and for most of the ten minutes I walked underground. Now after about forty-five minutes of travel from Chen's favorite Italian restaurant I end up in some Zen Buddhist temple. They must have shipped these big ass urns, statues, wall armaments and even the brickwork directly from China. I know L-Town well and a place like this would be a massive draw to tourists if they knew it existed. I've never read anything about an underground temple, Roman possibly, but ancient Chinese? Shiiiiit. I've got an eerie feeling that I've been privileged to be the first westerner, hell the first brother to set foot in this place.

The lighting is low, fuelled by burning torches. Cobwebs hang from walls like dusty veils, and in the recesses, I catch glimpses of the glowing red eyes of stray vermin. If I didn't know better I'd think that this was all an elaborate set-design quickly improvised to impress me, but my Triad homie doesn't have a flair for the dramatic or even, come to think of it, a sense of humor. What I can't figure out is why we need monks to beat the crapola out of this guy for his information. Praying over his twisted ass won't have any effect that I know. But, as always, Master Chen has a plan. The dude we'd captured was cold and calculating. I'm eager to see how well his gangsta shit holds up when these two babies start pounding on his ass.

I crack the knuckles of both fists and flex my shoulders. The corridor opens into a large chamber with ornate stone chairs to my right and left. Doors, which I guess, lead into other rooms or even more corridors, seem to be stamped into the walls.

Looking more or less the same as when I last saw him seven hours ago is my old adversary – chauffeur guy. He's stripped to the waist and, other than a few old wounds, looks no worse for wear. Man, I'm disappointed that he looks so good. No bruising, no swellings, the monks haven't tenderized his ass for my arrival, pity. Instead, a single acupuncture needle sticks out of the back of his neck. He's seated upright, rigid but immobile as if he's got a bomb strapped to his balls. He's alone in the center of the room. I smile at the metaphor. One solitary chair for one solitary ass.

The Shaw brothers step back allowing me entry. They don't have to ask twice. I'm already up close to the gunman. At first, I'm cautious, but I can see that the well-placed needle has totally immobilized him. I lean in feeling his breath on my cheek.

'This bitch right here, gets worse, turf boy.'

'It will, won't it.'

Chen said walking into the arena. Surprisingly he's dressed in a slick; silk traditional Chinese get up instead of his usual western suit.

'Glad you could join us, Chen. Maybe you can tell me why we're here?'

He motions to the chairs on his right. 'Sit with me and you'll see.'

Always the puzzle master, never telling the full story, all the better to jangle a brotha's brain cells. But I let it go. For the past week as we've pounded London's streets, he's both saved my ass and fulfilled all his promises. He seems to view this 'episode' as simply an entrée to the main course of risking our lives on this coming weekend at the Nexus Black Tie affair. Maybe he thinks that playing around with our inert captive will be satisfactory payback for the shootout at Jessica's place. Hey, if I get a piece of chauffeur boy, I'm happy to let him play out his hand. I sit as requested and wait for the lights to dim but instead Chen checks his timepiece then crosses his legs. That, apparently, is the signal.

The ornate seats to my right fill up with five somber-faced, elderly Chinese dudes in western suits. Chen stands, and I almost join him but think better of it. He looks over to them and bows. I've just witnessed my dawg showing respect to an obvious superior. This mo' fucker takes orders? What a beautiful thing to behold!

But the illusion of Chen being a lackey soon disappears because as he sits he growls under his breath in Mandarin. Questions run through my mind. If these men are who I think they are, why are they so interested in what's going on? Chen's got some explaining to do.

From the wings step two bald monks in orange robes, wooden beads strung around their necks. The older one walks behind the student who's carrying a wooden block made up like a porcupine's ass stuck with a mass of acupuncture needles. I'm gripped by the atmosphere as the monks pray over the needles. I lean towards Chen, who's ready to come out with some bullshit about Chinese superiority.

'This is an interrogation is in the Wu Wei fashion. Master T'Ang is an expert practitioner of the needles. By manipulating and activating the numerous magnetic meridians of the human body, resonating them just right, our friend will be compelled to tell us the truth to any question asked.'

'You shitting me, right?'

He gives me a 'do-I-look-like-I'm-shitting-you-mo' fucker' glare and focuses again on the spectacle unfolding before us.

Chen is a hard nigga to work out or maybe I've got the wrong idea about the Triad families. Word on the street is that these Chinese dudes laid down their shit hardcore. Steeped in ancient Chinese culture, they're deep as they are deadly. Axes, meat cleavers, and laser scalpels their primary choice of tools. Murder, extortion, and kidnapping, even within their community, all in a day's work. And yet here was a man more than reluctant to cause injury or take a life. It just didn't add up. Chen leans over to me as Master T'Ang sinks the first needle into the captive's wrists.

'Have you ever served time Mr. Campbell?' Chen's holier-than-thou-tone is pissing me off, along with his 'spring-mounted' eyes, alert and alive always never missing a trick. My neutral mood shifts a notch in the wrong direction. Self-consciously I tug my sleeve over the prison label embedded in my wrist.

'Yeah.' I say

'What for?' His question is innocent enough, but his initial superciliousness still lingers. I close my eyes as the memories wash over me, in no hurry to answer Chen's question.

Hollywood wives. Rich bitches. Sex. I fleeced them of cash and jewellery. Most wouldn't or couldn't inform Five-O because of their social standing, not to mention their husbands. It was a sweet deal, but I got too complacent. Careless in a town that wasn't as big as I'd been led to believe was a fatal mistake. I ended up doing three years in San Quentin.

I'd be a punk if I ever told him about Wang, my cell-mate, an old Triad OG from Hong Kong who showed me how to avoid a shank in my back when I refused the offer to become a cell-mate bitch. Wang showed me the higher ways of meditation, Tai Chi and reading. He even introduced me to an old boxer in the exercise yard who took me through my paces. I chuckle softly at the thought of the conjugal visits I had from some of the same bitches I fleeced money off. Maybe I should tell Chen that? But I decide against it. Why provide him with more ammunition?

'Fraud.' I finally say.

'Did Maria know about your past?'

His question catches me off guard making me hesitate. Bad move. I was a liar and a thief in the past life, right? Past life. Now I'm about to tell him the truth and it feels like some needy confession, crap.

'Nah,' I say, 'your sister was special. She didn't give a shit about my history, just the here and now. She had a thing about past indiscretions and our expectations for each other. She only wanted me for me. As wack as that sounds homie that was how it was. I wanted to tell her everything about me, she wanted to tell me nothing about herself. That was her style and I never questioned her reasons.'

'Our family felt she was special too. We knew she had a different path laid out to her than what was traditional. But still she was ultimately affected by what we tried to protect her from.'

I shake my head, my focus split between the spectacle of the monks and our conversation.

'Maybe you all didn't try hard enough.'

'Implying what exactly?' Chen questions me coldly.

'I ain't implying shit man. Just laying down the truth. You can take it or leave it.' I move in closer. 'The truth is dawg, you disowned her or she disowned you, either way, it doesn't matter. She wanted to live her life on her own terms, but deep down I'm guessing she still yearned for some contact with you and her culture. She never truly gave up, but you did.'

'It is never that simple. I wouldn't expect you to understand our ways and our commitment to them. Our traditions are sacred and have been adhered to by our ancestors since time immemorial.'

'Bullshit man! Wake up and smell the coffee! Are you listening to yourself? You're a goddamn gangster! Traditions mean more than blood and now she's dead, and you feel guilty, all of this is your way of making amends for what happened to Maria. You fucked up, your family fucked up and right now, you'd give your right nut to change shit, but it's done.'

Chen contemplates my words as the chanting of the monk's increases. 'It's never too late to right a grave wrong.' This is the closest he's come to admitting that Maria had been treated like a stray dog. But I'm not done. I had stuff in my craw he needed to hear.

'Remember when we met first and you tried to lay that superiority shit on my ass? Acting all how the fuck could my sister ever associate with a dude like me, rap sheet and everything? But you still wanted my help because you knew nothing about your own blood, didn't give a fuck how she lived until she died. Still thinking your sister could do better than me when she came from a family of gangsters herself. This street nigga stuck with her and became her family and is willing to lay it all down for her memory.'

Chen sighs, a sour frown on his face. 'Maybe I've misjudged you Adonis,'

'Misjudged me? Nah!'

'But suggesting we care more for tradition than my sister is not completely true.'

I ignore him.

'After my shorties murder, I doubted what I meant to her. Your bullshit added to that uncertainty but talking to the maid Ma Brown resolved all that. She confirmed everything. Confirmed how Maria felt about me before I met your sorry ass. Ma Brown knew because she was tight with Maria. You read me all wrong, man, sure I would have bailed on you after you got what you wanted, but it turns out I'm essential to getting this situation dealt with. My old lady, was much like your Confucius; she had a Jamaican saying for every Goddamn thing. 'The stone that the builders refuse become the head corner stone.' That's one of her favourites.' I finally shut up, done mouthing off for now.

Chen looks on with glistening eyes absorbing everything. For once he's got no comeback. The truth in the cold light of day is a bitch to swallow. But for all our disagreements and differences, if any man can stomach it Chen can.

Silence drifts between us and my entire focus is now on the two monks and their performance. They've placed all their needles except for one, all over our captive's neck head and shoulders. Finally, the acolyte pulls the last needle from the wooden block and hands it to the master who considers his final stroke. I'm starting to get apprehensive as the religious man draws out the climax before plunging the final needle into the assassin's jaw. It's my time to perform for the crowd, like the organ grinders monkey. The elder monk motions to Chen who acknowledges his skill by standing and bowing. In a harsh whisper, Chen tells me to haul my tired ass up and follow his lead. I comply, silently and walk over to the tough guy who's still sitting erect. He's lucid, blinking occasionally, his eyes alert, his breathing steady, beads of sweat on his brow.

I should have a volley of questions to sling at him, but the only thing on my mind is how quiet the place is. I inhale the calming smell of incense and feel the eyes of those old dudes on me. I try to muster some righteous anger, Old Testament fire, and brimstone but nothing comes. In its place is a calculated need to snuff out a life. The professional detachment of a contract killer runs through my veins. This is my first interrogation, and I was naively expecting blades, electricity, drugs, sleep deprivation, even bright lights. You know, the interrogator's traditional tools.

'You okay?' Chen is aware of my long contemplation.

'Yeah.' I lean down to the level of the Punto in the chair. 'You with me, man?'

He blinks in answer then strangely his Adam's apple bobs up and down like he's clearing his throat. His lips move, his tongue flexes in the dark cavern of his mouth.

'Can he talk?' I ask Chen, who signals to one of the Buddhist monks waiting in the wings. The elder shuffles over, and they exchange brief words in Mandarin. Nodding he approaches the bound hitman, observing the acupuncture needles with nothing less than delight in his eyes. He pulls two needles out of his neck and steps back, bowing to Chen.

'The subject is all yours,' Chen informs me.

I shrug and position myself right in front of him, close enough for him to feel my breath on his cracked lips. 'I want to know who sent you to kill my family motherfucker and I want to know now.'

22.

BERMUDA TRIANGLE

THIS VISIT IS OVERDUE. I'm in Finchley North London, and the leafy Englishness screams old money and upper-class pretensions. My ass doesn't fit in but I've never been the one to try and cozy up with any convention but my own. I'm wearing Outkast jeans, quarterback jersey, and an Avirex leather jacket. Ghetto gleam at a minimum, only my platinum diamond composite Rolex is on my wrist and my cloaking device dog tags around my neck. Crowning this fly shit is an Avirex doo rag and a New York Yankees baseball cap. The few people I do see are dressed conservatively, L-Town chic I call it and in a place like this, an outrageous dude like me provides a sharp contrast. But as unlikely as it seems, this was like my hood back in the day. I attended the best and most expensive finishing schools in the erotic arts thanks to Digital who never did anything by halves.

The place is just as imposing as when I was last here. It's an old boarding school with creaking joists and whispering walls, packed full of memories, history, and some scary-ass past student supposedly walking the corridors after four centuries of being dead. I'd spent five months here perfecting the art of yoga, tantric sex, projecting my sensuality, sexual technique, posture, and poise.

For a girl born in a little village outside of Warsaw, Madame Zorva, the lady who ran this joint, had done well. Without a word of hype, the hopefuls, from business people to street pro's were beating a path to her door ready to avail themselves of her services, hey, if she could streamline my black ass, she was the shit.

I'd called ahead to make sure that she'd have time to see me, in her busy schedule. This was far too important to do my usual turn up and hope for the best trick, but strangely her communicator was offline. So I'd called the school direct but still wasn't able to talk to her. Instead, Mandy her PA got back to me moments later with an invitation to come down any day and anytime this week. I wondered if Zorva knew what had gone on with Digital? Considering I was a friend as well as a former student my V-Comm was weirdly silent.

Shit went down almost a week and a half ago, and I've had a lot of stuff explained to me because I went looking for answers. But the bulk of my questions? Well hey, let's just say I'm still searching. What I do know, is my woman and my dawg Popeye were murdered – more or less before my eyes. Digital's HQ was blitzkrieged, his body wasn't found – and that left behind a serious question mark in my mind.

Madam Zorva was more or less the only confidante outside of the Sixty-Nine family Digital would trust. If there were more to all this bubbling under the surface, she would know, and I'd like to think that she'd share that information with me. Then again I was dealing with an old-world virtuoso. I'd just have to wait and see. In moments, I'm look up at the ivy-shrouded frontage, mount the steps and enter through the arches.

The Academy's systems detect me immediately.

'Mr. Campbell, if you would just follow me, please.' Mandy, Madam Zorva's PA, is plain looking chick with a personality to match. Ironic really. Considering where she works. All that knowledge and expertise at her fingertips. Life-changing principles that could make her into prime man-bait, if she bothered to put them into practice. Shame. But I'm impressed by the fact that she knows who I am before I've even opened my mouth. Maybe, I'd been too quick to judge. Perhaps she did have 'skills' after-all, even if they weren't the aesthetic kind. Just as I start to build a fantasy around her, we arrive at our destination.

'Just through these doors and on your right.'

'You sure this is a good time?' I ask.

'We've been expecting you for a few days now, Mr. Campbell.'

'Yeah?' I swear I see a hint of a smile break through her austere expression. I follow instructions like a good choir boy.

I watch her turn and walk away, habitually checking out her ass.

The door I open leads me into some atmospheric street scene, like something out of an Amateur Dramatics Club. This shit is vintage Madam Zorva. A real-life scenario created to enhance the learning experience for her students. Papier-mâché lamp posts, a broken-down wall with graffiti, a cardboard car wreck propped up from behind and a very shiny garbage bin. Subtle lighting comes down from the rafters, and smooth jazz funk plays in the background. I'm in the spotlight, center stage.

Damn! She punked me.

I smile to myself. I should have known better. I guess I'm a sucker for punishment because instead of retreating I take the challenge, hang loose and wait for the coup de grace.

The PA crackles into life. 'This ladies and gentlemen is one of my best past students. Adonis.'

I nod to the dark silhouettes in the distance.

'Play along,' Madam Zorva chuckles, 'I have some students who need your finishing touches.'

'Aight, where do you want me?' I groan.

The spotlight switches from my position to front stage that a moment ago was in darkness. Before me is a woman, butt naked, strapped to a bed by her wrists and ankles.

'Damn!' I whisper.

'That Adonis is Ms. Sabrina Ferguson. CEO of the Azalea fashion house. Don't worry she's fine. I'm quite proud of her, she's come a long way. This is her final test, a chance to prove that even in today's world of lost intimacy she can still show trust and true confidence, qualities necessary for true happiness in any relationship. Can she let go? We shall see.'

Sabrina is oblivious to what is being said. She lies totally relaxed and completely comfortable, a whisper of a smile on her lips. Sound excluders cover her ears, and her eyes are concealed under white light generators. The rest of her beautiful body is open for all to see. But even as I admire the curves of her lithe body, the ample breasts and the white light making her dark skin glisten, I hang loose and wait for the dime to drop.

Meantime my eyes settle on a trolley beside the bed, ice, fresh fruit, dildos, creams, oils, and vibrators. Essential old school bedroom joints. The PA crackles again.

'Adonis, bring Sabrina to an orgasm. The choice of weapon is yours. We will see how much she has learned when this is over.' I roll my eyes.

Not what I had planned, but hey, what the hell!

Two hours later I'm stretched out in Elizabeth Zorva's Roman lounge chair like a satiated panther. I'm relaxed and happy, compliments of Ms Ferguson and our orgasm experiment. Her private office is impressive. Her challenging upbringing evident in her treasured collection of refined trappings. Everything from her pens to the furniture that adorns the room are exquisite works of master craftsmen. I understand the need to compensate for lack, I even have a few of these babies myself. But after what I've just told her my 'toys' all pale into insignificance.

She points her fingers under her chin, thinking it all through with the calmness she's known for. The woman who taught a street smart, cocky nigga the fine art of seduction never buckles under duress but deals with whatever life throws at her with stoic indignation. I think she's handling shit well until the barrier breaks down and the cool emotions give way to unexpected tears. Love sure has a way of fuck-ing up your priorities.

'When was the last time you talked to or met up with Digital Ms. Z?' I ask even though I'm intruding on her thoughts. Her deep blue eyes are wide with grief. I'm not used to this raw revelation of the real her.

'Three weeks ago. A dinner engagement. You don't think..?'

'I'm not thinking Ms. Z; I just want to know where he is, if he is. If you can provide some clues to that question, then sweet.'

'You think he might be ...?'

'I have hope.' I try to gauge her reaction. I'm dissing an elder and that ain't right, but the situation demands it. If Liz knows more than she's letting on she's holding it down damn well. But if I have any doubts about the depth of feeling between herself and Digital the anguish in her voice confirms her pain is real. Maybe I should have been straight with her from the outset, but I had to present the facts and see if she would come to the same conclusion I had.

I let the enormity of the situation sink in, watching her frustration and confusion transform into something harder, coming from deep within.

'Richard was in a good mood,' she began, her voice low, contemplative. 'We talked, and as usual, he was great company.'

'What did you talk about?'

'The past, his daughter mainly and the future. Did you know that he was still actively involved with research into the disease that killed Melanie?'

I didn't, I'm thinking. But Digital was the kind of man who wouldn't just take no for an answer. He couldn't bear the thought of his little girl dying in vain. I took it as a given that Digital wouldn't stop until he could contribute something significant to this disease, I just never found out what. It was simply an example of the boundless love a father has for his kid. I could relate to that shit. Liz is still speaking. I hear the word worried and immediately tune back in.

'...there was something on his mind. He was concerned about you and how the business would stand up without him. He always said you were a quick study, and he had confidence in your abilities, but he seemed to be expecting something that would greatly test you.'

This is old news to me. I'm much further ahead in my enquiries.

'Did he mention any names; any organizations that he guessed wanted him or us out of the picture?'

Her laugh is short and bitter. 'You would know more about that than anyone else. He protected his friends from his world, apart from sharing the triumphs, but if he were worried about any aspect of his business, if there were any conflict troubling him, I would be the last to know. He al-ways said he had broad shoulders.'

'That sounds like a man who thought that the buck stopped with him.'

'No,' she shakes her head. 'I don't think that's what he was trying to say. I got the feeling he was concerned about your physical well-being amongst other things. Richard was a perfectionist; he wanted you fit and all the business systems in place, so that if necessary things could be operated with the least worry to you.'

'The least worry?' The relevance of her words makes the required impression.

'You think he was expecting this to happen?' She asks.

I nod.

'My God.'

'What?' Something in her voice makes me lean forward, my senses alert.

'He told me about an offer for Sixty-Nine.'

'No fucking way!' I blurt out. The only purchase that could be going down with Sixty-Nine would be a hostile one. Digital would never consider a sale, no way. An afterthought prickles my thinking and I wonder why my heart suddenly feels like a stone. 'Who were these cats anyway? Corporate types or independent operators?'

'Very persistent Chinese businessmen, who were most likely representing some interested corporate parties, were his exact words. At the time, he just seemed to think it was funny. Even said he met with them to see how favorable their terms were.'

'Digital?'

'Yes.' she confirms.

'Goddamn!'

A gut feeling tells me that my Chinese niggas have been keeping information from me about a possible connection. Sue me but I still have some trust issues with Chen to work out. I'm not playa hating cos I wouldn't want anyone else watching my back. But Chen was just one of the many cogs in the Triad wheel. A shit storm that he knew nothing of could be brewing in his head.

My stomach tightens again as I think of the upcoming Saturday night ball at Nexus headquarters. For all of

Chen's resourcefulness, I'm still not sure he's capable of helping me to pull this off, but he's all I've got.

Elizabeth and I talk some more, and I see the heartache taking hold. Her strength falls away in layers, and I decide to give her time alone. She's helped me as much as she can. I'm disappointed even though I'm not sure what I expected from our meeting. At the end of the day, the facts are straightforward. Dr. James Richard Marsden is dead leaving me with decisions to make and more mysteries to solve.

23.

BRAZILIAN BEDLOCK

ARE YOU SURE HE'LL BE OKAY?' Yvette asks, straightening Adonis Junior's leather jacket then carefully zipping it up,
'Little man is cool baby.' I say impatiently. 'We safe.' I ruffle his curly hair and he play acts a mini tantrum in objection.
Yvette smiles, reminding me of how it was before we split. The days when she was that sweet girl, content with how our life was going until she saw the light. Nothing to do with a new-found spirituality, just the ill advice of a group of well-wishing hood rats from her reader's circle.
'Where your man at when you ready to turn in for the night? What he doing that he not telling you about, girl?'
And so, it continued like a slow working poison until the questions became so intrusive, her doubts intensified and jealousy clouded her perception like an addiction. My metamorphosis was from a family man and provider to

philandering dawg, using working as a stripper as the reason to avoid commitment. Well, to Yvette's thinking anyway. Rumours and jealousy caused an ugly split, fuelled by her needless bitterness that eventually destroyed us both for good.

This time around Yvette had time to think about my actions without the comments from the penny section. After her anger had subsided, she was faced with the reality. She may not have understood why her life and the life of my son had been threatened. She may not even have understood why she'd shacked up with that dumb mo' fucker she'd called a boyfriend, who obviously didn't care for our kid but only worshiped her pussy. But she did understand that I would risk my life to keep them safe. You can't question motivation like that simply because it's more than a sense of duty, it's love, pure and simple.

Yvette has allowed me and Adonis Junior to go for a stroll like father and son for once. I pinch myself to make sure it's real. As recently as three weeks ago, this would have been unthinkable. I'd been in the middle of planning serious legal action against my baby mama for shared custody of my little cowboy. My priority was to move into Management at 69 incorporated and show the courts that I was capable and stable. Now it's all unnecessary. Everything my soul requires is happening in real time. Right now.

Adonis Junior grips my hand as we mosey up the high street away from Chen's safe house towards the local Mickey D's. For one beautiful moment, I'm oblivious to the world and its problems, enjoying the sound of little man's voice as he recites the entire list of treats from the fast food restaurant's menu. L-Town rejoices with me. The sun is high in the sky, and it's chilly but cloudless. Even Ariel traffic is sparse. I don't usually wax poetical or burst into spontaneous verse but playa I feel like I wanna to take flight. The hotties in their convertibles toot us as father and son catch an easy rhythm. The sight of me tenderly handling my son is sexy, and hey that's fine by me.

My little man is looking good in his tan Versace jacket, beige cords and brown Tiny J-man trainers. He's grown since I last saw him three days ago. If I'm not careful, this segment of his life will pass me by in the blink of an eye. I resolve to somehow make sure that doesn't happen.

I think of all the people in my life right now who've brought me this far. Chen, Jessica, Little man, my saviors, all of them. I need to survive this. I need to come back to these good people because without them I have nothing.

A car passes us by thumping out the melodic voice of John D and Adonis junior tugs on my hand.

'I know who that is daddy!'

'Who?' I ask, smiling at his eagerness.

'John Deeeeee!' He styles out the name in his signature kinetic way. The track name and album title follow in quick succession.

Damn, he's good. 'You're a music connoisseur now are you, huh?' This time my smile comes from pride.

'Con-nis-ur.' He rolls the word around, his toothy grin telling me like likes the sound and taste of it. 'Yep I'm a music con-nis-ur and I'm better than you.'

I give him a playful glare. 'You challenging me kid?' I say in my best Jimmy Cagney accent.

He nods vigorously as we approach Mickey D's and the sliding door opens.

'Best of five?' I ask.

And just like some super confident Tennessee gambler, he replies,

'Whoever wins buys?'

'Damn,' I say with Junior going ahead and me laughing all the way to the counter.

Two days later, I'm sipping a hot, comforting caramel Mocha in my First-Class cabin aboard the luxurious Orient Express. Only nine of these hybrid trains around the world that can function on steam and electromagnetism. Outside, speed, darkness and landscape all merge into one. The sleeper, replete with all the Mod com's any sophisticated playa desires including a large foldable bunk bed, hurtles towards Gare De Nore and although this is business, I still feel out of place without my Sixty-Nine family having my back. All I have as support is a dispassionate AI, making sure everything runs smoothly.

I sigh and place my Mocha carefully on the antique wooden table. I close my eyes and lean back against the wall. It's all catching up with me. My passion for my work is evaporating, leaving behind pure, bitter duty.

Two nights ago, the Shaw brothers had brought me back to Jessica's crib; my head was shit full of snippets from the assassin's mouth about why they chose us but mainly why they wanted me. Despite everything being on a need to know basis, for him to infiltrate 69, he needed some details. He was planted and began to try to destroy us from the inside out. When that hadn't worked as expected, they took off the kid gloves and proceeded to dismantle us piece by piece. I was the prize. The number one pain in their ass, the man Nexus Pharmaceuticals wanted, alive if possible, dead if necessary. The assassin kept talking about how I had something precious or maybe he meant I was something extremely valuable. They had no idea who their paymasters were they just knew that the remuneration was good. They just popped the marks and banked the credits.

So, my black ass was being attacked on two almost overwhelming fronts. I could feel Chen's need for immediate payback when the assassin snitched on his employers, not that he had a choice. He told us about a secret warehouse where the killers honed their skills and where the Dragon Syndicate was planning a proper surprise party for them. The Chinaman had it all worked out, feeding me only the essentials, as usual.

We didn't have a lot of time. It was my responsibility to make sure 69 continued regardless. Digital depended on me to keep his legacy together. I couldn't let him down, and I needed closure.

I sigh once again and open my laptop, beginning to finally understand the concept of creative problem-solving Popeye used to go on about. Lateral thought.

Most business challenges can't be handled with a right brain approach, he'd say.

I check my time piece. I've still got half an hour before I prepare for business. Enough time to fit in some battlefield planning. I stretch out on the ultra-comfortable bed and relax. I state my problem out loud.

'How can I be in five goddamn places at once?'

My thoughts tumble over themselves. Talking to that punk with the acupuncture needles sticking out of him had confirmed a few things. When Digital was running bizniz he had a marketing method that kept our clients trickling through for appointments at a manageable rate. Sixty-Nine could realistically only execute about three fully blown scenarios with a few of the most mundane encounters taking place in the space of a month. The organizational powerhouse watching my back wasn't human, and that could be a good thing. With a constant AI presence, most duties were covered, but the marketing creativity and the scenarios could only be accomplished by me.

I was on my lonesome unable to handle the work coming in. I was convinced that Nexus was responsible for making business better than ever but only because they wanted me to buckle under the weight. They had me trapped, and they knew it. The only way they could do such a thing is if they were familiar with our structure and had knowledge about our numbers. Mo fuckers had fine-tuned their research on us to a tee. Just one cancelled scenario would cause irreparable damage to our reputation. I desperately needed this initial storm to pass without incident.

I feel as though I'm floating, no shackles, no responsibilities, moving in total motion with the smooth vibrations of the train. Pity, I can't turn down the volume on my thoughts. Instead, I give them free reign, and when I've had enough, I decide to prepare for Ms. Ife Hughes.

Two hours later I'm standing outside of the First-class cabin number 1051. I'm twenty minutes early. Yeah, you heard me. So, you think a playa's slipping, right? Twenty minutes' leeway felt right, so I went with it. Okay, Sixty-Nine is renowned for its precision; its scenarios taking place only as specified allowing only for the vagaries of human nature. Yow, you know that my gut always points the way out of Dodge when shit gets chronic? Breaking protocol is exactly what the doctor is ordering tonight. I'd staked out the cabin as soon as I'd boarded at Waterloo. I never saw head or tail of the mark, but I had to be certain it was all cool. Try to understand why I'm tripping. This is the first time I've run a scenario from start to finish while being an integral part of its execution.

I'm cool.

Who the fuck you trying to fool, fool?

I'm nervous as hell.

I've disabled all the corridor lights. Consequently, I'm glowing like a fire-flies butt in my luminescent electrician's overall. My platinum dog tags jingle lightly reassuring me further. But I'm still edgy from fine-tuning the intricate predetails necessary for the success of this game.

Mr. Edward Hughes is an English multimillionaire who's made his pile from Data Strip manufacturing. He has everything any man could want but is getting on in age. 'A sprightly eighty-nine years old,' to be exact, his words, not mine. His wife was a stunning Nigerian beauty, who was a fraction of his age, celebrating her thirtieth birthday with me as her big surprise. She's a successful entrepreneur and the brains behind a promotion company operating mainly out of the Commonwealth of Democratic African States.

Hughes is concerned about the possible disparity in their sex drives. And although he had tech or bio-augmentation alternatives to improve his performance, to his mind they weren't the same. For a woman with everything, what better than her dreams of complete fulfilment being realized by the best in the business? I had to respect the old man. I'm not sure I'd be so accommodating towards some young buck spanking my old lady's ass, so I made concessions. I'm not a hundred percent happy about his request to take part, but the old guy was a voyeur who got his groove on by seeing his old lady getting pleasured.

Normally Sixty-Nine would be set the pace, dictating how everything should be handled but under the circumstances I've given some leeway. Mr. Hughes had stated the times his wife would be alone in the cabin. He'd also told me exactly what to say when I entered her private enclosure. After that, if we hit it off and things progressed to the next stage then the old man would take a load off in the best seat in the house. Front and center.

His being there wouldn't alter my game, just reduce my comfort zone. I prefer to ride alone.

I knock on the door, grip my toolbox of freaky shit and turn on my thousand-watt smile.

'Mr. and Mrs. Hughes, it's your cabin technician.'

There's no answer. A feeling of disquiet starts from the pit of my stomach. I keep it tight and go to plan 'B'; Open up this mother myself. The lock is a standard old school barrel in keeping with the era of the original Orient Express. In less than three minutes I turn the brass door knob, my shoulder gently urging it open an inch at a time.

'Mr. and Mrs. Hughes! It's your Cabin Technician.' I say again. 'We have a slight emergency, and I need to access to your suite.'

I listen keenly for a response but hear only sniffling. A weak neon blue light oozes through the opening, like I'm about to enter the Twilight Zone. I've given them enough warning, so I don't ask again. My balls are tingling, my gut calm, so I slip inside, loose as a goose, my situational awareness acute just in case my twenty-twenty takes a leave of absence. The cabin is a larger version of mine. Ife Hughes is seated trembling, to the left on the bunk bed. On seeing me, she belatedly and nonchalantly shrugs off her hurt. I flash my fake ID, apologizing for using my universal access key to gain entry.

'I'm sorry for barging in like this ma'am, but we have a gas pressure build up in our system and pipes are rupturing everywhere, just making sure the same doesn't happen to you.'

She smiles slowly, her new radiance throwing off the remnants of her earlier pain. Nevertheless, her eyes are red, the silk pillow beside her damp. Smoke from a lone cigarette twirls from a full ashtray on the bed. She picks it up and swings her long legs off the bed concealing her nakedness by rearranging her bathrobe and tightening her belt. My stomach tightens again.

'Mister...?'

'Jenkins.' I answer off the cuff.

'Mr. Jenkins,' she repeats, 'can you make your repairs in less than ten minutes? I'm expecting a visitor.'

Her voice is filled with melody. Even under pressure, she's pleasant and damned sexy. I figure she's normally an upbeat sister, but I'm also experienced enough to discern that there's some dark and despondent shit lingering in the background.

'Sure thing,' I answer. 'Is Mr. Hughes here?' I gesture towards the closed bathroom door. Her answer to such a harmless question is surprisingly a sharp intake of breath. Nerves?

'Go ahead,' she offers her permission for me to snoop around under pretence of my 'job.'

These cabins have been lovingly restored with the old-school sensibilities of the Victorian era. The toilet fixtures are gold-plated, with finishing touches of fine enamel and polished wood. I stare into the ensuite. Something doesn't smell right. I play Colombo, lift the toilet seat and look in the shower cubicle. The toothbrushes are dry, is the shower cubicle and the shavers are clean. The towels are unruffled without a strand of human hair anywhere. It's pristine, like an unlived in show home, nothing has been used.

'That was quick.' She comments as I re-enter the main room.

'All clear in there but I just need to check one more panel.' I smile at her. She's back on the bed while my twenty-twenty is buzzing, as always, I pay heed. 'You don't mind?' I lean over the bed and then crawl across it, stopping mid-crawl. I lean into her expecting flashes of fear seeing as she doesn't know who I am or what I'm about, but Ife fronts like she'd been exposed to hell before I turned up. The sense of discomfort lodged in my stomach heads south as I place my lips to a sweet-smelling ear. I reel off her vital statistics, academic qualifications age, star sign and her place of birth. Now she knows I'm not the engineer.

'Happy birthday.' I say, her lips move, but I stop any words with my fingers. I stroke her cheeks and put my lips to her temples. 'Don't say a word 'cos I know something ain't right.' Her relief came to a sigh of warm breath. 'Be natural, 'cos they can't know, I know. Just relax and trust me. Pappy wanted this to be special. Let's not disappoint him.'

I draw her close and wrap my arms around her. She melts into me, trembling with fear and excitement as the story begins and she gives in to me completely. Internally I'm sweating this shit on a major scale because I've walked into an ambush, willingly. But the threat wasn't just directed at me but at my clientele. The old man knew it was a matter of life and death or something close to that. Mr. Hughes signed the documents and in particular, Clause a3456; Never divulge to a client by inference or direct reference the enactment of a scenario.

It eliminates the element of surprise, the mystery is fucked, you lose your money and most importantly you've just forfeited an opportunity of a lifetime. It's a forfeit not to be taken lightly, and Mr. Hughes understood that completely. Whatever else Ife divulged would probably answer all my questions. You guessed it dawg, shit was about to get chronic and as usual, I was going to be in the eye of the storm.

24.

THE STEER

DIDN'T I TELL YOU NOT TO GO? didn't I tell your black ass you could get killed? The caricature of Chen in my head is goddamn pissed. The image is bright and bold in my mind's eye. It's funny how I'm picturing the China man sat in a lotus position, his hands clasped in his business suit like the Shaolin monk from Saville Row, cursing like the old cat from down the block. Chen was against this from the get-go. He told me to make apologies to the clients, cancel engagements, keep a low profile.

But I'm a hard-headed nigga.

'Maybe under different circumstances,' I'd say to him, but if Digital were in my situation, he would do whatever it took to get the job done. Now it was my turn.

Bullshit, motherfucker! My monkey brain chastises me. You're gonna get a cap in your high moral thinking ass just like Digital did. For real.

Ife's fully warned me about the honey trap I've just walked into. I urge her to chill. The warm blood coursing through my veins has been transfused with ice water and still a strange boost of confidence remains. I'm hyped up, aware of everything, no way to be flexing when this could be your last gig. So, like a good choir boy, I perform my duty. If I'm lucky, she'll get enough of me to allow anonymous observers to think that things are as they should be.

The lights fade, smooth R&B, comes through the system, and all my senses are engaged. Ife slips out of her bathrobe. Hot damn! Victoria's Secret lingerie has never fit a woman so well. Thick ass, skin gleaming tight, fu-fu fed, hill climbing, plump titty sister, coming from a whole generation of Venuses from the cradle of civilization. A jaw-dropping example of perfection and an immediate inclusion into my hall of fame sharing the top spot with a ghetto princess turned Lotto millionaire called Maxine, but that's another story. I soak up every square inch settling on the tattoo of an attacking scorpion; that rests in-between the crease of her ass and her spine.

'Adonis, Adonis, Adonis.'

I've got nothing against a woman being on top, especially when she's murmuring my name so sweetly. Ten inches of the Meat & Grizzle spreads her coochy wide open, probing hitherto unexplored depths. I'm on my back, propped up against the head of the bed, thrusting in rhythm with her gyrations.

Her breasts are real, all 36 DD of them, bouncing on my chest with an exquisite pliancy, which makes me wanna.... She whines like a pro, tantalizing with the warmth of her derrière spread over my groin. I'm not waxing poetic to impress y'all believe me. She's enjoying this with abandon, and if I can take her mind off what's about to go down, I've done well.

Ife has been riding me for twenty minutes, and my attention is caught between her and the doorway. I haven't experimented with anything remotely kinky but keeping that entrance in sight could be the difference between life and death, so I limit the sex positions. It was a bonus that Ife was turned on by the possibility of violence. She squats over me, her large breasts pressed out on my chest and thrusts her hips over my penis. Her stamina is impressive with control to match.

Focus.

The warning shoots through my brain. If I've learned anything about this hustle, it's that preparation is crucial. I take a deep breath, in through the nose and out through my mouth. I clear my mind, just like the great sex masters of China, then I massage her big, beautiful ass, one eye on the old-fashioned door knob while my third eye focuses my chi so I don't 'bust a nut' prematurely. I kiss her chest, the pillow propped under my neck giving me leverage and clear sight of my obsession. Ife shifts her position giving me her back, crouching over my erection, the scorpion tattoo at the base of her spine flexing its stinger. She makes her ass clap as peeps works that magic stick.

For one split second, I take my eye off the door and check out her clean-shaven pussy. I swear I see some movement, the knob being tested from left to right but I'm not sure. My eyes easily make out the details of the cabin, but even with clear vision there's no way I can know that someone is about to enter the room until it's too late. Normally I would have tethered the door with some early warning Tech, but I couldn't risk them being detected. So, unseen by Ife, I went old school and marked the gold-plated handle with a fluorescent white spot, courtesy of her lipstick that I'd borrowed from the bathroom. That spot had just turned clockwise, and this time I was certain.

My twenty-twenty goes ape-shit.

The doorway widens as the first mo' fucker steps from the darkness of the hall into the dimness of our cabin, his soft steps muffled by the background music and his suit adjusting to the darkness making him almost invisible. But my heightened vision clocks him easily. He stands uncommitted between both worlds. A deeper shadow flits across the tableau of the hallway that is suspiciously absent of light.

His partner hangs back.

My balls shrink in panic.

I can't make him out clearly with the door between us. I need to eyeball this cocksucker so I can gauge his next move. He's obviously in no hurry.

Shlick!

The sound of his heater folding out from the sleeve of his overcoat and into his hand is muted but I hear it all. He takes one step forward, silently closing the door behind him. I figure that underneath his big coat is a tightly muscled, wiry frame and some stealth technology masking the sounds of his movement.

The assassin's face is outlined against the shadows. He has an angular jaw, a boxer's chin, and a solid forehead all framed by ropey dreadlocks. Immediately I think that he's one of these out-of-business Nation of Ras Tafari terrorists they'd clamped down on months ago. I respect the Nation, but I'm also not averse to some black on black violence if it means saving my ass. I lock onto him wondering if he can feel the intensity of my stare or he was confident he couldn't be seen or heard. I've forgotten all about Ife, but she hasn't forgotten about me.

'Don't stop,' she whispers oblivious to what is happening, 'Please don't stop.'

Startled by Ife's words the intruder freezes, gun raised only realizing its pillow talk, and he relaxes. Instantly I regret coming here without Chen's help. I feel pain for my son, for Sixty-Nine, and for my future.

Let's do this.

I hesitate. Don't ask me why. Ife's voice has risen an octave; her vaginal muscles tighten as if she's on the verge of an orgasm. She grips both my shoulders with her strong arms and grits her teeth; her head flung back, riding me like a bucking bronco. The hit man leans back on the wall, apparently enjoying the sounds. His left-hand reaches for the light sensor but stops short of switching it on.

Motherfucker wants to see it all!

Ife's shudders, her face lusciously contorted with a hint of a smile, releasing a long drawn out grunt of orgasmic satisfaction and that's when I move.

I slide from under her and hit the floor. The cabin explodes into light, thanks to more of my earlier planning, but my eyes are closed, ready for the onslaught.

The dreadlocks steps backward, squinting, hands covering his eyes in vain, weapon pointed in front of him. When my eyes flick back open, I'm already airborne executing a round-house kick, slapping the gun out of his hand and sending it crashing to the other side of the room. In the next fractured second, he takes his eyes off the ball. Shit. He looks down at the pendulous swing of my flaccid dick! Whether he's gay and amazed or straight and amazed, it doesn't much matter 'cos, either way, he's gonna pay. I weave in and out of his reach, my strength and speed breathtaking. He tries to match my movement, firing his fists where he thinks I'm going to be but he is needlessly expending energy because nothing connects. While I'm three steps ahead of him, he seemed to be compensating for my movement, his blows coming closer. But the clock was ticking and I was in position, releasing a picture-perfect uppercut, the boxing legends would be proud of. The big right catches him on his solid jaw extending his spine with an agonizing 'pop' and putting the sucker into orbit. He flails around rising at least a foot in mid-air, his face contorted, before crashing back down into the vanity stool.

I make a b-line for the weapon I'd slapped out of the dread's hands, lodged under the bed. I'm rushing to get my hustle on because in my mind's eye the other guys got his weapon drawn outside, ready to storm the room. I make a dive for it, hitting the floor gracefully, ducking forward as my momentum carries me under the bed. I grab the weapon and spin on my stomach, pointing the barrel toward the door. An energized round hums in the weapons breach, cycling to maximum charge. The next thing I hear are shouts outside along with the suppressed crackling exchange of plasma weapons. Something heavy hits the door with a grunt.

What the fuck?

I slowly wriggle from under the bed, keeping my weapon pointed at the door. I freeze as someone knocks on the door.

You've got to be kidding, me!

I crouch low, checking quickly on Ife who's balled up in the corner of the bed, terror or a perverse pleasure in her eyes. I put my finger to my lips, and she nods. There's another knock at the door.

'Who dat?' I ask evenly.

'We just wanted to make sure everything is okay. Mr. Campbell.'

I recognize the Hong Kong undertones but I've still gotta see this for myself!

'Open the door slowly and step in with your hands leading. You got that?'

'Anything you say, Mr. Campbell.' Comes the reply.

The door opens slowly as instructed and a pair of hands is revealed. A body previously held in position by the closed-door slides partially into the room, the cadaver's chest charred and steaming. I look at the corpse and shake my head in disbelief.

'Son-of-a-bitch!' I say out loud. 'David Banks. Digitals PA!'

Lin Fu Sheng and Fong step in afterward. They see Ife in a state of undress on the bed and respectfully avert their eyes.

A sea of questions engulfs me but I stay calm, my big grin showing my happiness at being alive.

'So, Chen didn't think I could handle this gig alone?' I throw the question at the two Chinamen.

'Correct,' Fong says with no concern for my delicate ego. 'Mr. Chen had reason to believe all communication with yourself was being monitored, so we came prepared.'

'No shit.' I say.

Ife and I are ushered out as the Dragon's Syndicate clean up team move in ensuring no traces of my presence are inadvertently left for forensics.

Lessons learned from this?
A.   Chen knows best
B.   Chen is always right.

25.

JAMAICAN JIGGY

I'M HOLED UP IN CHEN'S SPACIOUS six-bedroom safe house in South London, an empty suitcase for company, feeling sorry for my disaster-attracting ass. Right now, this is the only place in L-Town where I feel safe. I catch sight of my reflection. My eyes are dim, and my normal proud stance has been reduced to a sulky slouch. It's as if my inner depression is being mirrored by my body. I take stock of my scant clothes, giving serious thought to disappearing and leaving all this behind. I slump onto the edge of the bed, turning away from the mirror. Thoughts tumble through my mind. How can I hold my head up if I bale? I've had challenges before, and although nothing comes close to this cluster-fuck, I stood tall.

Old man Hughes was in one piece thankfully, his captors dispatched like punks and Ife was shaken up but fine - and I mean that in every respect. In a weird and wonderful way, it had worked out, but it could have been worse. Only time would tell whether the couple would swallow my lame ass story that it had all been staged.

I'd have to wait and see.

I'm still in shock about David Banks. I knew the sucker was wrong from day one. I just couldn't say why and I had no way of proving my suspicions. Now it's all clear, he and Yellow Nigga were tight. The more I thought about it the more I believe this guy was the goddamn snitch who ultimately betrayed Digital.

I stare into the patterned interior of the suitcase a sudden wave of nausea washes over me, and I momentarily buckle. My legs turn to jelly, and I fall to my knees like I'm forced into penance by an unseen hand. I ask Maria to forgive me for thinking I could ever let this shit go without knowing who did this to her. And promise I would see this to the bitter end.

This ain't no road to Damascus boy. My monkey brain spits. Pull your trick ass together!

I stand and stretch, facing my mirror image full on, unafraid as I check my health Stats. I'm good but I can't help thinking its wrong. I straighten my shit up and correcting my body language.

I sit in silence, the only sounds coming from my rumbling stomach and my family beyond the door. What a prized collection of strays we are? Refugees from a dangerous puzzle I may have caused and only I can solve. Forgive yourself, my heart replies, and I allow the trickle of optimism to seep into me.

I know now what I must do. With my internal conflicts settled, and the fear of the unknown downgraded to a challenge, nothing will stop me. I think of calling my solicitor to make sure my Will was up-to-date.

But then I re-think.

I intend to make sure that in the end I will get a chance to appreciate life again with my family. Nothing else was acceptable. The smell of good food wafts under the door.

I join them in the lounge. Mrs. Brown is in the Kitchen producing French Caribbean cuisine for eight. Fong and Chang are playing Chinese Dominoes. Enough food is on the main table for all the famished family who picks at the fine smelling buffet amidst music, smiles, and good conversation. People from different walks of life, who hadn't known each other three weeks ago, sit and eat together, their cultures and viewpoints vibing. There's Jessica and Yvette in the mix. Jess knows I have history Y but she doesn't know the whole story. Still, she ain't trippin. Yvette is the inquisitive sort who just can't help herself; two other women under the same roof, one a grandmother, she can excuse that, but the other is a woman even more attractive than she is. Yvette is going to want to know who this woman is, her urge to control shit still strong. I suspect the lubricant keeping them chilled is Adonis Junior. The little punk has the same taste in women as his old man.

The Yvette is smiling. She's either accepting the inevitable or is just fronting. She thinks she has no options. I lived with the woman for three years; I know her swerve.

'Where have you been?' The question comes from Mrs. Brown as soon as I walk in. 'You okay?'

'I'm good, ma. I thought about closing my eyes for a while, but the smell of the food is keeping me up.'

She massages my shoulders lovingly.

'Don't waste time son, you go and eat something.'

Ms. Brown doesn't have to tell me twice. I make a full-frontal attack on the curried spring lamb, jerk chicken, corned rice, roast sweet potatoes and salads, fucking up a plate load of food in record time. I'm on my second helping as I touch bases with the loved ones I'm trying to keep alive. I feel better already.

Adonis Junior is the easiest to keep occupied. I'd bought him a Lego robot set with the newest artificial intelligence chip on the market for toys. That was done and dusted in two days, and he was already running his creation through its paces. I block his new robot's movements with my size ten's, chicken drumstick in one hand, fried dumpling in the other. I look down at his Android then at him.

'Whaddup little man!'

'Playing,' he grins up at me, a twinkle in his beautiful eyes. 'What do you think of the music dad? Stellar, huh!'
'Slammin! Old skool joints.'
'I mixed it myself!'
I'm impressed, but I need to know what else he's got. I point to his toy, which had already figured I was impeding it and was bypassing the obstacle,
'Well,' little man rises on his haunches. 'I'm gonna teach it how to look after mom and Jess. It can warn me if they're in trouble.'
'Hey, that's my job,' I say my voice cracking with fake ass hurt.
'I want to help, daaad.'
Damn! I hug him tight and tell him how much I love him.
My next port of call is Jess chill out spot. She's laid back like she's in her crib. She manages her multimedia magazine in one hand, while nibbling on cocktail sausages. Her dancer's elegance imbues each action with smoldering sex appeal.
'I missed you, babe,' she's straight and unabashed.
'Same here,' My gaze takes in all of her. 'If I didn't know better I'd be guessing you'd just passed through to see how I'm doing, ready to jet off somewhere exotic as and when you choose.'
'I wish,' she chuckles.

'For a woman who's been cooped up in here for a week, you look good, damn good, girl.'

'Your son helps. He's got a wicked sense of humor.'

'That, he gets from his Pop's.'

Jessica's daughter passes through my mind.

'Louise still by her Grandma's?' I ask.

Jess nods. She hadn't wanted her daughter around amid this fucked up situation.

'It'll be over soon. Then we can all go back to our lives again.' She says.

I see the hurt in her eyes at the pain of being separated and all I wanna do is make it go away. I nod with weak conviction, and she must have sensed my uncertainty.

Tenderly she pulls me to her and we kiss like we've just made love. I'm a lucky mo fucker to have a connection with this woman that goes deep. In fact, I'm luckier than most 'cos I had something special with Marie too. Two such women in one lifetime. What are the odds? I hug her and walk away.

The Yvette has staked her claim near the sash window. She's sipping from a glass of orange juice and looks exceptionally alluring in the sunlight, reminding me of what attracted me to her in the first place. Having a son hasn't altered her figure one bit. I can see why one of Chen's cats has been sniffing around her skirt tail, harboring some J-lo wet dreams under a blanket of professional concern. Can't blame the brother. I wait till he leaves for a piss and mosey over to her.

'You cool?'

Her smile is encouraging.

'Your Mr. Chen has covered my mortgage and bills. I'm comfortable here, and Junior is with me, despite whatever you're mixed up in.'

I nod, if she's trying to impress me, she's doing a damn good job.

'I wanna apologize to you, you know.... 'cos of how this shit is affecting you and junior.'

'I think I need to apologize to you about how things worked out with Morgan. I wasn't paying attention, took my eyes off the ball and junior nearly suffered.' She pauses to consider the ramifications of her words. The look in her eyes shows that it's not an easy thought. 'I was thinking more about my needs than his.' She goes on about her error in not letting me see my son, and I just let her talk. It's ironic how a bad situation like this makes her understand that I only ever wanted what was best for my family.

'Why couldn't we have talked things through like this be-fore?' I ask, despite my earlier resolve to remain silent.

'What in between all the arguments, fights, and cussing?' Her words are softened by a smile. 'I guess we're finally mature now.'

I kiss her cheek, and she holds onto my hand, looking into my eyes.

'Look, we've had our differences, and I'm still not sure if I can deal with what you do for a living but in truth it doesn't matter. When this is settled let's talk. Really talk.'

Damn! I blink making sure I'm not tripping. Suddenly the moniker Battersea Bitch seems inappropriate and disrespectful. I'm speechless with a newfound respect for the mother of my son. Man, it feels strange but good.

'Close your mouth!' She laughs.

I laugh too, hadn't even realized it was open. Yvette walks me over to the table where I refill my plate while making a silent personal promise; from now on I'm gonna appreciate the hell outta the people in this room, 'cos, they all I got left.

26.

STAR GAZING

I STEP INTO THE JOINT, MY HEAD HIGH, MY SHOULDERS SQUARED, my senses alert and straining at the leash. The room is constructed entirely from wood. Underneath the scattering of straw, which can't cushion shit, are neatly laid floorboards, lacquered to a shiny finish and held tightly in place with pegs and glue. The area is edged with wooden rails and is circular; something to do with the continuous nature of the universe, although I'm not too sure how much you'd care about such esoteric matters when you're getting popped upside your head. The ceiling is high and well lit. The walls are adorned with images of conflict, the only furniture a massive standing board bristling with swords, bow's, three-piece-staffs, nunchakus and throwing knives fitting every description.

This dojo has the vibe of a gym, kinda like the exercise yard at San Quentin but with a much more reverent air. The one thing they did have in common though was the prevailing scent of fear. You just didn't waltz into a place like this expecting to feel all warm and fuzzy inside. Here was a place of broken bones and blood.

Six cats circle Chen in the centre of the floor. My favorite Chinese dude is sweating, his free-flowing black Mandarin outfit - no trademark Saville Row suit today - is dishevelled, like he's gone through a workout and is anxious to conclude shit with some drama.

I watch the men prepare, my eyes veiled by thoughts the black-tie affair at Nexus HQ tomorrow night. Right now, my only coherent plan is to introduce myself to a Dr. Reed Richards at all costs. Simple huh? You'd think so, but even with all the anticipated cameras and advanced security, experience has taught me that if something can go wrong, it will go wrong. Law of averages or some shit. The thought of the unknown makes me nervous as fuck. But I can handle whatever is flung my way, for the sake of the people I've left behind in Mrs. Brown's Lounge, for the memory of Maria and Digital and Popeye, I must. I focus on Chen again, checking for the hidden clues in the way he's psyching himself up against these six dudes. Maybe, just like Digital, he knows something I don't.

Wouldn't be the first time.

I look around, alone in a room occupied by Dragon Syndicate where I'm the only key to the puzzle, and I can provide closure or spark a war. Who knows? I watch Chen carefully, my eyes half-closed, betting that the slick motherfucker is figuring some devious shit out. I smile at the thought of him kicking ass or even getting his own ass kicked. At my chaperone's bidding, I get comfortable at a small table with a fancy crystal water jug and two matching glasses. The chairs are far from comfortable, everything here is about pain, but they are the best seats in the house.

The six Chinese men aged mid-twenties to late thirties tighten their circle around Chen who stands with his head slightly bowed. I hold my breath in tandem with the new silence broken only by the occasional shuffling feet of the combatants. Someone, I'm not sure who, lets out a piercing cry and they converge in en masse, unlike fake ass choreography where only one man at a time attacks the star, this here is some real street shit.

Three men begin the assault from different angles, but, as if he's anticipating their movements, Chen blocks using both hands and feet, his movements so goddamn fast I have trouble pinpointing them. Deftly he twirls away, and the outer circle of men moves too, keeping him in the center. They attack in groups of three as Chen blocks, effortlessly standing his ground. As the next trio begin their onslaught, my man pulls out a sharp offense. With blinding speed and ferocity, he strikes the men with piston like fists, sending them reeling from the circle.

Puh - Pow!

The percussive force is like a small explosion flinging the dudes five feet across the floor, leaving them writhing in pain. Undeterred but surely afraid?

Group two moves in, ready to take him out. In a heartbeat, Chen adjusts. His arms revolve like propellers, a Chinese pimp slap and he puts one down, disdain written all over his face. I hear the sickening contact of bone against hard wood, and I can almost feel his pain. Chen goes into a flying roundhouse kick, easily dispatching the next oncomer. Landing in a cat-like crouch he sweeps the third man off his feet sending his next assailant crashing to the floor. The Triad boss finding himself on his back, skilfully flips to his feet, cautiously eyeing his trainees gather their wits. They looked like a rag - tag crew novices beaten by a master. They bow in unison, and it's done, giving me permission to draw breath.

Damn! So, this is his gangster side? The missing character trait, kept firmly in check in even the most intense of situations. I stretch in my seat, flexing muscles, my mind fast forwarding to tomorrow, Adonis Campbell's last stand?

After he's freshened up, Chen joins me for a little tête-à-tête. He's in gray sweats with a towel draped around his neck. His hair is tied back, and he's rejuvenated obviously by the violence. He lays a holographic projector down along with his Digi-Scroll, drops a pile of leather-bound files and pours water into two glasses.

'You going all hood on me now, homes? What's with the throw-backs?' I ain't said shit since he appeared, but I just can't help slipping one in.

Chen looks at me. The intensity of his stare telling me we're ready for business. I lean back in my chair and wave him on.

'Since last we met I've taken time to think about this entire affair, trying to find the path of least resistance. The bad news is there is none. What you may not have realized is that even with my resources, I couldn't do this alone and there was no way I would allow you to walk in there totally unprepared.'

'Ah, didn't know you cared dawg.'

'We both know that access to the building will be problematic, so against my better judgment I've had to request the services of Wu-Sheng Feng - Silent Wind.'

'The rock band?'

He flashes a half-annoyed look at my flippancy. 'Silent Wind is a band of Ninja's who have been under the Elder's employ for centuries.'

My laugh is spontaneous. For a moment, I'd forgotten who I'm dealing with and just what these Chinese cats are capable of.

'Normally they are very potent assassins but can be just as effective as spies.' Chen explains, 'Do you remember the old men who watched you interrogate the killer we captured?'

I nod.

'They are their handlers. At first, they turned me down until I travelled to Hong Kong personally to present my case.'

That explains it. No wonder my nigga is giving off a refreshed air. Spending a day in his homeland had made him, even more, Popsicle cool, while my tired and stressed out ass had been left to tenderize in hell.

'Eventually they gave me their blessing, after, erm, how would you say it...?' He waves his hand around in the air. 'I kissed some serious ass.'

I grin at his imitation of my accent. 'That must have hurt like a sonofabitch!'

'It did.' He concurs. 'I had some ambitious plans for their skills too, a Trojan horse manoeuvre at the top of my list. I should have realized the honored fathers would have conditions attached to the agreement.'

Chen seemed to have conjured up a picture of the old men denying him what he wanted. His anger was still burning hot, or maybe I should say sub-zero. The Chinaman sounded like he had been fucked by the only family he knew and consequently had a serious point to make.

'And what do the OG's want from the deal?' I ask, anxious to keep him on track.

'The Wu-Sheng Feng could only do reconnaissance of the building.'

'That's bullshit man! Do those old cats want to help or hinder?'

'Bullshit maybe, but that is all we have.' Chen activates the Holo projector, and a detailed three-dimensional image floats up between us.

'The good news is that Silent Wind acquired all the information you could ever need to know about the building. Oh, and one more thing. Once you get there, you are on your own.'

'Hell no!' The ingot of hope I'd been holding onto melts before my very eyes. I feel like I've been carjacked by stank ass thugs I'd previously called pussies after cutting them up in the aerial lanes. My fear of failure and the unknown stands on a soap box at Hyde Park screaming its goddamn head off. Just as I'm about to panic some more, Chen drops even more good news.

'I've already considered this possibility. I've asked the Wu-Sheng Feng to disrupt the building's security features; this should aid your progress through Nexus.'

'Now that's what I'm talking 'bout!' I holla. It doesn't take much to get my hopes up.

'.......digital viral nest was left in the buildings mainframe. It will disable essential systems - some for longer than others. The building's self-aware CPU will be out of operation for about an hour as a computer like flu compounds with the building's bad karma. After that, the organic components would have healed themselves enabling the building to be working once again at a hundred percent efficiency.' Chen is still going strong.

'Tell me there's more?' Bad karma gives me my edge, so I decide to lap it up.

'When you activate this, you will have approximately sixty minutes plus or minus three minutes before the systems resume. He slides over something flat and round, it looks like a key ring. 'Before you enter the building press and then discard.'

'Then what?'

'Then do what you do best.'

'And what do you think a playa does best?'

'He gets the job done.' Chen's fingers pass through the three-dimensional floating image of the Nexus building. 'And knowing how to navigate this fortress will decide whether you will get the job done or not.'

He punches in a five-code number at the base of the unit and the image changes.

From the huge main atrium where I would enter the building three highlighted lines of green, red and blue, show me routes through ventilation shafts which bypass whole floors. These routes would also lead straight to the fifteenth floor where my man will be making his presentation and where I'll meet him. He indicates six flashing points, two on each route on the virtual mock-up. Chen slips on his manipulator glove allowing him to interface with the holographic model. It expands into more detail magnifying even further but still not revealing what the flashing beacons are.

'Aight, so what the hell is that?' I ask.

I consider his ageless face, untouched by conflict or the gangsta life. Only his eyes tell of the pain he's endured and the deaths he's seen. I sink into them for a minute as Chen smiles back at me. An expression of triumphant one-upmanship and a goddamn miracle.

'I forgot to mention,' he adds, restrained amusement rounding his cheeks, 'the Wu-Sheng Feng left some items that could prove useful to your mission.'

'Oh yeah!' I say again, his meaning very clear to me. 'You tell them homies anything they need I'm on it.'

'They'll be thrilled but in the meantime, submit it all to memory, and we will meet at my London residence 18.00 hrs tomorrow.'

We eye each other with steely determination knowing there's nothing more to say and nothing more to do but to get it on.

27.

S&M

I'M A RED AND SILVER STREAK straddling a Kawasaki Thunder Quad. I'm rocking a matching Cyber helmet sans my leather skins, don't wanna crumple my suit. Dead or alive playas got to look smooth cos I've got a reputation to maintain. I'm cruising down the boulevard in an armored motorcade like an Alt-Right politico had come to visit the hood to apologize to black folks for fucking them over for all these years.

If I was still tripping about Chen's feelings towards me surviving this ordeal, the last two hours has drop-kicked the notion like it was the fourth down in NFL. It's all about trust. All the way into central L-Town I've been boxed in by Chen and the Dragons. Two Hummers on either side, a Mercedes 4X4 behind and a mean looking, fully tricked out Range Rover, its 26-inch shoes gleaming from the street lamps. I feel like a new born in the warm embrace of some prime plasma resistant steel, and although I should be coming to terms with my mortality, I can't shake the version of Chen that I saw at his crib earlier today.

Initially, I was welcomed into an expansive Georgian spread in St Johns Wood. Its marble floors, crystal chandeliers, fine art and the obligatory oriental honey's and a handful of guizi chicks positioned to show off their beauty, squealed gangsta. Then I was led deeper into the building to his private space. The image of him kneeling at a shrine before a hologram of Maria is forever branded into my memory. He'd held aloft two smoldering incense sticks and was praying to his forefathers for safe deliverance of her spirit. When he'd finished, he'd faced me with tears in his eyes, making no attempt to hide his grief. He was just a nigga in tune with his emotions and straight up; I was feeling him.

We'd sat in silence, Chen with crossed legs, me in the same position, drinking traditional Chinese tea from small porcelain cups, incense permeating the space between us. The whole thing had been surreal, but I'm painfully aware that it was both an honor and a necessity for me to be here. After a long moment of contemplation, he'd divulged shit that was totally new to me.

'My father, my father's father, indeed as far back as has been recorded, my family, have been a part of the Triad Society, the 14K in particular. My father was Lung Tau –

Dragon Head, the ruling authority over the society's business and operations. I grew up wanting to bring honor to my father by continuing his tradition, one day surpassing what he had achieved. Maria had her own ambitions and pursued them single-mindedly. She was allowed that privilege because of her pig-headedness. She attained a doctorate with honors in Biomedical Studies, and her first tenure was with Nexus Pharmaceutical. She was excited at the prospect of working professionally with Dr. Marsden. That was when the fireworks started, and they stumbled upon something that came to the Society's attention. It was so controversial they resigned and went underground. Not long after that, you came into the picture. Of course, I was asked to convince her that the Triad should be involved in her discovery, it was her duty after all, but my sister did not see it that way. The Fu Shan Chu accused me of not being able to fulfil my commitment. Allowing family to sway my resolve in a matter that could potentially net the Society billions. So, I was cold-shouldered, disrespected and demoted to Hung Kwan-Red Pole.

'I became their enforcer, but my father taught me well. Greatness cannot be hidden under a bushel. When they thought they were hurting me, I grew and so did their interest in my sister's work. But just as they took their eyes off the prize, I took my eyes off my sister's safety.

Consequently, as connected as we all are, other interested parties took our lax attitude as an invitation to hurt us. My sister is dead, and the Triad feel responsible. I, however, am responsible and I have to make it right.'

If he'd been trying to impress upon me the importance of what I was about to do, then he'd done that, in spades.

I'm about 400 meters from the Nexus building, my thoughts flitting between everyone I regarded as family; both the recently dead and those still with me. My automotive entourage peels off allowing me to complete the rest of the journey solo, just in time for my little touches to come into force. I look for parking, not too close to the actual building. I must make sure it's easily accessible from multiple entry points just in case I need to get away in a hurry. I pull into a parking bay, engine growling, drawing stares just as I want it to. I know my machine looks like it's from the dope pages of Ride e-magazine. The feline grace of Chrome and Ruby, with a threatening undertone of unparalleled power, just below my nuts. Hydrogen laced fumes pump through the bronzed outlets of the beast's guts. There are only fifteen of these joints in the country, but despite its exclusive ghetto fabulous allure, all the attention comes from the fact that it's such an unorthodox mode of transport. The other high rollers arrive in airborne Limo's that are chauffeur driven or wild whips that use plasma engines for propulsion at five thousand feet. Top marquee units of all descriptions that you would only see together in the Robb Report Nanosheets.

I want everyone to know that I'm different. If worse comes to worse and Five-O get involved, I'd be easier to trace, easier to remember.

Chicken shit mo' fuckers want me to go AWOL at this stage of the game?! Head to Jamaica with Lil Adonis, smoke some hi-grade and buss some Yard cherries? That just proves that they don't know shit cos sometimes you just got to stand up for what you believe in, no matter what the consequences. I won't let the side down, but if they do take my ass out Chen knows the truth. I'm confident he'll fight my corner and give it his all.

I log my details with the automated parking attendant giving myself parking freedom for at least twelve hours, and then I stroll over to the Nexus high rise. I'm in no rush to get inside the building that casts a menacing shadow over the district.

The entrance to the Nexus foyer is huge. A ring of glass rising from ground level gives a view of the internal workings of this mega structure. With no hard walls of steel and concrete, it's a marvel to the uninitiated that this building stays erect. I keep moving until I'm under the visage of a dragon hewn from a single chunk of crystal. I pause letting a giggling couple in front of me and reach inside my jacket, my fingers extracting the key ring given to me by Chen. It feels kinda like the key to getting the party jumping, only it's gonna screw up the whole computer security system.

Depress it and enter Naraka. There is no turning back.

I squeeze it, long and hard before discarding it into an atomizer bin. I whisper a prayer, eyes closed and hum two bars from Tupac's 'Thugs Mansion,' then I enter the gaping maw of the crystal dragon.

28.

BONDAGE

UP INTO THE BELLY OF THE BEAST JUST LIKE JOSH-UA or was it that Jonah dude, who gets swallowed by the whale? I'm not quite sure but what I do know is I'm out of my goddamn depth, being slowly digested in the guts of a luxury building which could end up being my grave. I swear I'm trying to stay positive, but damn it's hard.

Above me I see a criss-cross network of passages, as elaborate as a tarantula's web, linking interconnecting offices as far as the eye could see. My attention is drawn to an abstract sculpture made from pieces of metal, positioned to resemble a marauding dragon. I narrow my eyes wandering how they did that. Just below the sculpture is the security detail, whose station is shaped like a crescent, separating partygoers from the lifts. I'm not sure what I was expecting; bouncers built like brick shithouses bristling with modern tech, or fanatical company men eager to please their corporate overlords? Well, this ain't exactly that. I sum the hired heavies up in two words; plain ordinary. From what I've been told these are rent-a-thugs, not part of Nexus, here to look good while carrying out nothing more than basic checks. Wouldn't want them to risk annoying or upsetting the High Rollers.

I watch carefully, in case I'm fooling myself into complacency. There are six of them, standing with total assuredness, each movement a study in the careful conservation of energy. The attendees seem completely at ease around them, none of that awkward 'just pretend we're invisible while we search your person for concealed weapons' shit. It's all very genteel and polite. Too freaking nice in my estimation but I'm not the best example of cool right now. My heart rattles around my rib cage as if it's not anchored into position. I'm sweating and my mouth is parched dry, but you'd never guess. Externally I'm a long chill glass of Bacardi and coke ready to be pleasurably sipped.

Curious glances and, in some cases, outright stares remind me of how much I stand out. Hey, unlike my bike, it's not intentional, but I am six foot three and built like a pitcher. I'm also wearing the most recent Sean John dinner suit and exuding the aura of a Mandingo warrior with every step I take.

Security has noticed the crowd's interest in my presence. The change in their posture and body language is too subtle for the untrained eye, but I'm aware of how they're summing me up wondering if extra measures are required. Touching, huh? I tap into my twenty-twenty, but it remains quiet, letting me know that while they're not a cause for concern, the next hurdle could be.

I sift through a thousand things at once. How the hell do I get into the ventilation system from here? Even when Chen was detailing the Three-D presentation, I knew that until I arrived his directions wouldn't mean squat to me. My only entry point is on the foyer level in view of everyone and just to make this shit more interesting I had to get there somehow and not be noticed.

I step forward, confident like I know exactly what I'm gonna do, except that I don't. I hand the security guy my gold leaf invitation, he nods and guides my hand onto an ID confirmation grid. Warm light flashes over my palm and he look satisfied. The standard Biometric test was done, I stepped through the Halo and completed weapons check. My twenty-twenty is still quiet. You can't blame me for feeling self-conscious even under the circumstances. My dog tags, the personal stealth technology I carry around with me everywhere I step, had to be left at my crib, leaving me feeling as defenceless as Superman facing Kryptonite.

I'm handed a goody bag from an angelic hostess stationed just beyond the security detail. She recommends I use the SatNav card - also a part of the complimentary gift package - to find my way around. She rattles off the instructions like she could do it in her sleep. As soon as I can I check out the contents of the goody bag; Sex paraphernalia, designer stimulants, stacks of poker Chips, smart cards with massive discounts on top designer jewellery stores, prize draws for a week in the orbiting 8 star Eden1 resort, or get your sweaty hands on the latest Maserati floater. I did say High Rollers, didn't I?

The foyer buzzes with groups of people chatting or heading purposefully to the entertainment zones installed on various levels of the building. I need to move my ass, so I don't seem indecisive. If the building intuitive surveillance units aren't down yet, I can be logged and tagged for observation, and that's not something I want to happen this early in the game.

Waiters hover near, carrying trays crammed with exotic food and wines specifically prepared for guests with discerning palates. I need to move, be a part of the general activity, mingle and make friends quickly. I walk purposefully to the middle of the floor and find myself standing beside some dudes who favor the leather look. Just beyond them, my memory sparks with recognition, and in my mind's eye, I'm in Chen's 3-D model looking at one of the flashing beacons and the red conduit that wound its way to the fifteenth floor. That memory superimposes itself on the real building that confronted him. Chen had failed to tell me that the entry point would be in the ladies WC.

I eyes lock on to a Waitress stationed to my extreme right. She's catering to a small group of boisterous women filling up on vino and stimulants too quickly. I pop my collar and thug stroll in their direction, letting their look, their body language and temperament organically form questions that I would ask to endear myself to them. Just when I think that maybe my lyrics would take more time than I had at my disposal the universe gave me a helping hand.

'Adonis!'

My first reaction is fear, swiftly followed by uncertainty. I stop and turn, rewarded by Aisha's smile as she sings the sweet melody of my name. I shouldn't be surprised, but I am. Shortie stands with her clique near an Info point; she's dipped in minute flecks of what looks like molten gold. She's rocking a minimalist black Leroy Maltese dress which emphasizes her killer curves. Her right arm is adorned with a lavish Ghanaian gold arm bracelet, her dainty feet strapped into Jimmy Choo's Grecian sandals. I blink cos I'm suddenly in some ancient African court approaching a warrior princess of my people. She's a sight to behold and not for the obvious reasons.

For the first time, I smile and debunk the unwritten theory that states that if you scope a female trio in a club, you gonna get one hot chick and two ugly friends. These three sisters ooze glamor and sex appeal. A head-scratching choice for the most discerning of playas but I was at an advantage. Aisha and I had history, and the memory of her warmth, intelligence, and that coochy had me smiling.

Aisha dislodges from the other princesses, whose smiles say: 'go get your freak on girl!' She sways her fine ass and signature double D's my way. We meet in the middle of the atrium, and she melts in my arms subtly covered in a sensory stimulus aroma. Her perfume is close to five hundred credits a pop. And you can see why as the Amazonian psychopharmaceuticals send my nervous system into overdrive until I mentally grab it and alter their effects with appropriate breathing. I need my edge tonight. My hard-on builds. My brain works overtime at this new opportunity, even in such a precarious situation I'm feeling her, and I'm damn sure she's feeling me. I analyze her cool and slow, licking every part of her with my eyes. Ruffling up that perfectly coiffed image of hers.

'How you doing temptress?'

'I've been waiting to hear from you, still waiting.' She eyes me up and down, and a softness returns to her voice. 'What is tonight then Adonis, business or pleasure?'

'Strictly business baby.'

'Who's the lucky woman?'

'You of course.' I fix her with my intensity. She doesn't flinch.

'How so?' She asks.

'Cos you're gonna save my life.' I lay it out straight, so she knows I'm not fucking about.

Her laugh is achingly reassuring, sensual and confident all at the same time. Guilt wells up inside me like a busted sewage line. I'd have nothing to worry about if this evening's business was my usual field of endeavor but tonight is different. My life hangs in the balance as does my redemption. And yet, once again, I'm drawing someone into this web and a possible shit blizzard, so that I can get the answers I need.

Aisha has heart, and that's the only reason why what I must say makes any difference. Sex like we had left a lasting impression. You'd have to be a soulless bitch to think otherwise, and peeps are far from that. Still, it doesn't stop me from feeling like an eel, but my choices are limited so cut a nigga some slack. Shit, I'd pimped strolled in here knowing what I needed to do but not how I was gonna do it. I'm trusting that Aisha will provide the how with less friction as my plan 'A'.

'What's going on?' She asks and then in the same breath, 'How can I help?'

Damn. I've known her how long now? Three weeks and already she's got my back. I turn towards her and whisper in her ear: 'I need you in the ladies.'

'You didn't need to go through all this to get me in the cubicle with you baby.'

I open my mouth to answer but my twenty-twenty buzzes followed by a tingling along my spine. A resonating hum tickles the crown of my skull, and I stand to attention. My eyes fix on the reflexive surface of a spiral staircase, and I see the tall, muscular frame of a tuxedo-clad albino and his entourage of cut throats. Remaining gangsta when you're afraid ain't easy that I've managed to perfect the skill with years of practice. Knowing the object of your fear helps too. I relegate the internal turmoil tearing me up inside to the background, hold my peeps for the moment and give Yellow Nigga my back. Yeah, you heard me right. That cold hearted mo' fucker who tried to six foot six me, murdered my family then branded me as a biyatch!

I'm still holding my peeps telling her how delightful she looks, but I'm also observing the killer's reflection in the glass architecture and brushed aluminium. He's talking to the security men who gesticulate blankly in response. His posse is wound up tight while he's pacing and snarling, his head up like a wild dog sniffing the air for my scent. I pray to a benevolent God that we lock horns so that I can feel my fingers around his neck. Who knew that the urge to buss my four-fifths in a nigga would be so strong, even though I hate guns?

For this cocksucker, I'd make an exception, but under the circumstances, that's not enough. A life for a life, nothing more, nothing less.

But that's for later. For now, I bide my time. I gotta find this Reed Richards dude first. Yellow Nigga and his posse exit stage one in frustration.

I resume pushing Aisha's buttons, but now with more haste. She leads me by the hand into the ladies' toilets, anxiety in her eyes because she doesn't know what the hell is going on but she trusts me to explain everything to her later. Slipping into the toilets is easy as the CCTV cameras are out of commission, but I still had to throw any unwanted snitches off the scent.

I had to make this look good.

The toilet cubicle is small with just enough room to maneuver and, gangsta that I am; I still can't bring myself to mess up her perfect look. So, I lean her comfortably back on the toilet seat, reach gently under her designer skirt search for her panties to pull them asunder but nothing. Girlfriend has gone commando for this special occasion and my fingers tips are gliding over her velvet warmth. I shake my head and smile grabbing her booty instead and pull her to my lips allowing my mouth free reign. I start to use my tongue to spell out the alphabet – an old trick of the trade - but couldn't get beyond 'K' as baby girl was getting boisterous. I'm starting to wish I had more time as she moaned and squealed at my attention to the finer details of her anatomy. This isn't my usual not-a-care-in-the-world kinda gig, but the result is the same.

A screaming orgasm leaves no doubt what the hell was going on in the cubicle for the gawkers outside.

Before Aisha leaves the cubicle, she mouths the words, 'good luck' to me. Brandishing her ultra 100 sonic vibrator for all to see, she gently locks the cubicle door behind her, hoping no one knew or cared my black ass was left inside.

When the coast is clear, I remove the ceiling tiles and lift myself up and in. I wriggle through the network of air vents leading from the female toilets. Just as Chen had predicted, tools had been left behind in the water tanks by Silent Wind giving me access to the vents. The ninjas had even left me a Reflek jumpsuit with pull string hoody that would keep my shit crisp and ready to go when I crash the joint, whilst trapping my heat signature, cooling me down and making it impossible to be thermally or optically detected.

I move briskly through the maze and come to a dual lift shaft that will take me ten stories up via an assortment of small engineering lifts, ladders, and stairs. My ETA is thirty minutes before the virus I've force fed into the system is flushed out, and the security protocols are back in place. I look up from my precarious position feeling the warm processed air on my face and the reassuring way it buffets my body. I sigh and start my steady ascent.

29.

FETISH

THE VENTS ON LEVEL ten open into a well-proportioned steam room. I climb out of the duct and drop to the cool tiled floor. I find myself standing in front of three, rather large executive dudes, hanging loose all over the pseudo-Roman furniture, sweating and grunting like wart hogs. The svelte Donnas were providing eye candy to balance out this gross picture with their dime piece figures. They look at me with eyes wide and mouths slack as if to say 'what the fuck...?' I resist playing with the comic potential of the situation even though it's a zinger. Instead, I go for straight-laced misdirection.

'Is the heating comfortable enough gentlemen?' I inquire like I know what the hell I'm talking about.

Their initial doubts dissipate with my question. 'Absolutely wonderful.' One of the dudes with dark hair growing down his back and into his ass-crack, booms.

'We could do with some Ion charged towels, though.' This comes from the playa with the Sumo wrestlers stomach as if I look like his personal valet. But I nod and kick back like a good choir boy. 'I'll see what I can do, sir.' I say.

Dumb fuck.

I hustle out of there, wanting to get out of the suit before the heat overloads the cooling systems and anyway I've got a party to attend.

You still here ain't you boys? I feel for my balls. Yeah, we here.

I strip off the Reflek suit in the secluded locker room, keeping a constant eye on the CCTV cameras. Since activating the virus it's been fifty-five minutes, which means I've still got five minutes on the clock if the theory was to be believed. There's no guarantee of the exact time the Fung Yi virus could become quiescent, and anytime that happens I can't be caught dragging my dick. I need to be out of here and mingling. I join up with the rest of the party people and start thinking that maybe, just maybe, I can pull this shit off.

'Don't start no shit, won't be no shit.'

Is my mantra for the night, as I step into the Casino Room all thugged out in a blue tuxedo, four peak pocket square, and velvet brogues. As usual, Nexus has spared no expense. Roulette tables, Black Jack, Poker, Virtual Fruit

Machines, Digital Craps and even some of the more esoteric gambling passions are all in full swing. Credits are exchanged for the possibility of making much more or just for the sheer thrill of losing your shirt. The crowd is a mixture of the highbrow - intellectuals, scientists, technocrats and business people, hungry for the excess they would never experience in the worlds they inhabit. And then there were the HO's.

The HO's – Hangers On – were a consequence of the brilliance that was in the room. Like Remora fish they shared a symbiotic relationship with their hosts which was necessary but not always healthy. There were Pimps looking for talent, smoothers digging for political secrets, journalists fabricating fact and opportunist corporate spies. Then, of course, there are the extreme HO's, like the Lottis. I recognize three of them from the attention they attract.

These celebrities are leading Hollywood sex actors with Digital Random Coded chastity belts strapped over the goodies. Only those with access to the rarefied locales these 'A' listers inhabited had a chance. You needed deep pockets and the God's of probability squarely in your favor. Only then, you could become an instant worldwide celebrity and unlock a night of passion with the biggest sex symbols on the planet.

The sensory overload smacks me back into focus. I can't allow myself into playa mode although my whole being is ready to party. I weigh up my options trying to figure out the safest and most direct route to this Professor dude, Reed Richards. I check my timepiece; the award ceremony starts in two hours leaving me with two choices; Confrontation or simply staying out of harm's way. The second option makes more sense and yet I'm eager to get it on, deal with who needs to be dealt with, live or die. You're a prototype, kid. That was Digital's hype, and I was beginning to believe it. Maybe I can just walk up to this Reed Richards cat, I can solve this mystery with no repo?

I have no idea what's popping off in the other rooms as far as I'm concerned this is where the action at. I estimate about two hundred people in the space, with a steady stream of others from the swimming pool and lap dancing areas. I check surveillance. It's gonna be extremely difficult to keep tabs on anyone nestled within the crowds when shit comes back online. I decide to kill time here and then make my way somehow into the guarded awards ceremony, but I'll deal with that later, right now I chill.

I've made seven spins on the Roulette table, and I've won five times. What are the chances?

Ain't you supposed to be incognito nigga? My higher self asks me.

Well yeah, that was the plan, but the plan seemed to have changed mid-flight. I'm a reluctant winner. Well-wishers, amazed by my luck, stick to my ass like limpets hoping the ghetto shine will rub off onto them too. I decide to quit while the going is good but unfortunately, it's not soon enough.

Godammit!

Before I know what's happening, my twenty-twenty goes apeshit. Remember I hate crowds, don't like being swarmed. My intuition is the same; it can't get a bead on any posed threat to me through the confusion. Every survival rule that I've ever made for myself, I've broken this evening. I'm an open target, but it can't be helped.

I attempt to back out from the table but something hard and unwelcome twists against my spine and makes me think again. The heater that presses into my back is unmistakable, unlike the effeminate voice that accompanies it.

'That my brother is exactly what you think it is.' This pussy was really pleased with himself from the sound of things. 'If your body language even suggests that you're about to become difficult I will kill you. The collateral damage to these good people will be a bonus. Do we have an understanding?'

I nod resisting the urge to raise my arms just to piss him off.

'Mr. Campbell,' the high-pitched voice whispers in my ear. 'How the hell did you get in here without detection?'

'None of your goddamn business!' I snap back making some of the hangers on beside me look at me strangely.

He giggles, still pleased for some unknown reason. 'One minute we're wondering if you would turn up and the next you're here threatening to break the bank.'

'Who the fuck is we?'

'We are the men and women who put their lives on the line to provide a necessary service at a cost. For me, this is a satisfactory ending to a long hunt. Let's go for a little walk Mister Campbell.'

This cocksucker, expects me to jump up at his request, but there's one problem. I look down at my mountain of chips sitting on number thirty-two and get a strong urge to stay put as the croupier spins the wheel. The dime piece who's clung to my free side must have heard fragments of the gunman's harsh whisper or maybe she's wondering the kind of male competition she's facing for my affection. Her eyes gather venom, and her face darkens.

The Croupier drops the ball on a cushion of electromagnetism and it's fired at blinding speed along the rim of the lacquered spinning wheel. I've got a feeling about this spin, and I'm determined to see it through, even with the heater being forced into my back. But my shadow is impatient.

'Did you think I was pissing around when I said I'd kill the punters first?' He growls.

'Chill nigga,' I snarl back. 'I've already put all of my winnings on one number let me at least see if I get busted.'

He laughs, and I'm glad he sees the funny side.

'If you don't move, you'll be dead in a minute, and it won't make a difference. Either way, I get paid. Let's go.' He rubs the weapon across my rib cage like he's playing the xylophone.

I'm listening, but my eyes are on the roulette wheel watching the ball slowly settle into a slot. I'm leaning forward over the table with no need to change position because I'm comfortable. I feel his weight on my back. Laughing boy is stretched over me giving the impression that he also needs to see the action but can't. He's too close to me for even the best of friends. I can handle the extra burden easily, but his presence is off-putting. I know exactly what he's trying to do. He obviously wants to shoot me in the back and from the tension in his body he's thinking about it. As a consequence, I slow shit down. Narrowing my perception to a pinprick.

I stir, my muscles tense enough for him to anticipate my departure from the table. The ball hits the partitions separating the grooves, and for those few seconds, nothing else matters. The ball dances, jumping with a click clack from groove to groove until it hops into 32. I bet straight up odds of thirty-five to one and damn it's come in! I don't know what my adoring fans expect, but the number of onlookers has grown and so has my predicament. For my earlier wins, I'd played it cool, now that I've flipped the script; my shit is excited.

I yell with the satisfaction of an orgasm, as does the crowd and I use that euphoria as my ticket out. The roars muffle the sound of my elbow connecting hard with laughing boy's temple. The back of my head follows up impacting purposefully with his lower jaw and causing it to smash into his upper jaw. I piston myself into a standing position and shrug him off my back like a shirt that doesn't fit, just in time to see a whiplash of congealing blood trail from his mouth as he goes down. He's at my feet tangled in his own limbs. No-one notices or cares why. To complete the illusion, I gently nudge his energy weapon under the table.

Ba-da-boom, ba-da-bing, biiiitch!

I scrape my chips together, waiting for the frenzy to die down before I address the crowd. I glance disdainfully at laughing boy showing him the disrespect he deserves.

'I think my boy had a bit too much gin and juice!' The crowd around me roar with laughter. The Croupier speaks into a micro-comm embedded in his shirt cuff. I merge into the background with my immoral earnings and a promise to myself, Chen, Digital and Maria to stay in the goddamn shadows for the rest of the evening.

I transfer my winnings to Lil Adonis's account bolstering his small fortune before I look for somewhere less conspicuous. I wonder through the network of corridors hitching up with migratory groups of guest trying to mask my movement as best I can. Three rooms play a mixture of early millennium R&B, Dancehall, and Hip-Hop revival. Classic joints for early music aficionados swaying in the darkened confines of the R&B Hall, safety in numbers. The party is poppin! Normally scientists, technocrats, and business people give off a stiff and stuffy kinda impression, but these dudes aren't living up to that expectation. The revival sounds have got them on the floor enjoying the electricity and nostalgia regardless.

I sway in my corner, remembering the first time I asked a shortie for a dance. The smells, the sounds, the sights rush back from the days when I walked around with a perpetual boner, with all the confidence in the world but a woefully wack seduction technique.

I met Hector to my Achilles in the form of Sharon Sue Cunningham, a smart, sophisticated chick with the body of a pumped-up nymph and no interest in rubbing up against my big cock in our dimly lit High School auditorium. I learned the hard way; it's not just about your equipment but your technique. There we all were: girls on one side, dudes on the other an imaginary line between genders. The headmaster had personally arranged this to teach us social interaction. Little did I know headmaster had told the girls not to dance with us dudes unless we fulfilled a checklist of prerequisites; how we looked, what we said, our actions, how gracious we were, etcetera. All around me, the chat up lines of my homies were being shot down in flames to a backdrop of Neo Soul and the shorties reveling in the power they had against us, guys.

I was the first to crack the code, and I danced the night away as the social retards shook their chicken heads in amazement. But even after showering Sharon with my new skills I was still denied even a sniff of the pussy. It took me four long weeks to wax that ass and that was after relentless pursuit, patience and application. I developed a sound appreciation for the intricacies of the female psyche and the dating game. I learned that sometimes less is more.

Case in point; I'm doing my own thing when the crystal brilliance of her eyes catches mine. She'd drifted by me before amidst the other gyrating bodies, and I hadn't seen her too clearly, but now she's stationary, and I take a good look at her as she laughs with a companion. She has long dark hair, making her look almost Asian but for the glossy dark skin, full figure and the obvious, but subtle mix of Afro-Indian in her gene pool. I conclude Caribbean; Guyana or Trinidad.

A tune comes by R. Kelly, an R&B giant back in the day. The definitive pied piper of Hip-Hop soul still casting his spell. Peeps has soul to spare and her squealing on hearing the opening bars of 4-Play confirmed that. This music shouldn't be celebrated alone; it was just a matter of time before we connected. I catch her assessing my ass.

The hidden signals pass between us like a flow of electrons which rock me back on the balls of my feet. Soon we're in a close clinch. Music can do that to you. Instinctively we move as one, my senses clouded by her sweet aroma, everything as normal as can be. We don't need small talk; we communicate through our movements.

Three slow jams later I could easily dance away my remaining time right here but that would be too easy. My mystery woman has one strong arm around my waist and the other around my neck, her fingers stroking the striated muscles of my neck. Right on beat her touch maps out muscle and skin imperfections like a tactile sonar.

A glancing push to my back breaks the delectable spell, kick-starting my conflict perception. I experience an unusual wave of panic as my good mood has all but packed up and left the building. As usual, I adjust fast in the darkness, making myself as unobtrusive as possible. But Like milk in black coffee, I can now see the odd movement in the mix. Men in dark suits infecting the place like viruses. And they're carrying with them a vibe that is different from anything I've experienced so far. The warning slithers through me, leaving a slimy trail of uncertainty in its wake. Peeps feels something is up and it ain't my hard on. My body goes tense and I hope she doesn't think that the magical spell between us is broken because of anything she did.

The cozy dimness of my surroundings take on a murky and threatening vibe. Suddenly I feel more at risk than any time since I entered the Nexus building. A tingling at the base of my skull, tells me the threat is here but not immediate. Obviously, they've learned that taking me down is gonna involve more than 'smiling boy the bounty hunter'.

It would take some style and creativity.

These mo' fuckers had no style at all. Ten-a-penny wanksters found in any corporation big or small. Cardboard cut-out security contractors, spitting the same clichéd jargon and the same hyped up sense of urgency for the most mundane of situations. Overkill their motto, they'd bring a plasma rifle to a fist fight.

This time they've come prepared. Blinging with stylish Gucci shades obviously augmented for night vision purposes. I see with a clarity and depth of detail their Tech could never hope to duplicate so I ain't worried. But I wonder how long I can play hide and seek with them before I'm caught, or I'm dead. The thought threatens to mess up my step as well as my positive mindset, but I keep it together.

I slide my partner out of harm's way, happy for her to think that we're just looking for more space in which to party. The Men in Black are evenly spread through a mass of humanity getting their groove on, but I still feel threatened. Any minute now I expect the remote DJ to clear the hall, enabling a thorough exit search of the guests, myself included. However, that these cats are probably intent on flushing me out the old-fashioned way. Good customer service and all that, they were intent on avoiding the mess of upsetting too many High Rollers with big chips, big titles and big names who wouldn't take kindly to this shit.

I knew how these cats operated. They'd probably burnt my likeness into their short-term cortical memory, ready for a diplomatic body search. The prognosis for a man without a plan, namely me, isn't good. I think fast.

With a few choice words in my dance partner's ears, I convince her we need some down time, so we bounce over to the bar area, a temporary respite from the MIB's. I'm not trying to get another innocent involved in my mess; I'm still a romantic, obligated to making my partner comfortable because she's created a necessary and very valuable distraction, right when I needed it. Her calming influence has been the perfect foil for me to mentally kick back and formulate a plan.

I pass through the sound bubble with my muse, leaving the pumping bass behind me. We head for the few available seats, the strange muffled silence punctured by laughter and easy conversation. I lead her by the hand and guide her onto the high chair. The ceiling lights crisscross her exotic features. I wish I could spend more time with this dime piece. I order cocktails and engage in chit chat putting Tanisha – yeah, I eventually got her name - at ease.

The next bit is the hard part. My pheromone-enriched aftershave works its magic as I stroke the sensitive area behind her ear.

'You're going to have to excuse me for a moment baby, the little boy's room is calling.' I lie like a pimp being cross-examined, my voice lowered to a hypnotic baritone.

'Promise to come back?' She sings the question in her Trini accent. At least she's smiling.

'Sure nuff.' My eyes linger on her curves. 'Just don't move, baby T.'

I exit the sound bubble to the welcoming sounds of mid-21st Century R&B crooner Joe. Even though the hall is still full of dancers who can't get enough I keep my head low, fighting the urge to party along with everyone else. Instead, I blend in, shoot the breeze with strangers and waltz my way out of the visuals of roaming CCTV cameras into the John. This is the place to make my move. Throw them off the scent for a while.

I look around and decide on where I'm going to do my switch and think I've found the perfect spot. I don't know what it is that attracted me to this toilet cubicle, maybe space; undesirable color, a vibe that the Feng Shui was fucked or the dodgy plumbing. Not sure but I'm comfortable how it's positioned. I hang around the cliques, over hearing snatches of conversation and gossip, making sure that I'm positioned to get all personal with the right person. Finally, some skinny dude with glasses and a Tux walks into the lavatory I've staked out. I compliment a shortie on her dress sense and show interest in her profession as a Research Chemist. Moments later Tux dude leaves and the door closes behind him and he's replaced with two young women in rapid succession then another artistic looking cat with a love of white silk. That's when I see the match that I've been covertly waiting for.

He's my height and my build with an aight sense of style, a nice Trilby atop his well-proportioned head and tailored jacket, but an inflated sense of his coolness. A short sharp smile crosses my lips coz I know we can work. I excuse myself from my lady friend, take up my position and watch the dude saunter over to the lavatory. A cocky attitude emanates from him.

Man, he thinks he's some hot shit!

Hot Shit waits for the platinum pod to be free, as an overtly butch sister exits. I smoothly move in behind him as his palm flashes against the heat sensors and the door slides open. Too late he notices me. A firm push sends him inside with me hot on his heels. He protests vigorously, either he's straight so he sure as hell won't like me or he's gay and just don't like my ass either. Whatever. I cuff him on the back of his neck and watch him struggle for balance, then fuck him upside the head for good measure putting him out of his misery. Unconscious Hot Shit is still so cool. Even the way he crumples onto the toilet seat has a graceful elegance to it.

The change-over is a quick one. I snake inside his duds, folding my threads on his lap and positioning his unconscious body on the John like a still life art composition. Luckily for me he's hot on personal hygiene. No sweat or BO just a confusing blend of aftershaves infused into his clothing.

Aint complainin', just explainin'.

I check my timepiece, straighten my shit up and step out of the John with all the confidence in the world but stopped short looking at a dumpy looking cat in the shiny shirt, who's been waiting outside the door.

'Whoooo...weeee, playa. I wouldn't go in there just yet.' Fanning away the non-existent foul smell. 'A word of warning on the house. Stay the fuck away from the clams.'

I see his hesitation and breeze past him heading for the bar. But instead of hooking up with my dance partner, I admire her from a distance - it's safer that way for both of us - while contemplating my options.

I only got thirty minutes to go.

Suddenly the Nexus building doesn't feel as expansive as it did on my arrival. I'm aware of where I am, totally intimate and at one with my environment. I'm aware that hidden amongst every fixture and fitting could be some clandestine monitoring equipment secretly tracking my every move. Even the guests are a deadly curiosity that could potentially snuff out my life, and I question whether staying put is a good idea after all.

At the thought of what to do next, fear rears its head or maybe its excitement that's creeps up my spine like cold mercury. It's time to take a closer look at the hall where the awards ceremony scheduled to take place. Three-dimensional imagery is good, no disrespect to Chen, but can't beat the real thing. I'll see what's going on and then find somewhere to wait this shit out.

30.

THE TANGLED SPIDER

JOB DONE. I'D MINGLED WITH THE REVELLERS, flossing my new identity and satisfying myself on what I was up against from the fortified auditorium. Hey, I'd even checked my routes into the area and figured I wouldn't need a route out. With my kamikaze mission solid in my mind, it was time to reassert myself and apply what I've learned to the next phase of my non-plan.

Did I mention that I'm chillin in a fully tricked out Bio Bath, dawg? An infra-red heated, herbal infused, Jacuzzi. It has a genetically modified living anemone lining with a small residual electrical charge, feels like your ass is being tickled by a million minute tongues. This is the closest I've come to true relaxation in days. I accept this gift with both hands outstretched.

Because of the heat, electronic surveillance is practically non-existent, just a Security guy called Carl, a thick wedge of prime Jamaican meat from Peckham, possessing a thug life sensibility with enough ghetto finesse to make the idea of misbehaving in his presence suicidal. Baby boy is a part of a cadre of security personnel associated with the Nexus building. I'd already established they weren't privy to the Black Op's shit happening right under their noses and directed at me. Obviously, it's a need to know basis and these low-level mo' fuckers, didn't need to know. Nevertheless, we hit it off; he'll be my early warning system from Streatham, and I'm safe for now. I kick back and focus on the immediate task ahead; Chen would be proud of my attention to detail.

The ceremony takes place in Hall number one, the main hall. It's an invitation-only event with all the tables pre-allocated. Non-invited patrons will be witnessing the proceedings via Air Canvas™ in every room and open space. Security will be tighter then a clam's asshole and much less enjoyable to penetrate. I wasn't worried, though. Digital had my back on that particular aspect of the plan. What he forgot to mention was that having an allocated table was one thing, but casually waltzing through security to get to it would be another. I could just picture the security detachment tooled up waiting for my arrival. Overwhelming firepower and me bleeding through it all. I blink away the negativity. I leave room for the Karma to flow, can't afford the fatalism when I gotta stay sharp. Maria, Popeye, and Digital deserve nothing less.

Physically I'm humming like I've got a V8 engine under my hood. My senses are amped, and I'm feeling faster and stronger and with every passing moment becoming more and more excited or nervous. I'm like an emotional capacitor storing bundles of fear induced energy until action requires me to release it.

I sigh, adjusting my rear in the perfectly warm water and pull on a complimentary stogie courtesy of Carl while sipping Henny, the dual taste of tobacco and spirits merging seamlessly over my taste buds. One message flows through my veins; just relax. My body tingles all over as if I'm on the verge of an ejaculation free orgasm as I imagine a nymphet under the frothing waves giving me the most amazing Brain. I lean my back against the leather of the Bio Bath, feeling good but knowing that this too would pass. I had a job to do. I sigh again as that thought preludes the end of my solace. My twenty-twenty starts to stir as if it has just been awoken from sleep and slowly builds to a crescendo. I take one last drag on my cigar, blowing a cloud of nicotine and tar free haze to the ceiling. I'm ready for whatever is coming.

Let's do this.

Two men and one woman armed with heaters, silently enter the room housing the Bio Bath. But by that time all that's left of me is my still-burning cigar, a glass with a mouth full of Hennessey perfuming the air and a fluffy terry towel folded neatly beside it. Wish I could have seen the mean mugging going on around the Jacuzzi, but I was indisposed for a long minute. Information about my whereabouts had been downloaded into their implants from compiled intelligence, so can you imagine what was going through their confused minds. I'd laugh to myself if I could, picturing these straight-laced cats, personal initiative glands surgically removed from their square asses, asking each other, Where is he? What the fuck do we do now?

Two of the team spread out to investigate, walking around the room with weapons drawn. The female covers the entrance nearest the Bio Bath, her inquisitive mind trying to work out where I could have disappeared to. She leaned absently towards the bubbles issuing from the bath and scooped up some of the water, letting it trickle between her fingers. Her focus is flitting between her position and the position of her colleagues in the distance. Obviously liking the feel of the water on her hands she repeats the scooping ritual again. From my vantage point, it's a perfect gesture. I raise up from the water like some vengeful merman from a Brothers Grim fable, gasping for air, my lungs singing with joy at the relief of sweet oxygen.

Before she can react, I have one hand on her gun and the other around her throat. I leave the bath with her squirming and gasping for breath, the exertion minimal but should have been impossible. I just can't wrench the energy weapon out of his hand. And I start to figure she had a Bio-hack in place that has reinforced her grip.

She ain't letting go, and neither am I.

I slip on the slick floor and stumble backward, relieving the pressure around her neck but still trying to separate her from the weapon. Her grip is vice-like, lucky for me her aim ain't worth shit. She discharges a round into the jacuzzi as we struggle and it erupts into a geyser of aromatic boiling water at the point of impact.

'Shit!'

I use the curtain of steam as a distraction to pull her close and introduce her to the underside of my elbow. I watch her eyes roll back then Judo throw her over my shoulder; the Sig Saur Particle gun left solidly in my hand. I swing it in a wide, vicious arc the butt connecting with her temple as she tries to get up. And I just put her straight back down again.

The other MIB's who had spread out in search of me, came running at the commotion pointing their weapons in my direction with their arms and shoulders tense, tendons ready to flex around triggers at any moment. My answer is brief but explosive; I let the Sig Saur do the spitting, conscious that I'm outnumbered, outgunned and butt naked. They'd fired first thinking wrongly that I'm a sitting duck, but I'm on the move long before they anticipate it. I slip, steady myself and then propel across the slippery surface on my knees, firing as I go. The weapon in my hand bucks as an energy round hits the smaller of the two gunmen below the ribs, causing an untidy hole that spits blood and fire as it sends him careening backward like a flesh and blood comet. My next round is less accurate and leaves the last assassin nursing a shoulder wound that's deposited him against the wall.

I leave death and injury behind me.

My body is humming, and my senses are in the zone, grateful for every portion of luck, providence has sent my way. I hustle over to the lockers and slip on a baggy gray jogging suit, emblazoned with the company logo and retrieve all my shit. I wriggle my wet feet into form fitting trainers and check my timepiece, thoughts flashing through my mind like bolts of lightning as I consider what I need to overcome next. I reach for a compact Concussion weapon left by one of the gunmen, place it in the small of my back and wonder why they never used this Non-Lethal option when they came at me.

Really playa? My higher self asks sarcastically.

I shrug and head out into the big, bad world to make formal introductions.

My intention had been to get the job done with as little drama as possible. A job I've failed miserably at so far. But I don't let my scorecard halt my progress. I mosey on down the way, my trainers squeaking as I nod and smile to the few people passing. This part of the corridor is safe. I neutralized all surveillance in that area with my last EMP cherry that I attached to the wall. I'm still nervous as hell because I've been lucky so far and I got a feeling my luck will not hold. That's when my thigh starts to vibrate and pulse a weak purple light through my jog bottoms.

I fish out the smart card from my deep pockets - you know the one from the goody bag I received when I entered - and shake my head in disbelief.

'Son-of-a-bitch!'

My luck had run out.

An emergency of some kind has been announced, and they had sealed off the area I had planned to walk through to get to my meeting. I keep looking at the cards readout and watch as whole regions on this level begin to lock down. I see what they were doing, trying to corral me. Leading me away from my target, backing me into a corner and eventually when I had no place to go, taking me out. So, my next move, as Digital would have said, is inherently flawed but I make it anyway. Only a dumb mo' fucker would do what I was about to do, but I figure they don't know the crazy ass fool they were dealing with.

I'm super-hyped now, the threat of death breathing down my neck, my movements a blur. I'm making tracks for the self-same area they were closing down. I arrive at the corridor's entrance, and I see ground holograms of flowing arrows directing people away from the zone. Announcements are being made encouraging folks to leave as quickly as they can. I know the buildings smart system won't physically lock up the area until it's free of people, so I don't worry about getting trapped in here. I spot two sisters and an older cat making their way out of the hot zone in the direction I'm going, and I stick firmly with them. They don't notice that anything's up until they see the Concussion weapon in my right hand, accompanied by a determined 'gangsta swagger.' They realize what's up, in good time and cower at the threat I pose.

I'm about to explain to them that they have nothing to worry about when a cadre of men in black break the corner ahead of me at speed. Before they know who or what the fuck is up, my C-Gun screams, sending focussed pulses of sound towards them. Concussive waves shimmer through the air, slamming into flesh and bone throwing them around the corridor like rattled chess pieces. I sprint through the cleared path, jumping over the casualties. This is just the beginning, I know.

Soon I'm behind two dubious looking females whose dress sense was immaculate, considering their broad shoulders and muscular legs they were not the garden variety women. The transvestites had some runway experience from how they walked, and I was about to mess up their strut. I push past, sending them wobbling awkwardly off balance.

'Excuse me, ladies!'

Then my twenty-twenty hollers at me again. I skid to a sudden stop as two real women in uniform break around the next corner swinging Shock Batons that fry the molecules of the air as they waved them around for maximum threat.

Question; what kind of effect will a slap from one of those suckers have on my nervous system?

Didn't know but I was about to find out.

The second they lock on to my position they pull stances and charge at me with high pitched screams. I fire the C-Gun but the bitches are moving too fast, and I can't get a bead on them. In moments, they're half way closer to lighting up my world, so I turn tail and bounce. They home in, elated at the thought of me being a chicken shit, but I haven't just got brass balls I'm smart too. I propel myself up onto the approaching dead end, using it as a launch-pad from which to spin back around and execute a sweet round-house kick to the unlucky Dame who wanted to run up into it first. My heel connects solidly with a jaw, and I'm satisfied. I hit the floor in a slow-mo, cat-like crouch, giving into the force of gravity, readying myself for some payback. That's when bitch number two lights me up like a Christmas tree. My threshold for pain was impressive but didn't stop it from hurting like a bitch - every cell of my body was on fire. If I sound pleased about the experience of twenty-five thousand volts passing through my ass crack, well sadistically and philosophically speaking, yeah.

As Ma Campbell used to say, he who feels it knows it.

In other words, you gotta go through shit to know shit. You see once I took the burnt skin on contact, once I controlled my sphincter muscles, once I stayed composed as the current scrambled my insides, then I knew I could take it. Consequently, I didn't fear it again, you dig.

I'm down on all fours when the second baton strikes my ribs; I explode into the air and land heavily. I struggle to push up to my knees and eventually manage it. The girls are taking our confrontation personally as they tenderize my ass with electricity and sheer anger. I sup it up, my body already resisting the brutal punishment but I'm still aware. I flop to my stomach breathing like a man unconscious as the victors talk over me as if I don't exist.

'The target is neutralized,' the first chick boasts over the com, massaging the jaw I should have dislocated from my kick. 'I'm activating the tracking beacon, so come pick us up. We'll keep this wanker subdued won't we Selene?' She nods to the bitch standing over me with the shock baton and they both grin.

Big mistake.

I groan.

They fall for my deception hook, line, and sinker.

'Let me fuck him up some more until backup arrives.' The bitch's eyes sparkle, taut muscle tendons in her wiry frame ready to transform intent into action. All I need is a trigger.

Girlfriend flicks her hair ready to dismantle my black ass some more. She swings at me and with the speed and surprise of a rattlesnake I catch her wrist in mid-flight. Her expression says it all.

'Oh shit!'

I burst from prone to standing in one uninterrupted motion, my forearm smashes into her face, sending an exploding mix of blood and saliva from her mouth, but I want more. So, she's a woman, fuck that! I smash my elbow into her jaw again. Her body folds to the floor, but I hold her up. I notice that she still has a tenuous hold on her shock, Baton, like the thought of sticking a high voltage charge between my ass cheeks was worth hanging on to.

Bitch number two thinks different until I swing to face her with her incumbent colleague all rubber-limbed and incoherent rambling, blocking her strike.

Surprise! I think.

The bitch is a picture of slack-jawed and bugged eyed surprise. Sparks fly everywhere; the electro prods aren't designed to come into contact with one another and a localized EM pulse dims the light and makes the surveillance equipment falter. Her confusion gives me an ideal opportunity to get all fancy. Twirling the baton between my fingers I strike her three times in rapid succession, doling out excruciating pain with every blow. She stiffens, her muscles locked by the high voltage, before hitting the ground like a felled oak tree.

Damn! I thought she'd have more to say, but nah, she's too busy twitching on the floor to care. The barely audible sounds of their communication links implanted in their ears squawked for attention. They wouldn't be talking to anyone, anytime soon.

I face the dilemma of going forward. Back peddling would be pointless; I had to press on. I pick up my discarded C-Gun. The LED indicator tells me that I'll soon be out of cartridges. I never liked guns even the so-called ethical weapons, but I don't have a choice. I search the Sisters-Grimm moaning on the floor, finding four little parcels of metallic opportunity glimmering from their utility belts. I snatch them up greedily and move on, trying to blend in as well as a six-foot playa can.

In minutes' backup arrives and they don't look happy as they, assess the damage and wonder where my crispy ass has disappeared to. Mo' fuckers have come prepared too.

Aw shucks! They wanted me alive this time.

They carried Concussion rifles gleaming in time with the flickering of the overhead lights, even the shades covering their eyes take on a dull almost robotic luminescence. But what worries me the most is that goddamn thing they're dragging. The contraption looks like a restraining harness taken from the Spanish Inquisition and pimped with current technology.

The point man sees the fallen colleagues and holds aloft a clenched fist calling the team to a halt. Next, comes the realization that in the jungles of Chile they may have been hot shit but in this cramped corridor, they're sitting ducks. Too late for all that gung-ho military shit to make any significant difference to the outcome of this B-Ball game.

From my vantage point in the ceilings, I can see their movements courtesy of two strategically placed mirrors I'd borrowed from the fake ass chicks I'd fucked up. I let my right arm swing down and lob my first gift their way, bouncing the sonic grenades straight off the wall and into their paths. The best present I'd saved for myself; noise cancellation headphones. I duck down and wait for the explosion. Concentric waves of warm air engulf me; my headphones stick to my ears as the air pressure rapidly increases. I draw a deep breath and fall to the corridor floor, entering the mayhem with a half empty clip in my C-Gun. The scene is reminiscent of a bomb blast minus the blast. Collateral damage is zero, but the casualties are on the floor, writhing painfully. The few still standing are disorientated, suffering from sensory sound overload. I cut them down with the remainder of my clip. I reload from the surplus ordinance scattered around and head east with a shambling gait. I'm out of tricks, and this corridor is depressing the shit out of me. I need to get to the main area and fast. Getting past Checkpoint Charlie with all the wanksters waiting for me will be a bitch and a half.

Any sensible citizen wouldn't be rushing towards his demise like I was, but whoever said I had sense? I can see the finish line, and I'm determined to meet this motherfucker head on. If my life ends in the process, it will be on my terms but if there is the slightest chance of knowing why my family was butchered and dispense some payback, I will.

I'm in the huge atrium, the cylindrical heart of the building that runs from its root to its apex. I'm surrounded by reinforced glass which gives me a scintillating, panoramic view of metropolitan London. Small groups mingle while individuals and couples mill around making their way to other exciting portions of the building.

I join an easy-going crowd enjoying the festivities, playing down the pain I was feeling. My weapon was up, my sweats dusty; off-white, my muscles screaming with pain, my eyes wild, and intense like a prog fiend. I glance around and up. The entrance is highly secured, but somehow, I doubt they're expecting a dangerous madman to run amok. I've already started to reveal their duplicity. Busting open whatever secrecy, they had been trying to conceal and forcefully involving others who weren't and shouldn't have been in the loop. Consequently, what had been a simple job had got messy for them. But not everyone involved knew the truth.

I walk around, familiarizing myself with the surroundings, looking for a way to execute my plans. People move out of my way, sensing that I'm about to blow up their spot while wondering if maybe I'm a ham actor employed by Nexus to provide a diversion and keep the party jumping. They're all having fun, good for them. I see dignitaries still being ushered through into the auditorium. I check my time piece knowing that as soon as the human static clears I'll be standing open and unprotected.

Hell, of a plan, huh?

I count ten men and women plus Nexus staff, apart from the security detail at the entrance to the auditorium. They're carrying out basic customer service duties; manning scanners, checking credentials. This time there'll be no element of surprise, just one man trying to shoot his way through a unit of trigger happy company men anticipating my arrival.

I've done it already. I can do it again. My twenty-twenty tingles as I conclude the thought. Then there is a resounding chorus of discordant sound in my head that gets more intense, and it's not long before I understand why.

I'm reduced to small, ponderous steps towards the cylindrical entrance of the main auditorium because of the forceful insistence of my early warning system. Five cats in dark suits step out of the crowd oblivious to my presence, more concerned with escorting their chaperone forward.

Goddamn!

I blink twice confirming that what I see isn't a figment of my imagination. My twenty-twenty subsides a smile blossoms on my formerly somber face, followed by euphoria as good as my best ever orgasm!

Pay back is a bitch. Motherfucker!

Yellow Nigga adjusts the tie around his tree trunk neck. The albino looks slightly agitated, obviously, his security hadn't anticipated being hindered by a throng of people as they usher through their Chief Executive Officer Lorraine Van Horne. Neither are they expecting to see me standing between them and glory. I open fire on their punk asses with a growl. They try to slap leather, but I've caught them unawares. Yellow Nigga's mouth is wide open when the first wave of solid sound twists his torso felling him immediately, but he's too strong to stay down. The Piazza clears rapidly leaving just myself, Lorraine and some of her bullet catchers floundering on the ground.

One guy has time to fix up, adjusting his jacket, his gloved right hand disappearing in the folds of his jacket and then appearing again with throwing stars between his fingers. He lets fly a blizzard of steel in my direction. Even with my heightened reaction time I only just evade them. Unprepared another hail of shuriken streams towards me. I just can't get out of the way in time, but I bob and weave on the spot, making myself a difficult target. Two impacts drive me to the floor. One thudding into my thigh and the other in my stomach bending me over.

My twenty-twenty screams again and without thinking I extract both throwing stars with a grimace and return them to the owner.

They stream towards him twisting languidly as I watch them. Then explode on impact.

The conflagration takes out one more bodyguard and as the chaos ensues and I take the opportunity to lace them with concentrated sound waves, enjoying the theatre of pain they're trapped. When they recover, I'll be long gone, except Yellow Nigga that is. Oh, yeah, he's a special case. He's already told the CEO to take cover. Knowing this can only end one way. I watch him shake off the effects of the concussion blast and shakily pick up his plasma weapon.

He staggers towards me firing as he comes, and just as shakily I'm evading his blasts and firing back. Furniture, displays, and architecture are going up in super-heated explosions or shattering from vibration. Neither of us gets hit. In moments, we are face to face and weapons just seems useless. He lunges at me, and I'm ready for him.

Two weeks of running and hiding, watching my 69-family slaughtered, having a bullseye painted squarely on my chest, sleep deprivation, worrying about my remaining family and now knowing it was coming to an end.

I'm ready.

The big albino sends a glancing blow off my ribs, my defense ineffectual and I wince. He follows up with using his Plasma Rifle as a club, slamming it into the side of my head with both hands. I see red as the pain explodes through me and for a moment I lose consciousness. But then I'm back, righting myself before I hit the deck. Scrambling to close the distance between us, knowing he would use the weapon on me if he could but close quarter combat made it tricky.

He tries again, but my defense suddenly becomes offence as I block him with my forearms and then ram the stock of my handgun into the soft tissue of his neck. Yellow Nigga swears and crumples but not before he lets off a plasma discharge inadvertently or prematurely, I don't know. What I do know is I'm the intended target but I sidestep him, and the super-heated Terrenium pellet takes a flaming chunk out of the opposite wall. I ram him with my shoulders, take him off his feet and slam him into a metal feature that adorned the stairway.

It rocks in its foundation from the force. I step away from him a bit unsteady on my feet. He's groaning, his sense of balance scrambled, he tries to pull himself up by grabbing onto my leg, but he didn't have the energy left to complete his threat. I shake him off like he's a piece of turd on the underside of my kicks. I stand over him and crank my C-Gun up to maximum, nothing else on my mind except the thought of wrapping up his ass like a prize turkey. I stand over him as he lies on the floor, eyes flickering as he drifts in and out of consciousness. My nozzle hovers over his chest, I brace myself and fire. The condensed wave of sound lifts me five inches off my feet slamming into him, sending his carcass partially through the floor tiles. Bones crack; muscles tear as he vomits blood and fills the air with the putrid smell of his shit. Slowly I turn away, my expected hard-on absent.

Amongst all the chaos I see a pathetic figure, looking lost and disorientated, far removed from her seat of power. I'm on her like white on rice, just as the soldiers at Checkpoint Charlie are visually onto me. The fact that I have the crème of the crop tight within my grasp renders them impotent. To get to me they had to get through my shield, right?

Wrong!

The gloves are off as the mo' fuckers come out with all guns blazing, not caring or recognizing who I've got under lock down. Instinctively I take the CEO with me, the lounge furniture nearest me shattering as we roll out of harm's way.

Lorraine and I shelter behind an Information Terminal Point as shot after shot of energy slugs rain down on us. Debris and shrapnel rip through my clothes, tearing at my flesh, as our refuge disintegrates before my eyes. I scream aloud, desperate for them to hear me over the onslaught.

'You all crazy man. I've got your boss, Lorraine Van Horne here! Do you remember her, fools?'

The CEO trembles in my arms. No tears just fear in her eyes, her trembling lips belying her usual taciturn demeanor. Seconds feel like goddamn hours as I grapple with the real and present danger of my violent death. Here I am shielding the bitch that ordered the murder of three of the most important people in my life when I should just point her in the way of some friendly fire and have done with it. But she had to do time, no quick and easy exit for this witch. Only trial, judgment, and condemnation from her peers followed by virtual and miserable incarceration for the rest of her natural life would do.

Still had to prove it, though.

I look around frantically searching for a new place of refuge, any minute now the Info Terminal would be demolished, and It would be open season on my ass. If I was desperate enough maybe I can use her as a shield, or fling her to the wolves as I make a run for it. Fuck protecting her at the risk of my life! Let the bitch find her own means of survival. That was how I felt, but I couldn't do that.

An overhead volley of slugs makes my body hair stand on end, giving me more reasons to abandon her. Weapons are being fired from behind as well as in front. I spin around seeing a group of men moving through the rubble towards me. Smoky haze obscures my view, but I squint through it almost sure that I recognize them.

The Dragon Syndicate.

My dawgs have arrived, and only the dangerous reality of my situation keeps me from whooping it up. They're laying down some bad ass suppressing fire on my behalf! Chen, the Chinese enigma, the Yin and the Yang, ambles gracefully in from my left like he doesn't give a fuck about being hit. He and his team are shimmering from an ion field surrounding the lightweight composite body armor and ballistic head gear. I'm still wondering how they got in but thankful that they did. Our non-verbal communication is on point as brother Wong Cranks up a mean looking techno Gat, readying himself to squeeze. I grip Lorraine's neck firmly and holler again at her men at the checkpoint.

'Hold your fire! I'm not gonna be held responsible if you wanksters kill your boss.' I scream. 'Put your heaters on cock and do the right thing. Walk away.'

Either Chen and his boys make a convincing statement, or the authority and gravitas of my voice has the desired effect. Shit, I'd have put money on them recognizing her, but whatever, the volley of bullets and inordinate gunfire stops.

Silence descends like a warm blanket on what moments ago, was a cacophony of weapons fire. The urban cowboys at the checkpoint had cooled down. The only sounds were coughs, shuffling, sporadic cussing, fixtures falling to the ground and electrical sizzling. The CEO's voice was small but insistent. Maybe my hold on her neck wasn't tight enough

'Adonis Campbell?' The barbed edges of fear were inherent in her tone.

'Yeah, you know me bitch!' I chuckle darkly. 'Not as easy to kill as it was for my family?'

'Don't you think if I wanted you dead you would be? But you can still come out of this on top.'

Adonis cocked his head.

'I'm already on top I have a gun to your head.'

'Shut the fuck up, or I will put your ass to sleep, right here.' I snap not interested in her banter. I want this over.

I let her stand up first and soon after, I'm with her. I snake my arm around her waist and point a plasma pistol to her abdomen.

I start walking.

Men-in-black and rent-a-cops alike move out of my way like I'm Moses parting the Red Sea. I'm bleeding everywhere. I look back at the crew with a heavy heart tinged with relief that this could soon be over. Finally, there will be answers, and I'll be able to pour some liquor in memory of my fallen comrades and loved ones. I salute Chen in the distance and turn to the entrance of the auditorium. We step through the ornate doors, all eyes on me.

'Smile bitch,' I whisper in Lorraine's ear, 'you gonna be on camera.

31.

BACKSHOT

I'M STANDING IN ONE OF FOUR AISLES LEADING TO THE MAIN stage. I have been let in through a door that was reminiscent of a Bank Vault - seven feet thick, Tungsten latticed concrete with hundreds of tons of granite and steel encasing. The auditorium as luxuriously appointed as it was, for all intents and purposes was a bunker. I wasn't naive enough to think that this precious cargo with a gun to her neck would have allowed me access. There was no way I could get inside here to the gathered intellectuals and investors if what was at stake was the mere life of their CEO. This was about profit baby, and a market hit they would suffer if I spilled Van Horne's blood all over the Piazza wasn't worth considering. That would have been a PR disaster. They've been watching my performance outside on closed circuit monitors. I briefly wonder what they conclude from all this. I'm sensing I'm like a concert pianist who's forgotten his sonata, or a rapper who's lost his flow. My audience holds their breath, awaiting my next move. Their stares make me edgy. I wish they'd substitute the classical music playing in the background for some smooth old school R & B shit but that ain't gonna happen. I check out the rafters. Sharpshooters are positioned at four points, guns in safe mode, watching. More punks who want a piece of me but they got to stand in line like everyone else.

Lorraine Van Horne squirms as I change position and force the heater into her carotid artery. From this proximity, a blast would take her head clean off.

Whispered comments from the onlookers rise to a crescendo. For the first time in her miserable life she faces the prospect of being honest in front of her peers and it scares the shit out of her. I'm aware of the rent-a-cops tucked away at a discreet distance but nevertheless making their presence felt. My twenty-twenty hums; that I have this shit under control?

'I need to talk to Professor Reed Richards?' I lift my voice up and hope the natural acoustics will carry it. Then I wait. My request has been thrown out to the high rollers, safe and comfortable at their tables. Some of the patrons aren't even perturbed by my presence, excited, entertained but nothing to interrupt their appreciation for the classical music and their meal. I expected overwhelming silence, panic even, anything but this calmness. It's almost as if they'd come prepared for this shit.

From the corner of my eye, I catch a fleeting movement to my right. Someone is climbing the steps to the stage. He has Asian features and wears an elegant suit draped over a slim, diminutive frame. His presence sends out an aura of control and experienced authority. Reed Richards? Nah! Then I catch his smile and wonder what the fuck he thinks is funny about this goddamn situation.

My first thought is that this mo' fucker knows something I don't. After everything I've been through, secrets piss me off. He looks over at me with a look of relief in his eyes, instead of expected self-importance. Behind his designer glasses, his eyes shine with the gentle tiredness of someone who has suffering sleepless nights. I clock the suits sticking to him like a bad odor. All of them packing but strangely none concerned a diddly squat about the threat I pose. The Prof stands behind a podium shrouded in Nexus livery and waits for everyone's attention, like this was an everyday talk on his speaking circuit.

He leans into the microphone that floats up from the lectern and stops about twenty centimeters from his mouth. He taps it, grinning as the sound echoes from the hidden speakers around the auditorium. He takes a deep breath and bows low, holding the pose for about three seconds before rising again, looking his audience in the eye and speaking.

'My name is Dr. Makato Sasaki, or as my colleagues tease me with the title of Reed Richards.' His voice lowers with conspiracy and he grins. 'I think they are envious of my extensive original Fantastic Four comic collection, but I still will not share.'

The guests chuckle at his comment and watch his posture change to pure business. 'I know you've been waiting for the surprise announcement that we should have had before our meal but unfortunately, our star guest was unavailable.'

He motions my way, and I shuffle forward with my hostage, unsure of where this is going but recognizing that the Prof and maybe some of his guests have a flair for the dramatic. I'm feeling much calmer and with it comes an ebb and flow of pain that had been masked by my bodies adrenaline surge. This is some surreal shit. The Prof keeps talking, totally at ease with himself and this situation and I prepare for some revelation that was going to blow my mind - the metaphorical pimp slap.

'I would like to introduce our esteemed test subject, Mr. Adonis Campbell.'

Why I'm surprised, he knows my name I don't know. Test subject? What the fuck?

'Mr. Campbell has been an invaluable part of our Synthetic Organism trials which have exceeded all of our expectations. With the aid of my distinguished colleague Dr.

James Marsden, we have been able to make marked, almost hyper-human improvements in nervous, muscular, digestive and immune systems literally on demand. The cells were engineered from living components and manufactured nanomechanisms. The delivery system is nothing more complicated than a hypodermic needle injected near the Medulla Oblongata. The cellular assembly process takes a year to complete but what's more important are the results we have obtained.'

This is my life, they're talking about. They've altered me and I have gone about my business unaware. I should feel used but I'm more pissed that I wasn't told how to use my newfound talents.

'We have been very, very fortunate to have a subject with all of the genetic markers we required to proceed. There is only one in five million people with this make up. So, you became our only clinical trial. What we have learned from you over time can be applied to sixty-five percent of the human gene pool. Our findings say that we are now able to program cell behavior as easily as we program our computers. This is a phenomenal breakthrough which our reports will outline in detail. The many improvements in Mr. Campbell's overall physiology will make fascinating reading.'

The Prof looks over to my tired ass and my blank stare.

'Mr. Campbell, I would like to extend my thanks for your selfless aid in advancing human potential, you won't be for-gotten. You are the first in the line of human evolution we can control. You are Homo Praevalidus. Science won't forget you.'

I feel like I want to give him the finger, but he knows, and I know I was shanghaied into this shit, and the only reason why I'm not busting heads right now is that I know Digital had his reasons.

'We knowingly embroiled you in an unfortunate investigation of Nexus pharmaceutical that was running alongside our trials.' Dr. Sasaki continued. 'We felt it would be a good testing ground for you, but we just never imagined they would turn to such extremes to get their hands on the technology. Information about our experiments was gleaned by corporate spies who resorted to murder to give their employers a competitive edge in the marketplace. As you can see ladies and gentlemen, Mr. Campbell had to take appropriate action to be with us this evening.'

No shit, Sherlock. I think.

'Not forgetting the possible distress, I may have caused my associates and colleagues. And oh, Mr. Campbell,' he stares at me intensely, 'it's all over now.' He steps back from the podium and bows deeply.

The tension that has kept me taut like a bowstring is radiating off me in waves. I guess I'm sensing an end to this, the final steps to a long an arduous journey and I'm beat. Mentally, physically and spiritually but I still resolve to keep this bitch in my arms

My stomach rumbles as my adrenalin falls along with my energy levels. It takes me a fractured second more than usual to piece together what I'm seeing coming my way. The free-floating features of the woman approaching me are flanked by two suits. I sense no threat from them at all. I ease my hold on the CEO and guess the assured walk, and the fact that I haven't been approached by over-zealous Po-Po means they are an authority onto themselves – government I guess. Strangely, my eyes are focussed on her well-formed shoes at first, and then they travel up her form, to her face. I swallow hard and step back at the familiarity of everything about her. I'm tripping - literally, cos I know those eyes, those lips, that nose. The curve of her hips, that ass and those legs. I swallow and feel my Adam's apple bob down the length of my neck, and suddenly my mouth is as dry as the Vegas strip, and I'm sure I'm losing my goddamn mind. She brings out the Id. Card from her breast pocket to the palm of her hand. Faint light pulses from the dense memory matrix inside and I see her vital stats writ on the canvas of air above it as a holo projection is beamed from the card, accompanied by a professionally stark shoulder shot of her rotating on its 'Y' axis.

Agent Megan Ralphson
H Branch

MI5

I take a long ass blink as if I'm in some zero-gravity environment, but the image does not change. My angel Jessica is still standing before me. Still sexy, still with those caring eyes and those shotgun lips. Except the Jessica here and now is no stripper but Five-O. Goddamn!

'Adonis,' she begins, but the rest of her words fade, 'we'll take it from here. You need to give me the gun.'

I look at her with brows creased in confusion and it begins to sink in. This is all over. I take the weapon away from Van Horne's neck and let it fall to the floor. Armed men move in and cuff her before leading her away and ignoring me.

My angel and I exchange meaningful glances. I lick my lips and watch her take care of business with professional detachment. This was second nature to her; I could see it. But the many questions would have to wait. I'm tired and worn out, but still, my third leg is shuffling to attention at her commanding take charge attitude. I laugh like a crazy man. The playa has been played!

Jessica views me evenly.

'I'm sorry Adonis I'm going to have to send someone to interview you.' She reaches out to me, a gesture that was second nature when we were together. 'You don't look too good. You okay?' She asks.

I nod in answer to her question. Talking is difficult. Every injury, every morsel of sustained fear weighs down on me at once, a heavy penance for my weakness.

I want to curl up and succumb to my exhaustion. It feels like I've been sucker-punched by a pissed off super heavyweight and instead of being stretchered off I'm eager to see how this bitch, the fight - my life - is gonna pan out. I wrestle with the exhaustion, but it's hard. My world sways; I take a front row seat and just fall on my ass. Fuck it; I've done enough. I think.

Jessica screams out, frantically waving about for help and the frantic sounds around me have themselves succumbed to my exhaustion. They have slowed to an almost unintelligible drawl.

'I'm aight,' I insist. The medics murmur about blood loss, shock, and mild trauma but are amazed that my vitals are steady. Even though the chaos is going on around me, one figure stands out from the rest. Jessica.

'We're going to give you something to relax you, sir, to make you comfortable.' The medic says. I hear the harsh whisper from the big ass hypodermic as the laser stream punctures my skin and delivers its load into my bloodstream. From the look on his face he expects a reaction from me but I'm still conscious.

'I got a high tolerance to drugs.' I mumble to him and reluctantly after checking his instrumentation he hits me again. The double dose acts quickly and in moments I'm worry free.

32.

CLIMAX

AT FIRST, IT'S ALL BLURRY, LIKE THE COME DOWN I HAD from my first and only drug episode when I was a punk ass kid. A mask slowly takes shape as my scrambled senses struggle to place together abstract pieces of floating skin and muscle. I close my eyes, hoping my spinning bed would give me a break. When I open my eyes again I'm staring into the eyes of a dead man.

My homie and mentor stands over me as real as life can hope to be. My heart pounds in my chest and the reality of this dreamscape I can't distrust. The fresh smell of the newly laundered sheets, the softness of the pillows and my weight bearing down on the mattress. I look beyond the apparition standing bedside, hoping to catch a glimpse of Maria and Popeye too, but he is alone. Tears form and I try to wish myself awake from the torment. Just as everything comes rushing back, the spectre speaks.

'I'm alive Adonis.' Digital's voice is deep as if cured from cigar smoke and sipping Remy Martin.' They wanted me dead but I wouldn't let them.' He smiles for real, reaching out to me. I squeeze his hand a sigh escaping from my lips.

The emotional floodgates open like a busted dam weakened from loss and grief. I pull his old English ass close, relieved that he's alive. He pats my back for long moments our embrace never becoming uncomfortable.

'I know you hate me right now and you are justified.'

I shrug.

'Family fight all the time. That's what families do but at the end of it, we know we're family.'

'I owe you my life my friend and a heartfelt explanation.' Digital continued.

'I ain't mad at yah, man.' I try to swallow but my tongue sticks to the roof of my mouth. 'I know you well enough dawg, you got a damn good explanation for all this weird ass shit.'

'An explanation of why I'm here alive and why Maria and Popeye died for what I'm about to tell you?' He pauses with an uncharacteristic sense of deep loss. 'Damn it Adonis, it's shouldn't have turned out like this.'

'It shouldn't have.' I agree with him.

I adjust myself like a child getting ready to hear a bedtime story. I'd already got Doctor Sasaki's sanitised version, already been debriefed by MI5 but Digital's motivation was different, his explanation would come from his heart and not his head. I look around the bed for the alert button. Digital looks at me as if I've been naughty.

'Hey. I'm a recuperating VIP and I can do whatever the fuck I like!' I sigh at his pretend shock as I press the button.

A maternal sounding nurse answers and I order take out, playfully stating that she's got to bring it in for me personally. The kiss of her teeth was long and drawn out. She reminded me of Mama.

'She digs me really.' I say.

'Your energy reserves must be on low?' Digital asks with the concern of a father and a scientist.

'These cravings to get my grub on I've been experiencing are from the process I've been through, right?'

He nods.

'Your cellular adaptations require large energy on a regular basis. I'll be able to help you with that.'

I sense his uncertainty at whether I'm cool with the changes forced on me. After all we've lost, all we've sacrificed, his trepidation is justified. But from day one I've trusted him with my back, always felt secure with his judgements, lived up to his expectations without question. If I was in his position, I would have done the same thing.

I ask him.

'Was it worth it?'

His eyes lower in contemplation and then as he looked at me a fire erupted behind them.

'I don't know. But what I do know is because of you, because of all of us, a disease that could kill many millions will be kept in check, possibly even cured. My daughter and many others like her did not die in vain.'

Digital pulls out a red handkerchief from his breast pocket and daubs at the corner of his eyes. He looks at me straight and asks.

'Do you think we'll be ever able to get past this, truly accept that what I did was the right thing?'

I peer down at the landscape of my white sheet, the soft dunes fashioned by the cotton almost calling me into them. I look back up at him.

'I'm the new MD of 69; I'm alive and I'm cashy. I've got family and new friendships forged from some adverse shit I've been through. I got no reason to believe we won't get through this. Not yet anyways.' I look at him seriously a distressing question forms in my head.

'There ain't no fucked-up side effects I should know about is there? My dick ain't gonna suddenly fall off, right?'

'I promise,' Digital says. 'And I also promise you justice will be done if it takes my last remaining breath or my last credit in the bank.'

I know him well enough to know that was no idle threat but a promise.

'Where do I begin?'

He's either asking me that question or asking himself. I intervene anyway.

'Just Chill D and take a load off,' I nod to a chair beside my hospital bed. 'Start from the beginning and keep going until you're done.'

Digital matches my smile and, for once, takes my advice.

The End

ABOUT THE AUTHOR

Anton Marks grew up in Jamaica and was so enamored by its characters, culture, history and swagger that it inspired him. He began writing about the weird and wonderful fueled. by the island and its stories. His first novel began a trend of bestsellers that would transport readers to the ghettoes of Kingston, Jamaica in crime thriller **Dancehall**, futuristic London – **In the Days of Dread**, government agents in **Bushman** and the futuristic world of vice in – **69**.
His next offering will be a young adult Science/fantasy novel entitled – **Joshua N'Gon: The Last Prince of Alkebulahn**, the second in the *Bad II the Bone series* – **Good II be Bad** and a supernatural thriller based in a barbershop called **Headhunters**. Expect great things as the Marksman continues writing the most creative and exciting novels in the new Urban Fantastic genre.

Join the revolution at:
www.urban-fantastic.com

Printed in Great Britain
by Amazon